
MIDNIGHT
Of
HORRORS!

(Virgin Day Chain Revelations Explosive)

****

SANMI-AJIKI

ISBN: 9798573067179

Volume Three

NOTE: Continued from Volume Two.

CHAPTER 017

Abstract Mystery Is The Forest

Power base! Power pedestal! Power stand!
Power display in the power institution of the powers,
Stars fall in large numbers from the firmament of time,
Houses of wealth are destroyed; crowns of glory devoured,
Yet, the boundless appetite of the powers remains insatiable...

INSIDE THE FOREST, the wind blew hot and cold. Memory was lost in the house of memory. The memory was later found but it dangled in-between faintness and fullness. Greens called in love. The cool wind danced them to unheard beats. The shaded sky remained a spectator. Cocks□ crows honoured the new evening. The sun was journeying down into the land of the forgotten. Age counted its losses and gains.

Thoughts of regrets attacked Benlilo□s heart and mind. They were the toll of history, an unprepossessing account in the making. The era befriended, as it alienated. The deceitful season manifested false impressions. Life was the market of losses and gains. The losses were counted in abstract currency notes; the gains valued in plain and opaque vanities.

Benlilo confirmed his mother□s postulation that the human world was not a bed of roses. His conclusion confirmed that it was a well-planted and properly maintained garden of thorns. He recollected his pains; a roll call of his run of injuries raced through his mind. His head swelled double - he was still hanging about in the midst of forestry abnormalities. The irregularities counted in curses and in blessings. The blessings were natural like nature as at creation; the curses amounted to contorted naturalness at re-creation □ the mystery forest of conceptual mysteries.

For this reason, he now rebuked, in an extra expression of his mind, the naturally unnatural forest. But instead of his words to attract influence, the forest merely laughed him to scorn. He heard the laughing reaction of the forest. His hope had never in life suffered such a blow. So soon, the negative prophesies of the weeping ghost had been coming to fulfilment! He wept indignantly but instead of succour, he found sarcasm and more chastisement from an unknown voice spokesperson of his enemies, which said:

Emergency is crying inside woods:
Fugitive of our forest,
How fair?
You□re crying but you□ve seen zero!
You□ll want to cry blood

When water must have dried out of your eyes.

Be prepared! Coward, be ready! Be prepared!
Have you not been boasting yourself to be a man?
And were you not truly born intact a man?
Approaching events will prove or disprove the manhood

Your masculinity for
You are already locked in war against the powers □
The battle line has been drawn
Be set, belligerent boy □
The battle of the gods against your soul has just begun!

Though covered with dry and decaying leaves, the soil maintained its lousily demonic muteness. The piercing wind continued to dance the greens. The boy Benlilo stood trapped at the junction of dilemma. To step forward or to turn sideways became ill at ease. Exercising a reverse amounted to problem. He remained alone inside the mystery forest.

A momentary joy invaded his person. He discovered, to his sustained sorrow, that he remained inside the mystery forest of the unthinkable. The blockade of his movement was unseen. Later, it got broken down but the break-up was unheard. He turned leftward, surveying the forest afresh as if he had just arrived there against his will.

A tone of a night bird welcomed the unknown but approaching night. The nightingale□s mantra ministered deepest his being. Yet, the ministration was all meaninglessness. He could neither count his curses nor measure his blessings in pounds or ounces or dollars.

Some far-distanced rocks echoed the bird□s message through their hollows. The hero lost calculation of the calendar; he would not know whether the day was a Tuesday, Wednesday or Sunday. Some implied thoughts on the notorious yet brittle phenomenon called *life* beclouded his brain. They exhibited brutality and kindness, worthiness and vanity, sadness and joy.

The sky was busy taking census, in vain, of the stars that populated it. Age sounded its bell of commemoration. A fair of nought: the brutality displayed its wares, the kindness its increases. The worthiness proudly exhibited its virtues, the vanity its values. All the four exhibitions defined elaborate life in details. They mirrored night and day; they interpreted seasons and eras.

The forest, as a rich pasture, shepherded serpents and lambs. It pastured snails and pigs. It stocked lions and deers. It reared scorpions and goats. The serpents journeyed about in sourness of aggressions. The lambs hid themselves from the serpents. The snails fell preys to the pigs and their spirits fainted for rescue. The lions survived on the deers. Life remained inequity and injustice.

Time mothers history. History makes posterity. Posterity honours or dishonours humanity. Adage mirrors life to interpreting it. Proverbs also lend meaning to it alike witty sayings, otherwise known as *words of wisdom.* Symbol represents it, while metaphor educates man on it. Will is the power of life. Courage tasks and works it. Irony confirms its dubiousness. Yesterday cried for the injustice of being forgotten. Today yearned for satisfaction and, but, justified worry of rising and falling history. Tomorrow begs for fulfilment. Life means dramatic shifts of acts and scenes.

In quick succession, unheard and solemn singsongs of deliverance ran across the horizon. But where was the deliverance? Echoes of safety boomed through the land and by its sky but where was the safety? Benlilo gazed at the marked trees for yet another returning time □ they told him diverse stories of life. The stories were, solely, of sorrows and laments by actions.

The treetop greens caught his attention. He heaved a moan of respite but where was the breathing space? It crossed his mind, yet again, that he had never experienced this kind of situation before. It dawned on him that the house of his father was a beautiful place. The will of time might not be the best for man. The will of seasons and eras could be poisonous. The unfeeling danced clothed in the market place, behind the clothes was hidden the large quantity of his badness, his wickedness.

The kind showed kindness but he was repaid with evil. Yet, love swallowed sins; wickedness unveiled them. Where was love in the midst of the forest? Where was joy to overrun sorrow? The tell-tales of wildlife ran. Acute shortage of wisdom befell man in the wilderness of time - who would rescue him?

True, the deep called to the deep; the sky messaged to the space. Abstract interpreted life in madness and by sanity. The forestry region remained apathetic. Benlilo sopped a deep breath. His eyes roved the more to appraise the area. For the umpteenth time, he would not know why he was in the forest. The biggest problem without solution? He could not discern the sign of how he had arrived there and he had forgotten all about that. He was the ignorant pilgrim of life who lost his bearing. Yet, he symbolised hope, a very bright hope! His faith to survive in life did not dwindle in strength.

Inside the forest, insects survived on insects. Bigger birds of its air and bush fowls preyed on lesser birds and fowls to sustain and to nourish life. Therein, bigger animals hunted on smaller ones for food. The weather was amoebic abnormally. Night and day exchanged positions unarguably. All greens appropriated joy and sorrow of belongings.

Inside the forest, the dove sang of love and unity, peace and progress, while the vulture rendered hymns of filth of festival on corpses and through carcases. As the unknown voice in the beginning had postulated, the horse boasted of being mobility for war advantages. The eagle was an unsurpassed specialist in adventurous flights. *Elulu* the coucal and the cock were timekeepers for birds and fowls, respectively, as the woodpecker retained its position as the gifted carpenter of all birds.

The cattle egret□s clothe remained pulp-white contrary to that of the dirtily brown partridge. The snake prided itself in serpentine wisdom, in spicy enmity against humanity, unlike the tortoise in cleverness competition. The parrot served as the orator in the gathering of all birds, while the camel and the donkey said they had come to serve humanity. The domestic dog voted for the human home in sacrificial love of caring and sharing. This was unlike the wild dog and the wolf that had elected to inhabit the jungle as wild animals.

The wild cow swore that it would never serve as willing meat for man, no! not like the domestic cow whose generational members fell daily on the abattoirs of time. The sheep preached the gospel of obedience whereas the goat of disobedience. The gentle and genuinely loving cat chose the human home for habitation but the wild cat preferred the bush where it preyed and survived on weaker mammals. Inside the forest, the rat family recorded population explosion like ants innumerable.

All creatures of the forest were peculiar and clever or wise. They played and fulfilled their roles as apportioned to them by destiny and posterity in pools of contorted controversies. Life went on mingled. Ill and good fates took sides with the actors. Hope flew and it perched on the distressed tree of troubled and trouble-free time. Love did manifest in seasonal eras. Time rejected and accepted several forms of manipulations and actualisations.

The glorious star appeared again in the sky. A deer came into view not far away. The deer changed into a wild goat. The untamed goat transfigured into a rhino. The rhino raged. It transfigured into a lion possessed with a smouldering hunger. The lion roared at the star. However the lion of darkness and its negative action meant absolute nothing to the star; it minded not its unruly barking.

In shame but not in defeat, the lion stopped its roaring. It raised up its mouth and vomited a cloudy ball. Without wings, the ball flew inordinately towards the star with the ambition to attacking and conquering it. However, midway its journey, a touch of fire located the overcast ball and it was consumed out of existence. Beholding the straight failure of its attack, the lion began to shed tears. No one consoled it.

A new session of lamentation broke out in the enclave of darkness. The kingdom of light laughed the defeated dark hosts to scorn. The star celebrated the unreserved victory the best. Its laughter's roaring terrified the forest, the sky and the powers. The lad Benlilo continued to watch.

Several lamps appeared circularly round about the adventurously lonesome boy. The lamps' lights shined frostily. None of the timid lights was encased by glass. Equal numbers in multitudes of demons appeared. The demons were armed with their breath. One-to-one, they started to blow out the lights of the lamps.

Very soon, they had succeeded in extinguishing all the lights of the lamps. The lately mournful kingdom of the powers became cheerful for *the victories*. A prolonged roar of celebration rolled out in this particular primary constituency. That time around, they had *won*. The several lamps had been sons and daughters of man on earth. Their lights were their stars. How the lad mourned for their premature termination into the grave of non-fulfilment against all the beautiful things of life that had been divinely written concerning their destinies!

A hundred and seventy crowns manifested physically. A large team of leopards, tigers, jaguars, jacquards, wolves and bears bombarded the territory like warfare guerrillas! They attacked the crowns most sadistically; they devoured them. Only sixty-two of the crowns escaped the massive attack. The lucky ones had suddenly grown wings and flown away from the territory. The crowns were glories of men, women and children; the wild animals were envious and carnivorous agents of the powers, the gods.

For the second time in the adventure, the image of love, man's heart showed up. This time, it was suspended somewhere in the sky about a hundred feet to the ground. Yet another mystery marvel, no rope held the new image. It grew bigger and larger. Suddenly, it got entangled inside thorns. The thorns moved to choke the man's organ to death. In immense pain, the heart groaned at the mercilessness of this heaviest of ferocious attacks.

The band of thorns soon vamoosed but there was no reprieve for their victim the heart. It grew larger still before it turned into a hard stone. The heart had belonged to man; the thorns represented invasion of darkness, the most powerful cover for the powers. The stone typified the new state of the man's heart - having submitted to darkness and been transformed by it from flesh into a rocky substance.

The stone is the typical heart of the godless man. In this gritty state, it had developed absolute inaccessibility to water, which symbolised life and the truth. The forest is a mystery as the adventure. Shortly after, the stony heart became a well-heeled vineyard.

Among variegated creatures and plants, the vineyard was populated by scorpions, serpents, cockroaches, insects, frogs, toads, spears and poisonous arrows, vampires and multitudes of pests, weeds and the same groups of the thorns that had threatened to choke the heart to death at first.

Sixty-six stands of flourishing flowers made their appearances. The petals of the flowers were radiant purple, gold, blue, yellow and pink. In turn, they characterised royalty, wealth, love, success and greatness. The flowers were divergent brands of the beauty of life. They were the talents of men and women with which to beautify the human world - but what happened?

Sixty-six angry and hungry wild goats appeared from all angles of a jungle. They hurried towards the beautiful flowers. They attacked, conquered and devoured them, all in no time. Life was nastiness. In a response to the brutalities of the beastly goats, Benlilo shivered into the marrow of his bones. Undoubtedly, he was touched. Unconsciously, he closed his two eyes and, opening them a second later, what did they see?

They saw dedicated strongmen pulling down houses of wealth. They stumbled on expert arrow shooters shooting down fruits, which were human stars, to the ground from the tree of life. They sighted love of man waxing cold, even going dead and buried inside the soil of time. They discovered hate, envy, murder and other vices rejoicing. They multiplied and boomed like the ocean. Another time, Benlilo□s mind went straight to the barbed words of the vamoosed weeping ghost.

Furthermore, the lad□s two eyes caught sight of several wicked powers. They almost all carried the faces of humans. They were using their human workforce to set afire several treasure fields belonging to sons and daughters of men. At the roll-off of the latest series of horrors, Benlilo grew more appalled but the worst was yet to come. Those tragic precedents were mere child plays, mere preambles. Yet again, his mind of recall flashed back to the first voice and the hurtful words of the master talker the weeping ghost.

The night was coming, the day going. The sun was nowhere. Stars began to appear in twos and threes in the sky. The showering dew threatened to cease. Close by mountains and hills rejoiced in their tall glories, as wools of snow white clouds covered their apexes. The clouds were transportable. They moved and rolled but the hills and the mountains were never to be put to shame. They rejoiced the more by the passage of flying time. Oh, how they exulted remarkably! Life was joy!

A phenomenon called *age* cried and mourned inside a beautiful garden. The phenomenon was bedevilled with unhappiness and caution. It had to do with the murder of love on the street of unsympathetic time. That was not all: justice too was annihilated in a broad day light of nakedness without shame. Glories of living hid in the dugout. Beauties of life became eyesores. Man yearned for hope but gloominess overran his tent. He longed for peace but anxiety fell his lot. He begged for rest in futility: life was unadulterated vanity!

A part of adventurous Benlilo prayed to discover the life more; another inequitable part of the wayfaring boy yearned for an immediate evacuation from the mystery forest. The two partial half-hearts swayed between further exploration of the forestry zone and liberation into his family's *affectionate* home in Marpolio.

He remembered the truthful words of his mother Suiggaria:

"You will surely pass through the School of Life and the School of Life will pass through you. The colourful your glory is, the fiercer and hotter the battle. Yes, my beloved son Benlilo, you will suffer but at a point, the enemy's yoke shall be broken off your neck," the mother prophesied, both in the negative and in the positive.

He moved to recapture his lost independence from the mystery forest of mysteries, all because there is nowhere like home. Greens remain greens, the wind breeze in their orders of creation.

The wayfaring lad Benlilo looked forward. He fixed his eyes into the bosom of the forest but as a replacement for his two eyes to see some sections of it, a different setting arrested them exclusively. The sojourning boy saw a long African crown. The crown was a super-beautiful piece an epitome of unstained native culture and heritage. It was made of glowing ancient and modern beads of rotund colours. Gracing the apex of the crown were three homogeneous immaculate white feathers of *okin,* the mythological king of all birds.

Astonishingly and horrifically at the same time, observing Benlilo was further shocked to discover that the long beautifully beaded crown had no little peace. A big python coiled round it beginning from bottom to the top and the reptile was poised for war. Behold, its long tongue drew out as a mark of warfare alert. Furthermore, it was surrounded by voodoo-juju powers, in their multitudes, all seriously occultic. Except his extraordinarily bright star in the sky of the backdrop, a dove leftward and the crown, the scenery crammed with the paraphernalia of dark powers. In unity of conspiracy, they exhibited horrors and terrors ☐ avid enmity against the crown, the dove and the star.

Life, the forest, is made up of symbols and images. The symbols and images tell their stories in diverse of ways comedic and tragic, loving and hating, horrible and terrible. The long African beaded crown, symbol of success and royalty in nobility, was the voyaging lad Benlilo, as the cultic images stood for the powers of the night, his sworn-enemies. They were as clever as the tortoise and as fast as the bat flying mysteriously in the night sky. They were as fierce as the serpent and as deadly as the scorpion.

In sure confirmation of all those, as the boy explorer and discoverer persisted in his staring of the crowded scene so strange, a voice oozed out of the crown and it said:

"Benlilo, believe you these? You are the long African crown of beauty, as surrounded by hard-born enemies. It is all because your destiny is special, super-colouful! Nevertheless, you will move from minimum to maximum. You will move from nothing into something. You will move from poverty into prosperity. You shall move from shame into fame."

Although he had also received many divine revelations concerning his unique star, his uncommon glory and his enviable destiny, Benlilo had several reasons to doubt the prophesies of the departed voice. He prayed earnestly that he be removed from the forestry strange land into his father□s house in the City of Marpolio for the systematic fulfilment of the divine prophesies.

Raging controversy, yes! The crown stood for kingship but the unfriendly powers swore that it would not reign over them. How they lust to rob the crown of its glory but the crown too vowed never to surrender to his enemies. Eruption of struggles and battles for supremacy ensued. Military tactics countered military tactics, as warfare confrontations collide on the hot war fronts. It was battle of the gods in defence of their interests. The interests remain unchanging, the war prosecutors unrepentant.

Who will be the victor and who shall emerge the vanquished and the victim? Time lurked in the jungle of the season, by history and through posterity, to tell.

The mystery forest of mysteries spoke differences and indifferences. The differences defined the indifferences and they both combined to give multifarious life the very best of meanings. Life is battle and battle is life. Man is the sojourner on planet earth, even as the powers, holy and unholy, are his supporters and antagonists. The battleground is the life of the man with him as the warrior of fortune. It is either he sinks or he swims. It is either he survives or he perishes □ the choice is by fate in contradiction or in agreement of his prearranged divine destiny.

CHAPTER 018

Life Is A Proverb

The appointed night comes,
The root of transplantation exposed
Evening of uncertainty growing wild at ease,
While faith contradicts trust in the indefinite plane,
As hope wanders across and below the region for settlement.

□Where is the honey of life in the orchard of hostility? Where is joy to run similar to a river? Where is hope to flow smooth akin to the cool wind? Where is faith to fly skillfully approximating the expert eagle and ascend and descend in cool blues? Where is the confidence of *little* man of modest mind?□ a lone voice bellowed frighteningly across the forest.

The messages of the voice were direct and indirect exposures of truths □ but now, the inborn explorer in Benlilo was dying out. His entangled person existed in-between the land of hope and that of cheerlessness. More he earnestly longed to recover his lost self-determination.

There were hyperactive demonstrations of fireflies across the dark sky. The forest vibrated to its roots. Roars of thunder also banged. Benlilo shook like a coward at the appearance of death with its sharp claws fully drawn and carnivorous teeth at the ready. A ghost, half white and half black, appeared from the woods. It was one of the most fearful forestry encounters of the boy to date.

The ghost had on its forehead a long and sharp horn - also white and black in colours. The young man wanted to run but to where? The ghost roared its way towards his side. It was armed with a serpent in its right hand and a scorpion in the left.

□Coward □ *aahaaaa!*□ The ghost laughed Benlilo to derision.

Both creatures □ the scorpion and the serpent looked pale and ambitious. They hungered to bite someone and dispatch him from the land of the living to that of deadness. Benlilo did not imagine that he was their common target, their enemy. How could he have thought out such danger to himself? He loved himself passionately.

Time is the mother of events, beautiful or horrible. Age recounts tales by experiences. And, but why, there were often victims and victors? There were always tears and laughters, why? Oh! there were not forever successes and failures □ for what reason?

The half-white, half-black ghost intensified on its roaring venture towards Benlilo - its two weapons, the serpent and the scorpion, still fully drawn. The lad could not run; he could not hide either. The far distance between the ghost and the boy thinned off rapidly. A newly invoked round of jubilation broke out in some dark fortifications.

But instead of the beast to crash into the helpless lad, there suddenly appeared a transparent glass in-between them and the aggressor crashed directly into it □ and for the wounded defender, the glass, it groaned in durable pains. The ghost□s pets and arrows □ the serpent and the scorpion too got wounded but mildly. Scared, they both broke loose and disappeared by two different directions into the woods.

The wounded glass, nevertheless, held the wild ghost a helpless captive. In the gulag of the glass, the ghost struggled hysterically to free itself in vain. Benlilo, in turn, laughed him heartily to ridicule, to the great pain, further, of the watching powers. Life was the story of the vanquished and the victor.

The lad enjoyed his victory, as the creature endured its tragedy. The lad got a transplantation, while the ghost remained inside the glassy incarceration. Transplanted Benlilo met himself atop a high-rise mound hill of ecstasy. The syrupy experience made him to forget all troubles of life so soon. How this shift of base had happened he could not the least tell but he, in truth, started to enjoy it.

For here, sweet breeze permeated everywhere bountifully. The caressingly cool breeze danced the greens around and above and its flowing dancing beats could be heard distinctly. Life for him was pleasure. It meant triumph on the mountaintop of life!

Surrounding the mound hill was a vast area of a plain bush rearing several animals. A wild dog, completely white in colour, ran back and forth inside the bush. It stopped suddenly. It had smelled the hidden lad in the suspended open place. It lifted up its head to see the lad atop the high-rise mound hill and its wrath exasperated. It barked rowdily in order to pluck him down to the earth and devour him as a prey. To it, life was opportunity, a tough challenge.

The white wild dog could not bark down the seen teenager from the mound hilltop! It then invested in another means of trying to climb the hill but it could not. Here Benlilo received a new exposure: the damaged glass got flawlessly repaired by the wind and, for this, it rejoiced exceedingly. The forest and all environmental forces also rejoiced with the healed glass exceptionally. They congratulated it loosely.

The half-white, half-black ghost had earlier been released from its crude arrest and it self-effacingly roared down the slope into the woods - thanking its star for its regained freedom. The woods also happily received the lucky immigrant and congratulated it warmly.

It was then that it remembered its separated arrows and pets, the scorpion and the serpent. It sought for them, as they looked for it. They three met at *faithful junction* and it repossessed them fiercely, exactly like a fearless warrior of the gods. Life was unity and faith. It meant warring and winning together.

The failure pained the white-wild dog to no ending. It barked more rowdily and ran round about the foot of the hill - in distress expressions. Benlilo burst into a long-term segment of loud laughter where he remained atop the mound hill. The snow-white untamed dog became angrier. It ran out of sight, barking more rowdily and repeatedly. Life was entertainment of failure and success.

The forest became a great deal dark and frightful. Benlilo grew apprehensive. His ears, from the distant and near surroundings, could record some chirps of night insects. *So the night will meet me here, eeh?* he asked himself unbelievably. All greens of the darkening forest started to hymn severally different tunes disreputably beautiful and marvellously sickening in diversifications. Internally speaking, it seemed as if the songs were ushering him into another realm of the unknown, as laden with suspense and hanging surprises.

The night is fear in characterisation. It is the medium of the wicked. It is the passageway of the gods and goddesses. The roadway of the powers. That is why no decent human being trades in or with the night. The night is the harbour and ruler of all evilness; it is the night of horrors and suspicions. It is a night of fearful wonders when the unexpected happen. Love is lost to the night never to be found.

Hope there diffuses like the going light of the wearied hunter. Faith in the night shakes like the thin palm tree at the mercy of drought and windstorms. The night, strictly the night! the chain of transmitted thoughts rushed through the worried mind of Benlilo. For the very first time in the wild adventure, the powers had projected their views and conclusions into his thoughts.

The wind rose and fell. Greens danced in misinterpretations. The conquered sky remained unresponsive. Hope began to run a race of hide and seek. The fear became more mesmerising. For the lad, life remained a mystery, a scene of inscrutabilities.

A show of ten jolly associates rolled by: a sparrow flew out of the soil. A lizard crawled in the air. A chameleon materialised from greens. A desiccated wood vomited an insect. As soon as the insect came out of the dry wood, it began to grow rapidly and it soon enlarged itself into a hefty creature, still an insect but now very domineering and scary. A millipede dashed down from a tall treetop. The millipede was extensive.

The earth opened again and released a bush fowl. The fowl skated about on the ground in some circles of recklessness. The space sent down a wall gecko. The greens became jealous of the space, the air. They dispatched a fish down the earth's surface. The fish floated mid air down below as when in a deep. Therein it exulted greatly, issuing a song of love and hate:

Sacrifice is love in practice
Hope the river flow pleasure
And faith maintenance of life
At noon of sweat and breath...

The earth became more committed. Again, it opened wide its spacious mouth and ejected a ringworm. The worm stood straight on its elfin tail end and it danced to unheard beats. Finally, too, the wood responded to the challenge of double-dealing. It sent out an awe-inspiring demon-god to play the coordinator of the looming event.

Green in colour, the sparrow was angry; the lizard was yellow and anxious for nothing. The chameleon appeared in creamy white and it was cynically hungry. The millipede was red and agile in nature. The fowl, sapphire in colour, was hassle-free. The wall gecko was chocolate and it became visibly drunk. The fish, mud in colour, turned into a wanderer and it continued to swim inside the air pool.

The blue worm now danced to establish an acrobatic warning sign. Finally, the demon-god, clothed in royal purple and violet, crowed like a sun-up cock. But the earth became angry. It opened wider its mouth in a gap and, in twilight, swallowed up the total congregation of unrefined beings. Life was subjugation and blistering prejudice!

Benlilo preserved his adamant pose at the apex of the mound hill. There materialised an *Excellent Way* - an unusual path, as the crow flies, leading to a destination called *City of Holiness,* an abode of amity and joyfulness.

All day long, everlastingly, the inhabitants of the city rendered songs of *Halleluiah! Holy!! Holy!! Holy!!!* Perpetually, they traded in love and they invested in love. Their money for exchange in their trades was love. They lived in love, joy and peace forever more. Here Benlilo remembered the gloriously supernatural personality, and his almighty entourage, which he had seen at the inauguration of the adventure.

Three different heaps appeared in sight. The first one was a heap of dry snail shells, the second a mound of spent cowries. The third pile was of grey ashes. A lonely harsh voice of sensitive recitation relayed transversely through the forest:

□Behold every competitor for the gracious throne of life: rain, sun, moon, star and rainbow - all of them, individually, wanted to be king and reign over their one community. Their struggles and scrambles for the stool, nay the throne and the crown, started and persisted. Rain began to pour down in unmerciful torrents. It soon extinguished the glory of sun. Rain also killed the image of moon.

Power swallows power on the battlefield of ambition! Too, rain challenged star to battle and soon, it annihilated star□s shimmering glory. Rainbow, on its personal part, did not wait to war with rain before ravening clouds would black out its glory. In consequence, rain won the kingship and it reigned over the four brothers, namely: sun, moon, rainbow and star - all now subjected into hidden places.

A beautiful house rolled into view. *What! a house inside this forest?* Benlilo asked atop the mound hill. Eager as an investigative surveyor of incomprehensible life, he looked round about him to confirm whether he was still inside the forest and the confirmation was concrete. His sadness developed, as his craving to be home.

His heart got magnetised to the beautiful house, a bungalow. He was a great deal surprised to discover that the house was a prototype of his father□s house. *But how possible?* he remarked in questioning undercurrents. *But I am not home already; I am still inside the forest!* he reassured himself painfully. He wanted to run down the slope of the hill into the house but something held him back and down.

□Look, Benlilo, if you ever step your feet into that house, it is doubtful if you will ever be able to come out of it!□ an unseen voice warned steadfastly. Now overcame by fear, the lad stood still. Folding his arms and loosing them, the boy continued to watch in committed interest from his vantage position. Life was rolling scenery multifaceted.

Two heavy dogs were guarding the two doors to the house. Ten smaller ones assisted the two heavily built dogs. All the dozen dogs were witchcraft agents. Each of the two biggest dogs had six different legs and three dissimilar horns on its head. The horns were its combined weapons of war. Yet, the warring animals were clothed in arms and ammunition! They were anxious to war. The lad would not know who their enemy or enemies were. A little soul who could not tell the differences between colours of life, as the weeping ghost had said, how could he have known? Benlilo did not know that *Benlilo* was their chief enemy, oh!

The beautiful bungalow was a hijacked house! It was a witchcraft property, *an estate* of the powers. Round about it were two parallel lines drawn. The first line was cherry red, while the second one was coffee coloured. Mathematically speaking, the two parallel lines would never meet. One of them stood, in collective fate, for occupants of the house. The other one represented success. Life was a maxim. It was a food for thought; only the gifted wise mind could have understood and interpreted it.

It was very clear that the watching powers were very sad and angry that Benlilo had not rushed down the hill to enter the house. Some exchanging voices of steaming wrath roared against his person out of the house in turn:

□Rebel, you want to achieve what nobody in your family has achieved? You want to cross the ancestral borderline, beat the embargo, and escape the limitation. You say the family patterns shall have no impact on you. Over-ambitious rat, you want to rewrite your family□s history, well done! Your father Amaldia and his fathers lived inside holes but you want to luxuriate inside palaces and we are watching and observing. We are foundational destiny killers,□ said the first voice angrily and the second voice took over:

□Yes! by the established tradition, your family eats crumbs and remnants but you want to wine and dine with royalties. According to the first-fruit covenant of your family line, no first born ever prospers and you are the first child of The Amaldias □ or , Mr. Fool, have you forgotten? You are so desperate to destroy the machinery of governance in place hundreds of years before your birth □ how possible? Benlilo, have you forgotten? You are an offspring of witches and wizards. You are from the loins of occultic gods and satanic goddesses. You rightly belong to the gods but you are still wasting your own time, playing the rebel.

□You lust to break all the family patterns - you are a liar! But, then, be prepared! Be ready for your eyes to see what nobody in your family line has seen. Be steady to experience the worst that any human mind can imagine! Life is battle and we are professional war prosecutors. Be prepared □ you will pay more than the price!

□Because you are cleverly and stubbornly insisting on breaking the hedge, we□re assuring you, serpents will bite you! The scorpions will sting! You must pay the penalty - the fool on whose head the coconut is broken will not partake in the eating of its sweet flesh. Benlilo, you are the gory fool; we are the foundational star destroyers!□ Thus, the second voice of antagonism winded off and, angrily, the third one took over:

□Small mind, do you know - we are the greatest detectives; we are the unapologetic informants and prosecutors. Benlilo, you want to break the family tradition. You are so recklessly immoderate to open the closed door. You want to know the mysteries behind the closed door. You are hungry to know, to your own damnation, the mysteries of the power behind. You would have seen them, known them and made the shockers of discoveries but, by then, you must have been totally blind and mad and paralysed □ inside your decomposed grave for we are foundational glory annihilators!□ the fourth voice of castigation roared.

□Trail bracer indeed! You are the revolutionary, the reactionary. You want to tower above others. You want to excel □ why? How many of your ancestors had excelled? You are not a wise boy at all; you never know the type of family into which you have been born. You want to remove your name from our register and from our record.

□You want to break the ancestral covenant that had securely been in place ever before your grandfather Aloiki and your great-grandfather Hmnoikii were born. You do not know the venture of fire and of life into which you have already thrust your hand and brain. He who dares to do that which no one before him has done, his eyes must see what nobody□s eyes have seen! You□ve forgotten that we are treasure consumers,□ it was the fifth voice of revelation.

□Fire burns on the mountain; flood rages in the valley □ can you run? Can you swim? Can you struggle? Can you stumble or punch-up? Can you fight? Stubborn goat, Benlilo, I trust you - you love to use your personal experience for a case study □ well! Very good! You will know that the barking dog can also bite. The lion will not only roar and bite but also devour you! We are the powers.

□We don□t forget; we don□t overlook □ our records are ever fresh, constantly accurate and ever up to date inside our ageless yet ultra-modern and highly computerised libraries □ we are the ancestral murderers of fortune,□ thus came and went the sixth cruel voice of interrogation and threat.

□Look, this ignorant Benlilo, there are innumerable things you don□t know. Poverty is your inheritance but you are so wild; you want to break loose. Over two hundred years before you were born, we signed an agreement with your progenitors, that nobody in your family line will prosper, but you are a rebel! A rebel will always think and behave like a rebel. You want to contravene the agreement and prosper. Why have you failed to research into the truth and hold on to it? How many of your fathers have prospered? Have you not sinned? Is a rebel like you not a wretched sinner?

□Your ancestors have, long time ago, sold all members of your generation to us for a price and we duly paid the price. The price of your bondage and our contractual agreement we signed, sealed and delivered. Now, you are wise; you are very clever; you are fast □ but how can you succeed in your rebellious position? Even if you had wanted to, you are not capable to pay the price.

□Your ancestors had signed and sealed the everlasting covenant and contract of failure with us, and that□s final! It is settled - no power in heaven and on earth can reverse it! We□re the never forgiving powers! We□re specialists in turning winners to losers,□ thus the seventh faceless voice came and went.

□Benlilo, you are the shameless fraudster! You want to rise above your root □ impossible! You want to arise and shine; you want to walk and run and even fly, and you are actually flying - when your fathers have all been lame and crawling, and they cannot boast of a crutch for an aid. Your father Amaldia has been servicing the debt of his father Aloiki and his ancestors, but you believe that you are very clever and so fast.

□You are certainly of the modern and jet age, and you want to evade both the debt servicing and the debt payment. Born slave boy rebel, don□t you remember your foundation □ the manner of how your pregnancy was conceived, how your mother became a wife? What right have you to say that you will neither service nor pay the debt of your progenitors? You□re the child of bewitchment. Traitor, what boldness or legal ground have you to want to disobey and betray the gods and the powers?□ that was how the eighth unseen voice of chastisement rang through.

□But, Benlilo, why are you so foolishly hard-hearted like this? For how long will you continue to run away from the gods, the gods of your fathers? Benlilo, for how long will you continue to play the rebellious soldier of the powers? You have been predestined to lead the vanguard of the youths but, now, you are loyal to and serving a strange god of the foreign land! Come home, Benlilo - come to where really you belong, come and take your rightful position in the bosom of your father! Come home, my son, and contribute your quota. Come home and prosper. Come home and invest in the business of your fathers. Come home□,□ the ninth voice, of emotional appeals together with threats, reeled off. Thus the old man pleaded, almost in tears. But for the son, he wondered meditatively:

□Home! My quota□ investment in the business of my forefathers! Which business □ of darkness and wickedness?□ □ he queried. Soonest thereafter roared the tenth, last and longest voice extra-angrily:

□Who on earth can tame the wild witchcraft dog? Who can chain the roaring lioness of darkness? The lion and lioness will not only bark; they will bite and the hardest □ yes! We are the wild-wild witchcraft dogs! We are the dangerous lions and lionesses of grimmest darkness!

□Who can know the deep more than the deep? Who can tell the space better than the space? We are the afternoon of coordinated tragedies. We are the swallowing night of bloodletting catastrophes!

□Tell glory for me tarry on mount of blood sacrifice. Bid shame the portion of our victims in their extinction by fires quenched in the hottest cold of maddening rage. We are the reigning crown of calamities! We are the lords and rulers of the night. We are the kings and powers of the primmest night. We are the biting anger of vanity and the cutting wrath of doom-insured. Benlilo, have you forgotten? You are an offspring of witches and wizards. You are from the loins of occultic gods and goddesses. You rightly belong to the gods □ where then do you run to? Where do you hide yourself small brain?□

With the last voice winding off, something invisible a power from within moved Benlilo forward to rush down, again, the slope of the hill into the house but a contrary power held him back. He regained his lost consciousness. It was then that the boy had the courage to respond to all the challenges of the unseen voices. He did not know how it happened and his mouth shouted reverberatingly:

□Unseen and unknown cowards, you are all irrational liars! I am crowned with success, victory and wealth! I am the royal prince for prosperity! I am the tree planted by the riverside; whatever I lay my hands upon shall prosper. I refuse to live by your evil tradition, unwarrantable failure or wicked family pattern!□

Hearing the contradicting response of the boy, there were impulsive outbursts of hissing and spitting inside some hideouts of the powers. Then, their eight fold short and sharp but heavily loaded reactions rolled out:

□Pride!□
□Adamant head!□
□Pomposity!□
□Obstinacy!□
□Arrogance!□
□Stubbornness!□
□Self-importance!□
□Wrong-headedness!□

Benlilo heard the exchanging unkind voices, his own retaliating tone of anger and the invisible voices□ reactions but he did not grasp their messages□ imports in full. He did know that he was the one referred to as the *rebel* and *fool* but he did not deduce that the foundation of his trouble, complete with the reason for his transplantation into the forest, was his noble ambition as juxtaposed, contrastingly, with evil family patterns, embargoes and limitations. How could he have imagined, faintly, that his family, as a block, was operating under a watertight blood covenant with powers of darkness? Still, a salvo of enquiries overran the boy□s plagued mind of reasoning:

□What is the family pattern? The family tradition, embargo and limitation? What could the voices mean by saying that I was a trail bracer, a revolutionary and a reactionary? What do they mean by the closed door? Mysteries behind the closed door? The register! Crossing the ancestral borderline and experiencing what nobody before me in the family circle has experienced? That I am a rebel and an over-ambitious rat □ but what have I done?

□The hedge, what is the hedge? What family history? But my fathers lived and live in houses, not inside holes □ and they have never been beggars or eaters of crumbs or remnants from anybody□s table! My fathers □ they were never lame or crawlers but walkers and runners. The voices boasted of the scorpion, the serpent, the dog and the lion stinging, biting and devouring □ inside this forest? What do all these mean?□

A flying javelin, full of fire, roared into work. The parable of the parasite and the tree came for mentioning and for meditation. The tree had roots but the parasite had none. The latter relied on the former for survival in life, at the same time, as it is killing the tree gradually. Was life a parasite on man or man a parasite on life?

A dog went back into its mire. A wild bull renewed its strength from a fountain of darkness. An irate eagle flew past in glaring adroitness - in all liveliness and vehemence. The flying eagle□s excitement was not for nothing. The joy of beloved ones became sorrow. The sorrowfulness was free in the market of nought. Life was the market. Sorrow was an article; joy was another item. The sadness and the joyfulness portions belonged to sons and daughters of man.

Success and victory, along with wealth, were moreover their inheritances. However, they were the gold and the diamond - deep and deeper for mining with brain and brown from inside the soil of time.

But, first, the gold deposits had got to be located inside the soil. But where were man□s eyes to see the wealth□s deposits?

CHAPTER 019

The Paths And The Project

Magic has no end in the land of magic
Stage of actualisations swiftly unfolding
Magical wonders of the powers the surplus roll
In miscellaneously cold and hot exhibitions
Time smooth in tune with the well-ordered expedition.

A QUESTIONABLY-WORKING CANDLE appeared. The candle was tall and fat as a mature human being. Later, it grew all human body parts and roared like a hungry lion. The roars vibrated through the forest down its deepest basics. The lad was upset atop the mound hill; yet, he sought not a way of escape. A spectator on amoebic life, he stayed on there.

Therefore, in exultation, the woods applauded the roaring-away being. The giant-candle-human figure had been half-white and half-black in the two fulsome colours. It was the property of three fallen angels namely, *Cembim, Semphim* and *Celephim.* At this crossroad, the second heaven, otherwise known as the heavenlies, was rent open. A voice belonging not to it reverberated:

Trials! Trials! Trials and troubles!
Lesser wills, burdened courage:
All the trials and all the troubles!

Trials! Trials! Trials and temptations!
Weaker flesh, burdened hope dipping:
All the trials and all the temptations!

Benlilo looked round to behold the speaker but he could see nobody. The heavenlies was slammed closed. Thus would the beginning of a new beginning originated for his life, but in the super-creative morning of creation, he never bargained for these!

A compost of inexperience, he did not know that the battle of life was waiting for him ever before his pregnancy was delivered inside the quoted maternity of time. He could not discern the strict truth that, whether he liked it or not, he was already a commissioned combatant soldier fighting the battle in defence of his delicate but cherished life the treasure house of his star, his glory and his destiny, all rolled into one.

The treasure life remained, of course, his ambition to be fulfilled in life and contribute his quota to the advancement of humanity; his sin stood as before: insisting on crossing the family hedge, ancestry traditions and beating the inherited patterns. By this he had sinned against the gods and goddesses of the land and incurred their torrid wrath.

Aspiring to rewrite the family history was a sin that the powers could never forgive because they were strictly conservatives or call them conservationists. This was so because, as they had confessed with their own mouths, the powers kept all the family records intact and their memory never failed on their covenants with the family unit□s line. Wanting to rewrite the family history amounted to *a great rebellion* in the kingdom of darkness. The tyrannically envious gods would not tolerate it an inch. They detested merely mentioning or hearing of it.

One of the most dishonourable moments of the exploration rolled in. An extremely wild and weird personality called *Ancient of Darkness* made his ignominious re-appearance. He was all horror and fretfulness. He lacked tolerance and whatever peace or call it rest. He was full of arrogance and tedious rigidity. Cunningness mapped out his path through the forestry district, as unhidden hard-heartedness his trademark unsympathetically outlined.

His two eyes were constantly roving. He was all anxiousness to perpetuate outsized scales of evil. He wore an ostentatious robe of bubbling demonic cheerfulness as author of unlimited sorrows. He had no fragment of shame and he could not hide. He was filled with satanic expectations for combat, the most tragic of all battles.

He was a warrior, no doubt, and conqueror of souls. All the same, the highway through which he ploughed his ill-omened strength of character across the forest was filled with cowardly and quenchable smokes of untruths. How he roared like a wounded lion!

The personality was clothed in thick darkness, as his name had indicated. He was pavilioned in sadistic tempests and hailstones. He had a revolting crown of prickles gracing his head. His body was full of poisonous arrows. A shield of steel conviction rigidly negative protected his broad chest. His helmet of abolition was also iron, but it was perforated munificently by arrays of evilness.

The cart he rode into the forestry county was of flame and grimly in gloomy exhausts. His two-edged sword was dripping with blood, human blood. Seeking for whom he would devour, he was the roaring lion of darkness mentioned by the unseen voice of cross-examination at the origin of the forestry voyage □ Benlilo could remember. The evil personality roared out his personal-extol thus in caustic pains:

□I am Ancient and King of Darkness. I am the Old Serpent. I am the Evil Genie. I am the King of Pit and Hell. I am the Master Manipulator. I am His Satanic Majesty. I am Lucifer the Morning Star! I am the Thorn on the rock□□

Consequently, the boastings of the chief of the powers conquered the entirety of the forest. Then, in a puzzlingly swift rejoinder, there was an outburst of thunder light crossways the forest and the lily-livered baleful character vamoosed. Benlilo shook warmly where he was atop the mound hill. All along, throughout the duration of the self-confessed evil king□s appearance and demonstrations, the boy was clothed substantially with fire on the hilltop. This made him untouchable to the chief ruler and authoritarian commander of the powers. For this, the king hissed irritatingly and flew away.

Still, Benlilo could not descend the mound hill against his will. A dead hen lay on her ten eggs, burdened with the mission to incubating and hatching them? The whirlwind of life raged for victims. Men, in figurative droves, crashed inside a grave and therein they decomposed. Hailstorms of life ceased not. Victims fell like the sand of the desert place and they formed domes of the graveyard of unfeeling time.

A tree, totally barren of leaves, rolled in, in a dance of hey presto. The tree hummed like a thousand angry bees. An axe of lightening came down abruptly on the tree and it smashed its concave open. A thousand pigeons thus thereby regained their freedom. How they flew blissfully in the cool air, singing sweet songs of emancipation! Life was freedom from captivity. How sweet to savour, liberty! The pigeons were not pigeons; they were human beings, their stars and destinies, as defined by their talents and ingenuities on individual basis.

Benlilo persevered in his observation of the enlightening prospects at his helpful position on the mound hilltop. An insect flew in. The latest creature had a tiny head of man but two eyes of an eagle. Yet, the insect looked exactly like a model of a Singapore built merchant ship. It soon chirped rowdily and angrily and flew into the woodland.

There was an outburst of jubilation from the hosts of darkness inside the woods to greet its impressive action. There was life in a sense of belonging. The woods thus happily received their own. There was an outburst of jubilation in the kingdom of darkness.

From the northwestern side of the forest, a dove flew in. A wolf appeared from its southeastern part. The dove raced to the centre-stage, as the wolf also ran there to devour the bird but a mighty rushing wind overpowered the wolf and it was instantly paralysed. How it crawled helplessly on the ground like an epilepsy victim! The dove flew joyously away rejoicing and singing *songs of victory:*

Adage of time, victory
By battle fought and won.

Proverb of age, victory
With holiness the mightiest weapon.

Defeat for the enemy! His languishment
In the morning of roaring war!

Thus, the beautiful bird celebrated, colourfully, its triumph over the enemy. Victory acquired was exhibition of valour. Life was the defence of the weak by the powerful. Every victory deserved celebration. The persons of the powers also obeyed the rule.

There was jubilation somewhere inside the forest but the powers remained undaunted. For, at times, their defeat or tragedy had little or no meaning to them. A *black witchcraft* power landed at a centre stage in the forest.

A *red witchcraft* personality joined her soonest. Both the black and the red witchcraft beings were soon to welcome their colleague *white witchcraft* authority. There the three powers concluded an agenda for humanity with their programme called *Operation No Mercy!*

The three witches' ONM was further nicknamed *The Project. The Project* was sub-divided into seven different parts for effective operation at execution, stage-to-stage - scrupulously. The first was called *Marine Witchcraft.* The second part was named *Household Witchcraft.* The third part was known as *Ancestral Witchcraft.*

The fourth part was called *Environmental Witchcraft.* The fifth part was *Territorial Witchcraft.* As its name suggests, the sixth category was renowned as *Geographical Witchcraft,* while the seventh and last part had the identity, *Blind Witchcraft Power.*

The second part, *Household Witchcraft* was assigned to take fullest charge of what was titled, *The Benlilo Project.* However, they were to work in effective collaboration with the other six agencies, especially the *Marine Witchcraft Power.* Finally, the date was set and the operational curriculum for *The Benlilo Project* carefully designed and launched.

Thus was the bulky file containing all the affairs of the boy's life handed over to the concerned witchcraft division. The unit's operators had no iota of time to waste; they went to work immediately. Achievement, even with the powers, was by dint of hard work. Discipline spoke for success, as determination was the voice and action of victory.

The unit went to work straight away for, in that kingdom of darkness, business meant business. Time was more valued than money. Targets, for achievements, were pursued with bubbling vigour, rigid incorporation and intensive exploration - and there was no second of a given opportunity to lose or to waste.

There appeared paths for the boy. The paths were many and invisible. There come into sight giant and minor traps to police the scores of paths. The traps doubled the number of the paths for the sound reason that the powers would not fumble with chances. What they and their workers ostracised most was failure; what they cherished best was success, otherwise known as victory. They knew that wise or clever investments would profit them the investor. They knew that carelessness or laziness profited nothing but failures and disasters.

An egg hatched a twin of a scorpion and a snake. The scorpion crawled, while the serpent flew mid air, yet, they were working for the same personality, the Evil Apparition. Both 'workmen' crowed like cocks. They bleated like sheep. Too, they were all-agitation in the course to fulfilling separate course works. They were both clothed in terrorising darkness and they flew away: life meant demonstrations.

An anthill with propellers made its impromptu appearance. A gate appeared beside the anthill. The gate spoke many local and international languages. The anthill interpreted the languages in silver-tongued grammars. Dialectics co-habited inside the linguistic anthill with racism, tribalism, nepotism, regionalism and religious bigotries in fashions.

A river tagged *Flow of Sorrow and Tears* also came in lucid view. The river rejoiced in its flood. It had drowned a number of souls and they could not be prevented from freezing. Their wailing and weeping were swallowed by time. Another lone voice noised across the forest:

'The nut of courage is hard to crack. The harvest of success is difficult to make. Survival of will is not an easy task to achieve. The bread of victory is tasking to obtain and sharp tasting. The price for living is not effortless to pay. The wine of rest and joy is easier said than done to brew. Yet, you have to pay the price in order for you to win the prize — you are indebted to pay the price! No victory comes on a platter of gold; no true victory is without a price.

'Courage cries somewhere within the woods. Yet, also therein, success longs for a claimant. Will is never silent, only suppressed; it shouts for possession in all reasons. The table is already set with bread of conquest. Behold the price of living paid with pains. See the wine of joy in a bottle of gold!□

Yet, again, Benlilo glanced on all sides to see the author of those fortifying words. He could set his eyes on nobody. The forest remained unproductive of human beings beside him. Life was unwrapped discrimination.

The boy raced down the mound hill for it was another time to move. But to where? Where was west or east, north or south? As it had been from the not-so-distant beginning, time chose to design his itinerary. History voted for the itinerary□s recording. Posterity elected to treasure it. The adventure was the testimony. The testimony was the school of life otherwise known as, at this time accepted, the University of Tears.

Though his wakefulness did not connect altogether to this, the boy Benlilo was by now an undergraduate in the universally renowned university. He had been before now passing through the citadel of testimony, as the institution of wonders was passing through him. It was a twofold responsibility of fulfilment.

The powers stood on one side, while the adolescent was on the other part.

In the intervening time, the bungalow, that `prototype of his father□s house, had vanished out of sight. The mystery forest of abstract mysteries remained rambling and mysterious.

It was yet another sweet hour of celebrations inside the *Marpolio Witchcraft Coven*. It was just as a season of *wonderful testimonies* and all the witchcraft personalities were tremendously happy. It was another beautiful moment of truthful mind outpouring and every one of them confessed:

□See me see wonder ooh, the fool brought me a gift of a brand new car and I took it □ he believed that he can bribe me with a car gift.□

□Yes, why not? He is truly a fool and foolishness kills. Swimming inside his pool of ignorance, he never can imagine that we witches can never be pacified.□

□How can the sheep ever know the way and antic of the dog? The dog is the hunter for the greater hunter and it is clever, fast and deadly!□

□Sure, comrade □ at hours of deadly operations!□

□Echoes of the ignoramus□ bones sing songs on the rooftop.□

□And he remains ignorant inside his grave till eternity dawns.□

□Do you blame him?□

□No, I don□t blame him.□

□*Eeeahh!* For the second time, that ignorant idiot gave me a cash gift of thousands.□

□Valued in the land□s currency or in hard facts?□

□In the land□s currency of rags.□

□She is a fool.□

□She thought she was doing something good □ not knowing that she was increasing her sorrow by her own hands. She too could never have comprehended the spiritual working of us witches and wizards.□

□They don□t know that with their evil gifts, we have more access into their lives. And that we are better offended and worse positioned to attack and to destroy their stars and destinies.□

□*Aahahah!* Yes, with her own hand she gave you the money gift □ isn□t it?□

□Yes, of course, with her own hand she made the gift presentation.□

□And, my good friend, you took it with your own hand.□

□Yes, I took it.□

□Thus the contact was set - so that our capturing him could be easy.□

□Exactly □ that is the testimony of her undoing herself with her own hands.

□Henceforth, now that the coast is clear, her financial base must be massively attacked. The source of her finances must dry up and her unwise action has facilitated our attack and conquest of his economic house.□

□Yes, the car and the money gifts are our joint point of contact against the senseless maggots.□

□They are using their own hands to destroy, not only their present but their future as well.□

□Beauty runs errands for ugliness and errands work out fires for the messengers□

□For the sake of erroneous sentiment that we could be induced.□

□They don□t really know who we witches and wizards, rulers of the night are.□

□They don□t know who they are trading with inside the market of time cruel and candidly soulless.□

□They don□t know that we are the dark ploughs through alleyways of riches and wealth.□

□Magically working treasures of gold and diamond to become ashes.□

□In the night or at noon of flawlessly coordinated tragedies. Ashes for beauty and it is settled in the heavenly place.□

□Our victims, are crying but we are rejoicing. They must cough out blood. The scorpion sting to kill and compromise is never the asset of the fiery serpent.□

□Very unserious minds, they thought they could alter the decision of the gods.□

□We are the constant evil manifestations of all night.□

□The gods have passed their judgment but somebody somewhere is arguing unwisely. The powers have decreed a thing and someone doubts. Who can alter the conclusion of the night? Who dare to fault the decision of the deities?□

□The crazy one believed, most erroneously, that he can bribe me with his worthless gift of a car □ what a shame! He could never know that I am the slaveholder who it is impossible to satisfy. I swear by the gods, I will increase his portion of affliction. I will double the grip of my witchcraft rope around his thin neck and strangulate him. Enough has got to be enough □ he deserves an immediate strangulation! He must die!□

□Tell me, friends, who can bribe the sun not to scorch at noon? Who can corrupt the dry season fire so as not to burn and consume? We are the hungry and angry rampaging fire; we are the noon sun of anger and wrath!□

□Don□t mind the fool - he is the Good Samaritan of a farmer - sowing his seed of goodness for a witch in the vineyard of witchcraft.□

□Yes! in order to reap goodness and kindness □ but either he forgets or he never knows. Those of yesterday who showed us love, with what have we repaid them, brethren?□

□We have wined with their blood and dined with their meat □ *ah-eeh-aaaahah!* We have wasted their destinies and traded with their lousy stars.*"*

□She is the woman of conscience with a heart of love.□

□The Christian pilgrim going to heaven or is it Paradise?□

□The beautiful damsel dancing to the beat of death □ *walahi-talai,* I will teach her the greatest lesson of her earthly life!□

□To know that we witches don□t tolerate any nonsense from any quarter - whatever the opposite quarter.□

□Her bones singing the song of celebration on the rooftop.□

□After the delicious flesh and her syrupy blood are gone in the pathway of our bellies.□

□I will strike at her the very hardest □ she will fall. There will be an outbreak of mourning, lamentation and sorrowing in his household but we shall celebrate and rejoice. Or who is she by the way to survive the witchcraft attack?□

□We are in the season of wickedness and immeasurable cruelty mixed as a strong wine. We are the slaughtering warriors who toast with the sweetest wine of blood.□

□In witchcraft cocktail parties of callousness and evilness □ yes! as a mixture of raging indignation.□

□Blow out her heart! Roast it on the fire by the altar and it will smell sweet □ oh, very very pleasant! Incredibly appetising and enjoyably good for your body.□

□You trust, colleagues, you can bet with your life on my behalf! The beauty of witchcraft powering is in killing human beings for food; the witchcraft glory is in settling of scores □ better in sacrificing to the gods of the night.□

□Yes, by this, comrades, the investments of the night will multiply. The will of the gods shall be fulfilled and their judgments confirmed.□

□The night will remain the night and absolutely nothing shall change the day to become the night. The day is a coward but the night is the fighter. For at wisely coordinated night of networking, heads of fools roll off their necks and their bodies are butchered in abattoirs of soulless time.□

□We are warriors of the valley and of the game □ driving our forces of chariots of flames into human treasures. We are the hardhearted destroyers, annihilators and crucifiers.□

□Tell the fools to continue with their *goodness,* I mean foolishness □ we remain evil as far as we are con concerned. This is the way we are and nothing can change our permanent nature. We are the leopard that can never change its spots.□

□Comrades of the night, let□s celebrate for our victory won through the spiritual contacts, the gifts of car and money □ lets rejoice in the god and goddesses and go straight to work.□

□We toast to their devastating destructions.□

□*Yee-yee!*□

□Kudos to the never-failing-power of the witchcraft cult.□

□All hail our Mother the doughty Queen of the Coast.□

□Hip-hip-hipipip!

□Hip-hip-hipipip!

□Hip-hip-hipipip!□

□Hurrah!□

CHAPTER 020

The Trapped Woman

Entraps are set and they collect propitiations;
Animals of the forest are the targets of the traps.
Dearly beloved friend, beware of lust for quick riches
For poverty masquerades as prosperity in the market of money,
While mercy and peace there flee far from the lost money-monger.

AFTERNOON TIME. RAYS of the burning sun perforated greens to heat and to burn flesh like fire. Still, the scorching sun was comforting to the greens □ what another brand of natural mystification! The greens rejoiced in good radiance. Life was sunshine and rainfall. Space longed for belonging. The floating breeze commemorated in accomplishment; time recorded all the developmental stages for posterity.

At alternating episodes of concise or lengthy disclosures, the lone voice, true representative of either or not of the powers, never ceased to travel cater-cornered the forestry quarter. This time around, the revelation was that of an elderly storyteller. It rolled through a distasteful labyrinth of a storyline:

□Son of man, dregs of riches and wealth of money are filthy,□ the voice sounded plainly in the ear of Benlilo. The narrative ran furthermore:

□There was once a pretty woman trader but poor. She was married and the matrimony was blessed with, surprisingly, five hale, hearty and brilliant children □ three girls and two boys. She, her husband and all the five children lived inside a one-room apartment in the suburb of the city. There, always, they fed on the bread of malnourishment.

□By her petty trading, the woman was a hawker of oranges and sweet potatoes on the streets, while her husband was a factory labourer on a miserable monthly earning. Long often therefore did sadness and grumbling tarry in their home. The downbeat voice was that of suffering. This was so because failure is the most tragic aspect of the human life. Poverty is a curse. It is one of the mightiest evils of all ages!

□The poverty-stricken woman had an intimate friend in the trade. The close colleague would later disappear, without forewarning, off the orange and sweet potato hawking scene. She later re-appeared inside an expensive four-wheel runner jeep □ gorgeously attired to the envy of high society ladies of the time. Her complexion had won a glittering look. The hair on her head had grown long and beautiful. In brevity, she was now all elegance - how manage?

□The first woman became inquisitive. Her inquisitiveness was tasked the hardest. The totality of her life got hooked to the challenge, the depth of which was shrouded, to her, in a mystery - mystery of the other side of life. Flashes of deep questions and answers raced through her restless mind. She became literally mad when she got to the ultra-modern mansion of her friend in the most expensive and exclusive area of the city □ where the wealthy, the richest and the royalties of the society were livingly luxuriating. After much an exercise of eagerness and probing, the second woman promised to introduce her *good friend* to her new trade and she was all gratitude.

□The appointment date and time were fixed. Thus would history set for her another *brand new opening.* The poor woman hawker was greatly relieved. She was all thankfulness to this personal friend. She was full of scintillating expectations. Songs of hope expelled those of despair from her tongue. Optimism for a better future started to flow like a big river in her heart.

□The appointed date and time came quickly and their limousine soon marked its way into a impressive castle worth billions in construction. The people who opened the main gate for them were different from the people who opened the door of the jeep to welcome them. Those who ushered hem into the palatial mansion were different people from those who asked them for their choice drinks and refreshments. Those servants who did that were different from the security men who took their positions in and around the magnificent palace.

□Both friends met themselves inside a palatial sitting room luxuriously furnished. Differently uniformed male and female messengers appeared from different directions and they were treated to choice drinks and classical food items. Later, they were invited into another flamboyantly furnished sitting room where they met with a man who, with wooing smiles, offered them his warm welcome. The first woman knew fully what was happening but the second woman did not suspect that the man□s toothy smiles were a trap, more of hovering fatality!

□Here the big business started. Yet, an incubating egg that was yet to hatch should not have been celebrated. It could hatch into a vulture instead of the expected dove: life is full of wonderful surprises. It is the market of the blind. Of pleasures and embarrassments.

□Snappily, the male host interviewed the second woman guest in regard of her newly chosen area of interest, business-wise. She was interested in the distribution of some imported materials. The other chapter of the real business got opened□

□For, right in the presence of the first woman, the man moved closer to the second woman on the sofa. He held her left hand and pinned an injection needle into her flesh to draw blood. The woman groaned aloud but she was helpless □ by now captured! Her two eyes opened, she had and with her own two legs, walked into a trap, an enemy□s captivity - so soon.

□She could see clearly that the man was not a nurse or a medical doctor. By the way, was she in the place to receive medical treatment or to seek a way to the land of fortune in emergency riches and wealth? She was yet to suspect that blood was the highway to the land flowing with quick money and sudden wealth. Dire premonitions! A surge of anxious terror raced through her mind. Her heartbeat jumped rapidly but she was helpless; she had embarked on a journey of no return!

□*This is strange!* The man drew his own blood and mixed it with that of the woman. The second woman would not understand the new state into which she had optimistically walked. The first woman watched with casual interest. She had grown into an experienced hand of a recruitment officer in the trade. To her, the unfolding scenario had little meaning now. She looked on. The ritual exercise had just started.

□The man drank a little of the blood and the second woman was made to drink a small portion, while the remaining quantity, inside the bottle, was taken into an inner room for keeps by the host. The purpose of the third part of the blood was to henceforth serve as a *remote control* against the life of the second woman in the mounting business arrangement and management, more of a deal.

□What this means is that should the woman dare to □misbehave or betray□ the blood covenant in any way, she would be dealt with the most ruthless way cultic. Any evil or good done to the secret part would affect, in whole, the portion working either in her disfavour or in favour.

□A creepy silence of loathsome glorification continued to rule the air. The man soon re-appeared, now only in a woolly-white towel wrapped around his waist □ smiling like a new bridegroom for an additional soul that had been gained for darkness, the middle point of the initiation ritual had been reached.

□The new initiate, the woman could not have rejected any of the deadly options because inside her heart, something continued to whisper that her life was strictly on the line. The atmosphere smelled wild occultism. Two young men and a rascally dressed lady, in their twenties, walked freely about the place. The men were nattily suited in all black, including dark glasses, and ebony-shinning shoes. They had their short powerful guns visibly drawn, as two double-edged daggers, each inside its sheath, were hanging tidily on their bodies.

□From all indications, the two young men and the hooligan-looking lady were no-nonsense killers! For this, the only available option before the defenceless woman was her highest cooperation with the human powers inside their dens.

□There was absolutely nothing to be ashamed of. The man stripped himself naked before the two women. He moved nearer the second woman on the sofa and started to undress her. Smiling like a boar pig, he first removed her head tie and placed it somewhere gently in a demonstrative act so amusing. In reaction to this, the first woman laughed coolly.

□Then, the man detached the second woman□s top wear and wrapper before her under-wears. The friend who was introducing her to the cultism of moneymaking had donated all the wears freely to her. Had it not been that she was capturing another soul for cultism, she could never have given her the native wares, including a pair of costly shoes.

"The woman shrieked but her salvation was far-gone. In addition to her *enjoyment*, the second woman continued to watch the □beautiful situation and sensation□ as they were unfolding □ life was a theatre □ real show business of the silly. As dear as they were, she had never seen the nakedness of her friend; now, she could boast of it. She too had gone through the same ritualistic process as introduced by someone else, another *friendly* woman. Watching them in the *interesting* act, the first woman sang:

Master sexist, make sure you satisfy my friend.
My friend, make sure you satisfy the master sexist,
Life is mutual understanding in the accord
Blood covenant of the highest seal.

□At this point, the woman was already bewitched and both her and the man were down on the rug engaged in hot love-making right in the presence of the first woman who was drinking choice wine as fish drinks water inside the deep. And while the man and the second woman were engaged in the sizzling sexual game, the man and the first woman conversed, smiled and laughed hilariously, truly the satisfied African village boar pig on a heap of filth.

□With the man operating under the influence of hard drug, they soon went into the second round of the sexual exercise and then into its third and concluding stage. They finished and the second round of the initiation was satisfactorily achieved according to the lustful taste of the man. Thus was the blood accord written, signed, sealed and delivered.

□The third stage of the overall ritual theatre was performed when the latest lovers were back fully in their clothes and the man issued to the woman a small note addressed to someone, a Lebanese, in the heart of the city. Her friend, the first woman was to lead her there. She had now become a full-fledged member of the money cult and every new soul she could bring in would earn her a promotion or at least a bonus of wealth.

Meanwhile, having now regained her consciousness, the new initiate was fraught with highbred irritation in awful regrets. While on the way inside the limousine jeep, she burst amidst solemnly streaming tears:

□Friend, but why? You never told me all those?□ she asked in swanky frustration.

□Good friend, yes! because you want to become rich like me. How dare I? Did you know the source of my money and riches? Have you ever asked? But, now, you□ve known! Where□s the clean money? Do you not know that dregs of worldly wealth and riches are dirty and maggots filled? No fool of a woman friend would tell you. I am not a fool and I will never behave like one.

□Dear friend, experience is the best teacher. I also underwent the same routine □ just normal!□ the first woman answered with an all-tone of irrevocability, throwing away her face like a heartless harlot. All the same, the first woman was weighed down by wild embarrassments. She cried in untold anguish:

□Oh, friend! you say just normal?□ she queried.

□Yes, just normal!□ the friend answered and quickly added, □Or what□s new under the heaven?□
Silence!

□The trapped woman was horror-struck. Far therefore from satisfaction and writhing inside of her the mud of irksome pains, she remarked lamentably:

□But, friend, I had thought that you would be taking me to a church!□

□Ah, church! To go and see a Pastor or a Reverend Father? To fast and to pray? To seek and to knock? *Aaahaaaah!* Church! How funny and childish you are, friend! You irritate me, really! You are not mature at all! You have not yet become the ideal city woman of substance. Far-far from the society lady go-getter. How negative you are? Do you find money in church? Inside the house of God? No, my friend, no! You find money inside a dirty place. You can only discover and own wealth , worldly emergency wealth right inside the house of Satan and where I have taken you to is not the wrong place. It is the right place: house of Mammon whose surname is Satan,□ submitted the first woman cultist.

□But, still, friend, I never expected all those horrible things!□ the second cultic woman reacted angrily and agonisingly. In response to her submission, her friend became angrier. She barked into her face:

□You had expected good from inside the house of Satan? Ignorant woman! Offspring of the lamb! Never-satisfying-daughter-of-Eve, tell me, what exactly did you expect? You had expected showers of prayer and magical baptism of money! *(Now aside in a commune of a kind, carried away and worshipping her god of money:)* Oh money, my dearest god □ you□re the mightiest cord of unity for the human world! You□re the most important and almightiest deity of the human universe!□ The estranged friend thought she had finished reciting her eulogy of money but she was mistaken.

□Man made money and money makes man □ which is more important? Who will elect not to be a friend of the rich woman? Where is the foolish person who will nurse enmity with money? Money answers all things. Money announces its possessor□s arrival. Seeing is believing, my sister. No laudable ides comes into fruition in the absence of money. My dear friend, the realistic truth is that poverty is the worse evil that can befall a person □ deadlier than death, *aah!*

□Money answers all things; money makes the youngest to become the eldest in the family. Money reformulates the slave to become the master. Money constructs the way where there is no way. Money answers for everything everywhere and anytime. When you have money, you are queen but when you are poor, you are the slave. When you have money, your voice will weigh heavy, in tones □ not in ounces or pounds, but in gold and diamond in the gathering of men and women of substance. Money □ oh my darling money, you are the generator of boldness, rest, comfort, joy and abundance.

□As for me, early in life, I made up my mind never to have anything whatsoever to do with the evil called poverty. I made poverty my enemy and it promptly made me its archenemy. To be economical with words, I reject poverty in its entirety.

□Money, oh money! The greatest human social invention. Is it not you money, my god, which says, □Let no human being deliberate or conclude on any important issue of life in my absence?□ The senior money-trader-for-souls had talked as if she was swimming inside a pool of blissful recreation. Then,

□My stupid friend! where□s the free gift?□ she asked a question, which she swiftly answered by herself: □My sheep friend, I assure you, there□s no free money anywhere in the whole human world, search out - north, south, west, east or centre!□ You pay a price to have something and especially money. There□s no free money in the market of human life.□

□The senior cultist woman had burst into a session of sneering laughter before her last frank explanations. Her core message to the friend was that she had already bartered her single life, her soul, for emergency wealth and riches. The gods had captured a faithful. A conjured stillness took over the atmosphere. They progressed on their journey.

□The fourth and last, for now, segment of the business ceremony was concretised when the two women *friends* arrived the premises of a multi-national company where the Lebanese was director of affairs in their chauffeur driven custom built jeep. They were almost immediately ushered into the presence of the managing director, who had been eagerly expecting them, right inside his large and luxuriously furnished private room. He offered them his *warm* welcome. He wasted no second. He asked in the appropriate cultic slang:

□I believe the Patron has matured our dear friend?□

□Yes, of course!□ it was the first woman who answered, smiling gratification.

□I trust!□ the man smiled merrily in return. He moved near the second woman visitor and pulled up her clothe by the armpit. He also brought out an injection needle and drew blood from there. He drew his own blood and mixed the two together. He drank three drops and gave his newest visitor three drips and he kept the remaining quantity. The initiation ritual of the blood covenant fully completed, the overall chief executive then issued a note to her. The note was jointly addressed to the company□s warehouse controller and the chief accountant.

□All night long, the extraordinarily spacious warehouse was always filled to the brim with finished goods of thousands of brands from all countries of the world - every one of them neatly packed inside their suitable cartons. Without an exception, the goods were manufactured in a satanic factory beneath the Atlantic Ocean by the Port-Harcourt axis of the Nigerian Nation. The suppliers were workmen ghosts from the dark world. All the operations formed a network of pure magic - very difficult to believe but the unprocessed truth.

□*All for free,* the controller was to disburse five thousand cartons, each, of sixteen brands of imported products to the second woman, while the accountant would give her a cash of five million notes of a particular currency. Life was thus renewed for the once-poverty-afflicted woman.

□That was how she *luckily* crossed the land of poverty and melancholy to that of riches and prosperity, so dramatically. She soon had fat local and foreign bank accounts, investments, buoyant company shares and landed property all over the city. To her, life was opportunity, even in the wickedest way but where was the profit?

□She had gained a microscopic portion of the world only to lose her soul! Meanwhile, she had purposely quarrelled with her husband and divorced *the poor man.* She told the man that he was no more her match and that she would henceforth have nothing to do with poverty till the rest of her life. She replaced the prefix *Mrs.* of her name with *Ms.*

□The price of conjured success is high! Highly unreasonable! For unknown to the enriched woman, the blood covenant was to be sustained with bloodshed, one of her five children every year, as the wealth had the life span of five years. That was not all: every night at a particular time, she was to dine and wine on a particular filth pit somewhere in the outskirts of the city.

□In addition, she was, for the remaining part of her life, to nurse a large sore directly in her private part. Finally, she was billed to die on the very day that the blood covenant would complete five years. All these made up the price for the emergency wealth of money.

□She is very much in lust to become rich like me and I will help her. She must know that imitation is the greatest killer. Myself I am seriously regretting ever trekking this path but she□s so eager to come on,□ the friend and first woman had concluded, crowned with a bitter laughter. The gods and the goddesses nodded their heads in concurrence. They exchanged agreeable looks; they laughed.

□So therefore, because she had been so much desperate *to fly out* of her poor condition into riches, the whole deal had been negotiated, signed and completed on her behalf by her *good* friend, ever before their journey. The friend had settled for her a contractual agreement ill affordable, at her peril and the gods had been happier. Trading with the devil could be that expensive, eating at his table was for her more than death. The poor woman did not realise that she was flying out of peace and out of life. She never imagined that she was courting wild enmity with joy and with hope.

□The satanic price was to be paid on an instalmental arrangement but often in advance. So immediately the quick wealth and the riches manifested, the virginal sore did not hide itself and the eldest child, a son, of the now wealthy and divorced woman became the only casualty of a ghastly motor accident. The estranged ex-husband mourned pathetically.

□The woman wailed and wept and mourned but her wealth multiplied. Her chain of sorrows got elongated when the first year rolled by and the sore magnified and her second child, a daughter and four hundred level undergraduate student of Chemistry major at the university, died mysteriously. When the mother could no longer bear the raining overlying burdens, mid the year, she lost her senses and she started to vomit abominable confessions at a public square in the heart of the city.

□Her colleagues in cultism were unforgivably embarrassed; they vowed to settle for nothing else but an act of vengeance. One night of horror mercilessly exercised, therefore, the woman was kidnapped and she was never again to be seen in life. The price of living is too exorbitant for the wicked.

□The chief prize of life is contentment in godliness, the greatest achievement of the wise. It is only the fool who envies the wicked!□

At the end of the report, Benlilo shook his head a couple of times dismally. *Wealth and riches are honourable but the lust for them is tragically dishonourable!* He promised himself never to play the ignominious role of a money-monger in life.

□Money will be my messenger; I will never, in my lifetime, be a messenger or slave or lunatic of money but its manager and controller,□ the young man guaranteed himself in all self-confidence.

CHAPTER 021

Compound Field Of Tragicomedies

A populated field of speculations, this life,
Flying moments of jokes in all seriousness!
Success cries for belonging, failure echoes,
Life plain and deep to the mountaintop flies
With man between cheerless day and peerless night.

THUS THE UNSEEN voice narrated the tragic story of the *trapped woman* and the anecdote winded off. Not long after that, another voice echoed and Benlilo re-adjusted himself. Having now been used to the routine of hearing, he remained a bundle of attention, as the new message wobbled out:

□Inside a forest, one finds big and small trees. One discovers little and huge fishes and other sea creatures inside the deep. Both giant and tiny birds and fowls ply the skyway that is so spacious. Hence oppression and suppression rule the sky, as well as the forest and the deep.

□Animals devour animals in the forest. Birds of the sky oppress, suppress, attack and eat one another. Fishes swallow fishes inside the stream, river and sea. Men and women are lovers and haters. They profit and consume one another in the human planet: life is injustice and unfairness.

□Time is the master of events. Money authorises majority of man□s needs. The weeping and talking ghost is right: money has emerged the most popular god of the human race! Age is lower than rage. Greatness is endearing to civilization. Courage conquers all fears. Hope dwindles in the channel of horror. It flourishes on the mountaintop of heroism. Cowardice is catalyst for death □ man is dying because he is afraid of death.

□The very hour that man conquers the fear of death is the very moment that he conquers death. It is the exact minute he begins to live. For the major gateway to the death□s enclave is timidity. Familiarity is the best trainer. Philosophy is its definer. History feeds on the flesh of eventful life. Favour is baptism of mercy. Love is the crown of all laws. It perfects all things in words and by deeds.

□Who can unravel all mysteries? It is only Mystery who knows all mysteries. Darkness recognises darkness and it appreciates light and trembles before it. The light honours light and chases away the darkness. The day is twenty-four hours □ twelve hours of darkness and twelve hours of light. It is the same twice over dozen hours of testimonies of good and evil.

□Proofs abound in the land flowing with rejoicings, tears and mourning. Glories wane and wither in the homeland of negativity. Beauty there fades as a labourer□s spent uniform in the workshop of cruel season. Beware! wasters of life have run amok. They devastate talents □ mean human resources. The deepness of the pit of life has no gauge. It is ever insatiable. It swallows stars and glories by careers and destinies. Helpless owners of those talents weep and wail uncontrollably. They are all victims robbed of their endowed intrinsic worth.

□The night vibrates to overthrowing the anointing of the day. The price of war is too exorbitant for the warring man to pay. The dry season threatens to swallow the wet one and erase all traces of its achievements. Hate conquers love without concession. None of the elemental forces competes with the soil because the earth is the mother of all - ask Laala. The night is far-gone; the new morning is near with its groundbreaking messages and expectations.

□The sun soon shall rise to shine, to scorch and to burn. Yet, afternoon is precious. The evening, too, is pleasant. Memories of the past night transmit shivers into man's spines. An envisaged reminiscence of the coming night robs the man of the peace for which the Creator ordered the night in the first place - all because the night has been commandeered and abused by the powers and the gods.

□Who can argue against destiny? Only the fool - only the wicked argues against destiny. The work that has been completed and perfected, who can alter or stop it? Only the fool, only the wicked would try it. Whatever the Almighty One has decreed to happen, who can decree it out of existence? Who can alter the courses of the stars and rob the moon of her illumination? Who can cover the glory of the sun and drain the ocean of its water? 0nly he who can do this can fault the Almighty Creator!

□Victory is gold for the victor but defeat ashes for the vanquished. The dog that journeyed into the den of the lion and came back is surely destined for greatness. The cat of grudge crawls along the story path - yet, it is as fast as lightening. The journey of life is wearisome. Still, the same life becomes two for half a nonentity.

□Yes! there is death lurking at the corner along the journey. The death is preceded with a battle. The battle heralds birth. Before the birth was an abomination. The abomination was an inheritance. The inheritance runs from generation to generation. It forms a foundation. The foundation withstands all things fine and it succumbs to all stuffs bad. It echoes songs of success and mantras of failure. It crows hymns of defeat, as it hoots rhythms of victory.

□There is a field called *mystery*. Thereon, a fowl swallows an antelope. A rabbit vomits an elephant. An insect eats a bush cow. A cricket threw up a snake □ life is a two-way action - the ending competes with the beginning. Life is a dual carrier of minus and plus. It is a straight of dilemmatic mystery, going by calculation.

□Fear rules in the street. Yet, *joy* beckons man to come and dwell in the street. Terror rules the season, as horror the era - yet, ambitious man longs to own both the season and the era. The grave labours in pain of plenty and in glory of vanity. The drain cries for vengeance. The pond bemoans its stinking state. It groans under the burden of creation. The dry well remains dry; the rain has not failed in its season.

□The plain wields its power in plainness. The mountain remains unsatisfied by complications. It hungrily longs to reach heaven but Heaven will not permit an unholy competition. □Stay your ambition wild where you are,□ the Heaven orders the go-getting mountain. The mountain has no choice other than to obey. It was a mere creature; the commanding voice was that of the Creator. Holy embargo is no sin, alike righteous limitation. Only sacrilegious family patterns are evil.

□Lies flourish in the garden of sinful time. Treasures of life are difficult to find and much harder to mine in a season of hunger for wealth. Tales perpetuate for men to cherish in the land of the living. The unenthusiastic lords itself over the enthusiastic. Era befriends and it defrauds. □The beautiful ones are not yet born□; ugly children of men filled streets in elegant arrogance.

□They knew nothing but they claim to know all things. Then, there are roars of jubilation instead of echoes of lamentation. There are rivers of cheers instead of flows of tears. There are reverses of goodness. Failure trademarks the path of honour, as success eludes men.

□Foolishness wars with wisdom and it overcomes. The lost is found and lost. The dead rises up and it swallows the living because the living is not actually living. Benlilo, do you know that several great men and women of the world are swallowed up at infancy? If in doubt, ask the grave. Probe the cemetery. Yet, the bereaved refuses to be sorrowful. Life is shallow and deep. It is liberalism and extremism.□

That was how yet another voice would come and go. Over again, the lad Benlilo looked round but he could behold nobody. A rainfall loomed in the sky. Thick clouds darkened the firmament. Flashes of lightening roared across the same sky. He wondered audibly if the looming rainfall would meet him inside the forest.

The lightening flashes whistled different tunes of possession to hail and to herald the dim clouds. The earth waited intolerantly to receive the heavenly blessing. Greens made merriments in all anticipations. Plenteous harvests awaited the land. Life is sowing and reaping.

Another experience: the door of day was opened; that of night closed. The gate of success got flung open; that of failure shut. Shouts of victory rent the air against cries of defeat. The dugout sank into greater harassment. The plain venerated in triumph. The mountain remained now contended. Glory was born at creation. Hope stood lost and found with man. The season sided and it betrayed; life remained a two-edged sword. It is really a tale of tragicomedies!

Three differing butterflies appeared in sight. They were irately aggressive. They flew round and about in a fierce competition. The first butterfly was golden red in colour. The second butterfly was yellow, while the third one appeared in rose colour. They sang a homogeneous song of war. The lad Benlilo would not know who their enemies were.

The three butterflies were warriors. They were all able and disabled agents of the powers. They would not accommodate any baloney or insignificance. They were the conquerors of the weak. They were spirits in forms of butterflies. They were all, individually, as big as mature bats. They were fierce eagles of the striking season. Doing battles was their vision and mission.

The lad met himself by a riverside. The river was dirty and stinking □ maybe it was the river he had seen in the beginning of the trouble. Wild frogs populated its inn, as they hymned a uniform tune very unpleasant to the ear. The wild frogs too were celebrating the gift of life.

The river was wide and it flowed sluggishly down a slope. Waterleaves and low shrubs covered its banks, overshadowing uncountable heaps of mud. There were various odd and cool sounds of water creatures from the deep. For Benlilo, it was a memorable morning.

The boy, alienated though he was, stood by the river shore and he surveyed the new environment. He burst into a sort of over-elaborate smile, not knowing any reason for it. Again, he stood still and gazed into the river as if an event was about to emerge from there. Premonition stood him still by the river and he stably gazed into it.

A completely new chapter of the storyline of his life was about to be opened and posterity stood to be the beneficiary thereof. The adventure schemed to manifest its proper colour. Though, ahead of that, a newest voice of the anonymous ran through the moody forest:

Life runs in good and bad revelations
The beauty of life is the ugliness of it
Morning of love and hate rolling by
Deeds of suspense and surprise arraying:
It is the groundwork of things to come,
History in the making, posterity in build-ups.

Life is an irony for an event did, in actuality, emerge from the bowel of the river. Within one hundred and twenty seconds of Benlilo□s constant gaze into the big river, a monster came into view from it. The water was greatly troubled. It breathed heavily, as the monster was rising up from its distance downward.

Observer Benlilo heard some human voices eulogising the beast, as it was speedily making its magnificent but ignominious appearance from the depth of the river. Human voices echoing from the bowel of a river? Unbelievable! The boy could hardly believe his ears and eyes. For this reason, he was resolutely arrested to the scene, as the human voices relayed their message:

Warrior of warriors, soldier of soldiers,
Welcome onto the battlefield of life
Welcome! Oh welcome!

Valiant fighter of fighters, welcome!
Great your commission, the battle you□ve won
In no time the fool destroy and devour!

Benlilo became frightened with the worrisome wordings of the song; no doubt, it was a volley of arrow into his brain and his mind of reasoning. He wondered what the human voices eulogisers meant by their warfare gobbledygook! Again, he wondered worriedly how human voices could be booming from the inn of a river!

Afterwards, he remembered that he was still inside the mystery forest of mysteries.

With those eulogies, the rising beast became better energised to record its appearance from the water. Upon its appearance, the monster's head was like the iron-cast of a lion. It had two sharp and pointing horns on the head. It was equipped with three unalike big eyes. The first two eyes were positioned beside the nose, while the third one appeared in its forehead.

The first, in its left side, was blue and white in colour. The second, in the right side, was yellow and pallid, while the third, directly in the forehead, was diamond-like with a golden bisect. In brevity, all the three enormous eyes radiated and transmitted hate and live fire as signals. They all scared to death!

The monster's mouth was that of a wolf, while its two fore limbs had many fingers with terrifying claws, all as sharp as shaver blades. Its whole body was that of an enormous leopard and it was graced with minuscule thorns — all also with cutthroat sharp ends — thirsty for flesh and blood? Yes, of course!

The long and fat body too boasted of a very long tail of ash colour. It very much resembled the tail of an imposing Australian crocodile. Above all, the beast looked hungry and irate a madcap carnivorous animal. It was undoubtedly poised for war and it had no atom of time to waste. No endurance to exercise. No conciliation.

This is death, callously soulless death! the conclusion raced through Benlilo's jumping heart. The terrified lad's look got distorted on the spot. Nevertheless, he re-affirmed his chief goal in life — not to die but to live.

He ran—

Through rough and smooth
The forestry journey of life—

PART THREE (A):
THE ADVENTURE

The green snake bites
The black scorpion stings
The brown insect chirps
The white bird sings
Yet, love is sweeter a thing
Than thousands of kisses— rings.

CHAPTER 022

Gun Shoot! The Race Starts

Race of life tougher than a child□s imagination,
Beauty of survival hidden in ugliness of its battle;
The genesis of horror is like a comic story of fun
Beginning of history between benevolence and malevolence
With nature and elemental forces serving as their viewers.

Yes! BENLILO COULD not be manly enough to wait for the beast to emerge fully from the river. For his person not to experience realistic evil, his total body parts must serve as the collective solution □ he quickly reasoned out the conclusion. Accordingly, he commanded his standing-by two feet to carry him to safety, whatever safety, as fast as possible □ and they obeyed him.

But more than that, at this most rebellious moment of his life, how he had wished he could grow the wings of an eagle and fly out of the forestry danger zone into safety □ the safety of his father□s house! He was hostilely saddened; he could not grow a wing! He remained a human being on the ground. Helpless but without losing a bit of hope. Neither did fear of the emerging beast hold him down, nor did his reasoning fly away from his brain. The invisible wind spoke a seemingly meaningless paraphrase and Benlilo could hear its voice specifically:

Through rough and smooth
The forestry journey of life□

As the gigantic monster rose from the water with its two forelimbs up into the sky and ready to leap out of the water and pounce on him, Benlilo did not shout for help. In fact, there was no such around. No indication of human existence inside the mystery forest of mysteries. He simply commanded his heels into a swift action; thank goodness! he was a leading star 100-metre runner in his school. His only consolation was the realism that if he had no wings to fly, he had two legs to run with. And he was right. The two legs became light. They waxed eager to do what they knew best how to do, as at foretimes.

The boy ran manically for his dear life. The fearsome river beast pursued him fiercely. Yet, he was completely lost. He could not understand the competition going on with him an active partaker. He could not understand the reason or reasons behind it. Nevertheless, he increased his speed, as the monster doubled its. The race soon graduated into a matter of life and death. The whole forestry environment became terrified. The foundation of the forest gave the impression of being in danger of extinction with stimulating and demoralising vibrations.

Inside and outside, as the eulogistic song had declared, the monster was fortified with and propelled by the raging hope of capturing the lad quickly and devouring him at once but it was mistaken. The little human soul Benlilo was resolutely determined to keep his life intact, as the enemy was at robbing him of it. Thus, the race, as a game, began and it intensified, whereby the greens and other forestry feature served as spectators.

As the show progressed, there were no cheers but silence - uneven quietness of nonchalance and concern from the natural and unnatural audience visible and invisible. The trees became cheerless. Their greens remained in their positions however. The sweet breeze never ceased to flow. The running boy was soon covered in sweats. The pursuing beast too faced an uphill task, as its anticipated hope was not materialising quickly.

This, all the same, did not mean that the pursuer was in any way discouraged □ no!

Benlilo stole a flashy look at the monstrously carnivorous beast that, like an angry elephant, ploughed its way through the multipart forest in order to catch up with him. He was confident that, despite the enormity of its size and high speed, the pursuer would not be able to catch up with him □ even as time desired to prove him right or wrong.

He invested more efforts, whirling through the shrubs and trees, as the lion-like monster too manipulated its way unbelievably all the way through them. For its sheer size, the shrubs and small greens looked as if to give way like little children awe-struck at the passage of a cavalcade.

Soon, Benlilo met himself again by the bank of a *bigger* river. Something told the lad that it must have been the same river in a transformation of deception. The water of the river was now gem clear like spring water; unlike before that it was dirty and fetid smelling. The river had coiled through the forest flowingly.

The river-flow appeared cool and loving. It showed no sign of anger whatsoever. Now, it crowed not, neither did it whistle. It paraded no cone show as a trademark of its predictive hazard. It flowed smoothly down the slope in a curvaceous style of all natural friendliness but it was all lies! The boy got to the riverbank, as the monster approached agitatedly.

He weighed, for a minute, the option of jumping into the river, shallow or deep, and finding his way to the other bank of it. But, immediately, he remembered that the monster had emerged from a river in the first place. How dare he willingly jump into premature death? He reasoned that the river could be an enemy after all □ the same enemy. Alternatively, if a friend, why had he released such a fear-provoking monster after him in the first instance?

Therefore, he discarded that option of jumping into the river straightway. One must dump foolishness and embrace wisdom, □once bitten, twice shy.□ He sped along the bank and then ran back into the thick forest through an inlet of four trees in a row. The four trees formed a traversal opening. The lad had concluded, rightly, that running the race on an open place would be advantageous to his inhumane pursuer. The trees lost their coldness, as he so did. They now cheered him happily to the damnation of the beastly pursuer.

Yet, the eulogistic voices would not stop to boom from the bosom of the river, now far away. In fact, it seemed that the human voices of energy were accurately trailing the runners, as they ran their races through the forest. Louder they showered their eulogies on the lion-like monster:

Beast of beasts, never you be discouraged!
Beast of sure nation, power! Might! Power!
Lion of the tribe of darkness, lose no hope
Your smooth way you must have thorough,
Your moment of war exercised for worse -
The fool slain and devoured at the go!

Again, the beast was unspeakably invigorated. On the other side of the barricade formed by the four trees, Benlilo stood at a distance. He watched the fearful beast struggle to get him with a finger that the little opening could accommodate. The monster seemed to be hung thereon. It struggled at a loss. At this, the trees and the greens, even the wind □ all burst into a rousing session of condescending laughter.

The lad, too, burst into a brief session of derisive laughter of a victor. Nonetheless, soon, he realised how childish he had been. He quickly came to term with the naked reality that this was not a laughing matter, that it could not possibly be the end of the struggle for survival. Therefore, he turned sideway. He discovered a narrow footpath running up the forestry line. He followed the path, walking as fast as he could, while looking backward at the trapped monster at short intervals. At a point, he resumed his race. He was inspired to do this by sheer fear.

The trees and the wind all appeared to be on his side. They applauded the boy-runner Benlilo. Their greens started to wave to him as their own contribution of encouragement. In addition, the wind did not stop to flow coolly to dance the forest - but he was soaked in running sweats. Again, Benlilo glanced back in a flashy moment. The monster was still battling for its passage through the trees.

Oh! how the boy had wished he was armed with the double-barrelled gun of his father, who was a professional hunter, straightway he would have braved a go-back and a head-on collision with *the stupid thing* and pumped severally strategic bullets into its skull through its big mouth! He laughed. He found a consolation in the fact that the trees were his friends - hence he believed and hoped that they would continue to hold the enemy lion-like monster foe their hostage. For the umpteenth time, he remembered his father's house. He picked his sizzling race again and ran, and sprinted

He saw a mighty mahogany tree. He ran towards it and he soon disappeared behind a big, flat shoot-out-covering frame of its stem. He stooped low, peeping from the down-below cover in all manifestations of worry and curiousness. The invading fright overthrew the curiosity. It became more terrorising and gripping.

Meanwhile, the irate monster had freed itself from the blockage made by the trees and had successfully traced him to the foot of the mahogany. It became more angry, madder and poised for war. Its hunger and anxiousness to pounce on and devour the lad grew more avid. It was now a complete representation of steaming and gushing anger plus death!

It now ploughed rowdily through the immediate environment in order to locate him. In the process of doing this, many of the small trees and shrubs on its unmarked path were damaged or uprooted completely by the raging beast. All the wounded and uprooted plants and shrubs groaned. The entirety of the immediate forest watched the horrid development in fearful glare. Meanwhile, the eulogistic voices for the lion-like beast had stopped. It was now all suspense and concentration, as the powers watched to know what would happen next.

The ruined plants and shrubs rained abuses and curses upon the raging beast relentlessly. No power could silence them. But what concerned the beast with those natural ones' enmity in conspiracy? It swore to capture the boy and to make a public show of him in shreds that was its main concern of priority.

At last, the beast could smell the presence of the boy within the vicinity. What only remained was locating him at his exact position behind the tree's stem's flap and bulldozing its way thereon and seizing him by whatever part and devouring him without wasting any second. By the aid of its nostril intelligence report, it seemed it was now having its desired breakthrough and it was soon rampaging its beastly self towards the boyish target like mad.

Sighting this and sensing that his life was surely near to finish, Benlilo's person, from head to his toes, was invaded by measureless trepidation anew. He bolted out of his hiding place. He ran energetically upward the land like a desperate man closely pursued by a wild lunatic who was armed with a bloodthirsty machete. By a small cone-shaped mound hill upward the forestry part, the running boy turned right and negotiated a sharp corner by two fat trees' stems, gold and pink in colour, and he raced on...

The carnivorous beast seemed to be caught unaware by the boy's action. It became more terribly angry for what had just happened to its disadvantage. An uneasy silence ruled the atmosphere. The lion-like monster quickly regained its balance from the invasion of the rude shock; it pursued the human target more ferociously. At this, the forest became better concerned. It held its breath, watching the scene, as it was recounting in breathtaking suspense.

Benlilo ran further southward, then eastward whirling his warped course through the shrubs and plants and in-between trees. The lion-like monster too would not give up. It pursued him unwaveringly. But as the lad turned rightward, again, he met himself at the edge of a swampy groove. The groove surprisingly reacted in a masculine voice and said:

Welcome! Come right in Benlilo and take your place, it invited him into its inn but, silently, the lad rejected the invitation. He well remembered the evil invitation of the river, the fire and the gulf in the beginning of the adventure.

He stood still at the edge of the groove; his two eyes surveying everywhere like those of a disturbed eagle while, at the same time, re-invoking his pledge not to die! He backed this up with determination and willpower. The determination resided in his mind and brain; the willpower dwelled in his feet and sprinting talent.

CHAPTER 023

The Groove And The Gorge

Participants of weird life come and go
On the forestry stage chameleonic in colours.
Innumerable characters populate the play of life
Time, era and season swapping poses as actors and actresses
Beyond the understanding of man in hasty assessments.

THE ATMOSPHERIC CONDITION of the groove land spoke evil. The invisibly flowing but prominently felt breeze interpreted it shoddier. The groove itself yearned for evacuation and advancement. Funny enough, the adjoining forests, in unity, countered □No!□ The season was repressive unlike its higher-ranking counterpart, the era. Incongruity mapped out every one□s identity, courtesy of time.

They all spoke out in saccharine and pungent tones of love and of hate. Life became a parable of a web of divergent interpretations and malfunctions. The atmosphere of suspense became thicker. Blood ran rapidly in the flesh and bone stratums of the lad. His soul lay at the border of delight and grief, anticipation and hopelessness.

There appeared a hungry and angry looking lean buffalo. The buffalo looked pale and fragile in breath and in strength. It appeared exactly like an AIDS (the Acquired Immune Deficiency Syndrome) victim. Benlilo□s hair strands stood stretched-out as if he had suddenly met himself in the land of the dead.

Brownish red in colour, the buffalo was possessed inconsistently with the spirit of elevated anxiousness in its passively immobile state. It limped. What baffled Benlilo most about the wild animal was the fact that its head suddenly changed to that of a ghostly vampire. The head became enlarged and terrifying. The boy□s body shook all over feverishly.

The ghostly vampire□s mouth was a short but intriguingly bulky beak of an inexplicably big bird. It started to crow gutturally like a three-year old village cock. The lad got terrified the more but he remained on the spot. It did not occur to him to move as of yet. He could make or offer no explanation on this.

Balanced on the buffalo□s head was a basket full, to the brim, with wide-ranging kinds of minor and major curses. In isolation, all the curses were multi-dimensional and restricted in nature. Like a vibrant liquid gas of carbon dioxide, they all issued out of an open cauldron positioned and balanced at the middle point of the basket. The basket was filthily sandy in colour. The evil pot was buttery ashen, while the issuing smokes of the curses were black by outlook.

When the ghostly buffalo saw Benlilo, it endured all pains and fragility and fled out of display. Still, neither the cauldron nor the basket fell out of its place on its head □ astonishing! These were darkness□ doings and they were marvellous in the devotedly watching lad□s sight. The buffalo was soon completely out of sight; its laughter could be heard clearly in the far expanse. After the laughter session, it burst into an uncharacteristic song accounting to its identity:

Benlilo□s roving eyes caught hold of another quarter of the groove. Inside the vast groove was a trough. The name of the valley was *Defeat and Sorrow. Valley of Defeat and Sorrow* was a dungeon wherein several earthly geniuses ended their lives tragically; therein all their fancy hopes perished forever and redemption, under no circumstances, raised its head.

This was the gutter where golden talents and out of character fortunes were robbed of their owners at gun points and the fortunes caused to perish or be transferred, ever before their stretch of fulfilment could reach, by envious household wickedness. Succinctly speaking, this was the furrow of catastrophic diffuseness and death but an abode of wild celebrations, ad infinitum, for the powers.

The valley was oversize and limitless. It was barren of all living things such as vegetation and animals, except the powers. No amazement, it was filled to the brim with fresh and aged bones wet and dry skulls of human beings. The human being owners of those countless bones and skulls were past and recent victims of some supernatural powers. The conquests of those unfortunate destinies had been preceded with massive attacks and counter-attacks, re-enforcements and systematic re-groupings.

With their full-size wings, as fulfilled birds of the night, the powers flew rowdily and hovered lowly above the valley, as they gladly sang songs of off-putting victory. They were celebrating their overall mischievous victory over the vanquished souls and spirits that once owned the fresh bones and raw skulls. It was all obscenity but what concerned them? The greater the number of casualties the healthier fulfilled they were.

A big hen with her fourteen chickens scanned, gratifyingly, through the bones for fleshy remnants. The impatiently hungry hen and chickens too were gaily celebrating their victory over man. In reality, they were not fowls but all witchcraft powers. Human beings □ women and men in physical flesh, bones and blood but evil spirits in the spiritual realm of power, whatever power!

An ebony black domestic cat also searched through the bones and skulls for soft tissue bits. Too, it represented a witchcraft power in a fulfilled action. Now, a mudfish, empowered with two tattered wings, flew across the low sky of the vale deftly, all in calculated intolerance. While in this act, the two wings echoed thriving ovations. The applauses were all in honour of *the prevailing powers.* They also rendered eulogies to *dedicated night workers:*

However, a lightning roar disrupted the winged fish□s flight across the dry sky of the conduit. The flying fish vamoosed but its wings□ resounds of the songs could be manifestly heard in the aloofness. With time, they thinned off into a waiting and wailing oblivion. Life was tarrying and worrying. It was sorrowing much and joying squalid in an all-night of dulled surprises by sky-scraping apprehension.

The moon appeared in sight nearby. It lighted up everywhere around the gorge like, □no woman□s business!□ The sun and the stars also registered their attendances. As collaborators, they too were rejoicing and celebrating their triumphs over those hopeless souls □ men, women and children.

For, earlier on, those three groups of elemental forces had been wooed, enthralled and won over to conspire with the powers against their would-be victims. Thence, many evil benefits □ the crown of which was premature death, were programmed into their lives.

Even so, on their part, the fatalities□ flesh, bones, blood and skulls refused to be silenced. All-day and nightlong, they groaned in pains and wailings unlimited. They cried incessantly to the Righteous Judge to avenge them speedily of their enemies.

However, their cries wobbled into the free sky. The reason was that they had nearly all died in their iniquities. Hence, their weeping was empty and rowdy barking of dogs in the ears of the Almighty One. Had they been saintly martyrs, he would have answered their prayers or in fact, there would have been no need for those prayers.

They cried; they thirsted; they hungered for salvation that was never again to be. They yearned obsessively for resurrection but alas! it was too late. The life-battle had been fought, lost and won □ lost by them and won by the powers.

Yet, the sufferers had all along been faithful on the side of the powers, oh! How great was their disappointment! Their loses How imposing the god□s□ path of betrayal! However, in the first place, why did they expect good from the land of evil? Why had they been expecting blessings from a cursed ground?

More evocatively, the powers□ cultic drums sounded for it was festival time. They danced better lithely in their gruesome flights in the ominously obnoxious sky of the outlet. The valley was the *valley of valleys*. It profited its trade by swallowing and devouring giants of giants and high breed talents in the camp of men.

Surrounded by others, the same cesspool invoked the past to smite the present in order to dismantle the future. At intervals, the powers changed their tunes and *new songs of victory* oozed:

Hereto is victory won and lost
Hereon is life lost never again owned.

Hereon are several destinies hijacked
Hereto are fortunes bastardised.

Herein are uncountable treasures set afire
Hereby are numberless talents set apart.

Hereby are innumerable stars killed
Herein are multitudinous glories buried.

Deep-down inside our valley of defeat
Down-deep inside our dungeon of sorrow,

Haaaahah! In the morning of recreation
Eeeeeheh! For eternal night of all perdition.

Benlilo turned rightward and ran. At this point, he had been lost to the lion-like beast, as the beast was lost to him. This was however far from saying that the monster had given up its search and chase of the lad. Far from it! By now, it continuously ploughed its way about the forest, lost eastward, in hunt for him.

More the elemental forces and territorial hosts laughed it to scorn. They would not know what had happened to its nose organ, for quick discoveries, but it would not mind their negative reactions! Its determination to locate the fleeing lad and deal most ruthlessly with him became stronger.

Having learnt his lesson, that anything was possible in the mystery forest, Benlilo was persistent in his running. He met himself inside a vineyard of barren trees. Flowing through the vineyard was a stream. The streaming one vomited curses and abuses without conclusion. It sang by its swaggering flows:

Age of curse, moment of affliction
Counting rages of the whirlwinds
Beauty of honour above and beneath
Season of actualisation in the region of revenge!

The lad would not know who the angry stream's targets or sufferers were. By and large, he only knew that they were sons and daughters of man. Remarkable enough, he did not see himself as belonging to those beneficiaries of the streams' curses and abuses – yet, he was an integral part of the humanity.

He was that deluded!

CHAPTER 024

Soulful Singers Animalistic

He stood to stare at the singing group
Yet, watching wonders so negatively entertaining:
Hymns of death, too, are beautifully sweet in the ear
When, by capacity, abolition is insured with captivity
In a phase of fascination without a grain of love.

THE STREAM FLOWED northward and not southward. Its water was blood red in colour. A boar pig cheerily bathed itself inside it. Later, still having its body buried deep inside the muddy water of the stream, the pig lifted up its long and titanic head and, in the language of man, began to sing a *song of joy in sorrow:*

Bewitched day! Conjured night
Life in the vale a payable right!

Invoked night! Expelled day
Overflowing joy here without a jot of ray!

Benlilo was baffled beyond all human descriptions. He heard the song audibly but he could hardly pick a meaning out of its wordings. He had heard and read fables of animals speaking like man but, now, face-to-face with the stripped reality, he could not the least figure out what was happening before his own unveiled eyes: *A pig singing in the tongue of man? More than mysterious!*

As he was about to flee from the scene, the water of the stream bubbled, raucously shooting to the low sky and there was an eruption in its bowel towards the surface. Thus was his attention better reverted but he kept his distance. When serenity eventually returned to the stream, the huge pig was seen no more. Yet another mysterious manifestation, the stream had swallowed it into its mystery belly?

The adventuring lad was further baffled. He jumped over the stream in a spark panic only to hurriedly recommence his race upland the forestry sphere. For shilly-shallying of the unseen, he would not even brave a look backward. He continued to run for escape but where was the getaway? He did not know that hope was far to the direction of the land of cheerfulness. He knew not that the night was far distanced to his morning of salvation.

Outlying northward, the boy arrived at a spot where the bush hummed and cleared before him on its own accord, but unenthusiastically, in continuously murmurs and hisses. He halted his race when he stumbled on this new scene. He gazed curiously at the virgin area round about him with a deep measure of renewed amazement. Still, he would not understand.

At the far end of the bare ground stood a small rock. Brightly blue-green in outlook, it shined like a diamond in the sun. The rock magnified the more and shone better admirably. Life was beautiful after all. A treasure of rainbow colours. A gemstone of glittering sparkles!

But, without any notice, the rock opened at the middle and a ghomid jumped out of its bowl-shaped womb. The ghomid□s countenance was, simply defined, unconditionally wicked. It was armed with a spear. The spear was as black as the nut of an *ake* apple but it had its pointing end as white as snow.

This was a contrast. Benlilo was petrified beyond what the mouth of man could tell. Still, he remained glued to the spot. He continued to watch the peculiar creature in its own peculiar act. Life was only one of its kinds. He had no choice. Peculiarity of an event lasted with the event.

From its neck downward, the ghomid had the body of a human being but its two legs were those of a well-nourished Nigerian Fulani cow highland the big Niger River Basin. It was barefooted and its only dress was a circle of sketchy layers of fresh palm and raffia fronds around its waist. It was bursting of muscles with all its body veins gruffly visible. Its head was a big piece of ripe palm kernel bunch.

Not an eye could be located on the head, yet, the ghomid being was seeing. It was not deaf but no physical mark of the ear was represented on the head. It was very sensitively smart at smelling things, living or dead, around it - still, its nose was untraceable. No mouth could also be located anywhere around the head but the creature could sing loud and clear. Life further sustained a multifaceted chain of mysteries for the wayfaring lad.

Further, still, the palm-kernel-bunch head oscillated coolly like a perfect Japanese machine, in a complete circle every tenth second. The ghomid never minded the trifling presence of the lad, *a mere mortal*. No! it had no time for him. It was being pursued by haste □ rash and rush of another version and mission, respectively, of the mystery. For in the realm of darkness, with the powers, missions differ and visions are defined unbrokenly according to professions by specialisations.

Hurriedly, the ghomid ran eastward the forest surface in a terrific agitation. As it raced on, its voice echoed thunderously and angrily across the region in the remote distance, diminishing with the passage of time. Its terse message of an inconsiderate warning:

In seasons cold and hot
In all eras odd and even -
Beware of life so sweet and sour
Beware of life so gall and honey
Beware of life so wild and meek
Beware! Beware!! Beware!!!
Beware of night and day, beware!
Beware of seasons and eras, beware!

Benlilo received the message but he could not understand what the ghomid had warned its hearer or hearers to beware of. He could not fathom any considerable connotation to its communication. He forgot all

about the creature along with its *meaningless message* forthwith, and focused all his attention on the journey —
his way of escape out of the forest. He had seen enough and his body was getting tired.

He could not understand that out of six full hours in the encoded adventure, he had spent a little above one hour. He still had nearly five better-quality horror-packed hours of familiarity to pass through, *waoh!*

He arrived at a junction where the path spilt into three. He hesitated a little while. After a few seconds, he took his decision and made for the one on the right, neglecting the middle and the left side ones. He resumed his escape race with energised heartiness and ran for his dear life. All along, instincts urged him not to think that the danger was over.

He ran to the foot of a small hill. The hill glowed like a piece of solid snow. He promptly climbed it. He was about to survey the new environment when he looked forward only to behold a fat cat and a he-goat. The cat, whose gender he wasn't able to judge as yet, though it gave out a rather feminine impression, was a very beautiful and impressive one.

It appeared in immaculate white with yellow spots and blue stripes. Its white tail ended with a cap of aquamarine blue. Its two eyes, set on a head continually bisected with a rainbow combination of colours, were immaculately blue and white. Its tail never, for once, stopped wagging.

On its own, the he-goat bore a very close resemblance to a he-goat owned by one of his stepmothers back home. It appeared in a combination of dust and golden-brown colours. It was prominently labelled with a small goatee and it looked vicious. To cap it all, it was a portrait of perfect unattractiveness. Its body was restless like the cat's tail.

Benlilo was taken aback. The beautiful cat and the ugly he-goat were engaged in a 'free fight' when he stood face-to-face with them on the snow-like glowing hill. He moved nearer in an attempt to mediate peace between them — *blessed is the peacemaker...* But, rather surprising, the two animalistic fighters stopped abruptly. With their joint reaction, the lad had halted his walk towards the two supposedly domestic animals and he began to watch.

They both stood at attention like local police officers in a training session at Kano Police College. Side by side, they looked Benlilo straight in the eyes as if he was their trainer from whom they were expecting an order of instruction. Then, more surprisingly, both animals burst into an unusual song very confusing to the lad in contents:

The green snake bites
The black scorpion stings
The brown insect chirps
The white bird sings
Yet, love is sweeter a thing
Than thousands of kisses' rings.

A young adult, Benlilo did not know that the song was nothing but a proverb addressing his beleaguered person. He was awfully shocked and visibly shaken, from head to toes, to see and hear these two little animals sing perfectly with human voices, another familiarity of sort in the adventure. He wondered on why the forest was full of so many uncommon wonders, which he had hardly heard of before. He called to remembrance the realism that the forest was called *mystery*. He could now re-mould the name into, 'The forest of amoebic mysteries.'

The two animals sang so beautifully like the famed professional singers of the Queen of Heaven. Their voices were not cracked or dry but thin, cool and echoingly rhythmic. They were full of invitation and invigoration. They were filled with assurances overloaded with fraudulent outlays of a manipulation but the boy was too naive to know. He sincerely believed that the two animalistic singers and dancers were genuine entertainers.

They sang as rarely talented earthly singers and, yet, mystical. As they sang, they moved their bodies in a quaint accordance to the rhythm that only angelic singers of the heavenly place could have mustered. How the watching boy had wished that Michael Jackson and all American professional singers and *marvellous* dancers could learn their musical and dancing lessons from this mysterious cat and the he-goat! How he had wished that these extremely talented creatures would be employed as guest artists in specialised music schools around the world - to teach millions of young folks the arts of music and dancing!

For, as expressive singers and dancers, they were simply fantastic! Their singing and dancing outputs were in reality pleasant-sounding testimonies of ingenuities and not of western education. Passing through the ears, emotively, their songs touched the three components of man: soul, spirit and body. Its magnetic contact to these organs was sharp as well as they were stirred gratifyingly.

Benlilo remained genuinely arrested to the spot where he was firmly rooted. This animalistic singing and dancing group of two was more than a thriller! Birds□ singing, yes! This was surely the second time of seeing animals sing in the manner of men, and they danced so super-marvellously! He was terrifically amused. He smiled excellent contentment, as he stood still, watching the two melodic animals perform their twofold pleasant-sounding acts.

For the time being, the young person had forgotten all about the pursuing monster. The superb singers and dancers knew what they were doing however. They were nursing a goal; they were grooming a hidden agenda towards maturity time. The ploy was to arrest the lad□s attention and slow down his movement through the forest. For with the dark powers, more than a few things *were* possible. Simply put, they were good tacticians. Excellent strategists. They treasured surprises by suspense killer blows; they cherished employment of variegated methodologies and warfare lines of attacks.

Whenever it seemed that they had reached the end of the song, they picked it up again and sang more tellingly, and danced better arrestingly. Soon, alas! another entirely new dimension was added to the rock□s top setting of the animalistic festival of rare music and golden dance. The second round of their singing and dancing was appropriately accompanied by warmly musical outplays of lyrics so majestic in orderly outpouring □ another quick invention by interjection of darkness.

Benlilo could not identify where these had emanated from. He did not know that this, too, was part of the powers□ roundabout game-play. Unmindful of his presence, the cat and the he-goat rolled out the second stanza, an unrelated piece, of their salient song:

The sun is a good friend
The moon is a dear colleague
Stars of heaven are very lovely
Like the forest and the breeze
Oh, like the sky in a cool season,
Just like the striking snow at fall!

Thoroughly entertained Benlilo could not express the billowing gratitude of his mind to the two animal entertainers. Their entertaining and invigoration rhythms had been most appropriate as expellers of weariness from his being. □An ignoramus per excellence,□ he could not have imagined that he was coming to hate the two animals intimately.

Rest assured, oh journeying soul!
The forest is beautiful!
The season is beautiful!

Further the two animal singers sang to entertain the boy. Yet, a snaky-stream seemed to be encroaching on his person from the same within. He could not, the smallest amount, trust the two mystifying but domestic animals and their outlandishly exciting show of artistic music and cultural dance!

This truly was the mystery forest of breathtaking mysteries!

CHAPTER 025

A Cafe, The Forest And Darkness

What the unseen end from the beginning
Hurried decisions outside norm and rationality -
From frying pan to fire, so the free captive runs,
New seasons in bolder higher manifestations
By time running in quick-witted testimonies.

FEAR INVADED AND wrapped up tighter the heart of Benlilo, the one-man-spectator. The animal singer arresters and dancers repeated the second stanza of their song with all the accompanying instrumentation in faultless synchronisation.

Still, he would not know and could not see or imagine the source or sources of the complementary musical instrumentation. He remained transfixed on the spot but the great singers were not jesters. Every opportunity utilised and appropriated mattered most to the powers and life was opportunity seized, exploited and acted wisely.

They were out to shock him further. For, all along, they had been very friendly through their entertainment and seraphic poetry. Working to precision, to them, the time of entertainment for their alien visitor was fast lapsing. It was now time to be very unfriendly and nasty. But, alas! not without a known but forgotten re-enforcement - what happened?

The lion-like monster re-appeared and it was roaring its way up the hillside. The two familial animals pretended as if they knew nothing was in the offing. Talented actor and actress, they continued with their fabulous show of pleasingly musical and cultural entertainments. They had expected the lad to suspect nothing - but they were flat wrong ☐ he suspected something.

Sighting the monster that was now a portrait of wicked eagerness and anxiousness rolled into one, after looking back showily having suspected that, may be an elephant was around; Benlilo was terribly dazed beyond expression. Like a monkey nearly in the throes of death, *fuaam!* he jumped over the cat and the he-goat in a re-invoked flight.

Most surprising to the lad, the two lesser animals abandoned their singing and dancing altogether in that second; they started to pursue him. Shockingly, their determination terrified the watching greens in their silence; their ambitious movements injected the still air with hidden but extensively felt disruption.

Embarrassingly, the heaviness of the sounds of their heels roared behind the lad like those of two uncontrollable elephants. The roars of the heels alone were enough to terrify him into a fall. The powers believed this warfare strategy too could work out something positive and they had invested in it.

Here it became manifestly clear that both animals had actually been expecting their master the lion-like monster to appear before they would join in the race against the targeted Benlilo□s person. This was the reason behind the incessantly tautological repetitions of their *beautiful* song.

In actual fact, though all-along seriously engaged in their marvellous singing and dancing extravaganzas, they had been communing or communicating with the lion-like monster. The two animals knew that they had not the muscles to tackle him on their own. The powers disliked disappointment or failure with perfect aversion and they never encouraged their warriors to give any of them a trial. They hardly gambled; they actualised. They are not theorists; they are practicalists.

The gruesome lion-like monstrous ogre continued to plough its way like thunder towards Benlilo□s direction. The beast now looked hungrier and was boiling with greater rage and wrath. It had its speed increased along with its boosted determination to capture the lad and devour him without wasting any time whatsoever.

The boy raced through the bushes more speedily than ever before. His three pursuers chased after him with bolder efforts and consistence, even as the dead series of earlier eulogies recommenced to the disadvantage of the boy:

Energy is power, power is energy;
Beauty of victory starring us at the face
Oh glory, we□ve won the battle so soon!

Catch him! Stop him! Fell his tree of life
With your axe cut it to its roots and leaves,
As vegetable for your stomachs, oh hungry beasts!

The three carnivorous animals were seriously worked up by the transmission of the magical wordings of the song. They invested more efforts, as their flesh and bones matured stronger. They could see that, already, their sponsors the powers had concluded that the battle against the boy had been won point-blank so early in the adventure.

The cat got to him first. It became very frantic to climb, claw and bite him but Benlilo turned round and about dramatically, like a highly talented mathematically athletic footballer on the field of play. He stopped suddenly and with a farm boot that had suddenly appeared on his right feet, gave the cat a terribly accurate kick directly into its face.

The wounded cat cried *Mieu! Mieu!! Mieu!!!* three pathetic times - its voice going down by each one cry. It rolled on the grassy ground and cried. Its two eyeballs turned round and it seemed that it was about to give up the ghost. It groaned loudly in the pains, as it wailed. Blood and mucus gushed out of the wounded animal□s nose, mouth and ears.

The he-goat, on its part, was scared. The monster beheld the picture not so far away but it seemed unconcerned. For the *brutality* that the boy had meted to the cat, it became more intolerably angry and badly charged. What mattered to it was nothing other than capturing the boy and devouring him. Its determination grew rocky.

It got consumed in a burning ambition to avenge its colleague the cat of the enemy Benlilo. For with his latest *negative* action, he had had his sins against the powers augmented. The lion-like monster had overtaken the he-goat and the lesser animal was now trailing on its path in a red rage. The injured cat struggled doggedly to be on its limbs again. Benlilo continued to run, as the cat groaned and cried in pains and it wobbly pursued behind.

The boy sighted a tremendously fat and tall mangrove tree not so far away. Right from its foot upward, the stem of the tree appeared in royal blue colour. He ran towards it, as the three pursuers pursued him tenaciously. Surprisingly, they roared in a new session of wild jubilation. The source of their joyousness was an envisaged optimism for negative victory over the hotly pursued schoolboy. They had that destructive hope so booming like the ocean in their hearts. For Benlilo, he was surprised at the latest cheerfulness of his three pursuers.

Getting to the foot of the tree, the boy whirled round it only to meet himself by the mouth of a big café. From inside the café was an echo of a *sweet* voice, which said, □Welcome.□ Without giving the voice□s greeting a crumb of thought, Benlilo dashed inside the café, as its only opening got sealed off immediately.

He had so hurriedly concluded that, that was the only option before him for now. He did not know that the available option had meant a brand new prison and elongation of his sorrows in further assurances of suspense and unimaginable surprises. Then, in turn, some mosquitoes announced their presence with some sirens of irritation.

Arriving there, the three hot chasers saw a hilly mound rise and not a café. They bustled about the mound hill and the tree many times confusedly. A rage of fretful agitation invaded their persons. Their earlier optimism gave birth, by vigour, to pessimism. They quickly probed the immediate environment with their eyes but they could not locate the whereabouts of the boy. Yet, they avowed never to give up.

Physically and meticulously, they combed all the nearby surroundings to no benefit. They surveyed all the treetops, also with their eagle eyes, to no reward. Had they sighted him anywhere on any of the treetops, the cat was duty-bound to climb up with the speed of lightening and pluck him down, in all viciousness of madness, into the waiting mouth of the lion-like monster.

They sank deeper into anxiety by depression and were enveloped by greater misinterpretation in adaptations. Still, they were not tired, far distanced from the land of frustration. Discomfort had no place in their hearts. Neither doubt nor an arm of weakness. They remained resolutely determined than before. Their rigid faith did not wane. For no tenable reason by human judgement, the faith was now stronger and bolder.

The cat smelled it that the mound rise had harboured the "abominable" lad underneath it. It transmitted the message and the he-goat quickly confirmed the suspicion that the heap hill was a conspirator. In a spree of volcanic reaction, therefore, the third and elderly actor in the animalistic triangle, the lion-like ogre ploughed itself against the new enemy and adjudged collaborator - the mound hill.

All trees and greens of the environment watched in arrested interest. They watched as if they had not seen warriors in action before. Beastly caterpillars, how powerful! The mound hill□s soil gave way and it was soon scattered but its base seemed solid as a rock's table, wonderful!

The three mulish animals began to scan the rubbles for their prey, Benlilo. It looked as if they had all run crazy. Nonetheless, they soon retired, but not tired, in abject dejection. They would not just appreciate how the prospective prey had vanished so mysteriously. To them, it was the challenge so difficult to meet! The most demanding mystery to unravel along their hunting expedition so far.

Meanwhile, the light of the once well-lit café had gone off immediately Benlilo stepped his feet inside it. Therefore, he had no atom of opportunity to examine his new environment. The echoing and welcoming voice had only sounded once and ceased □ he could not tell whether it was that of an enemy or that of a friend.

The suspense of his mind relegated into a raging misconstruction, seeking for a restful place to settle. His earlier-on treasured hope dashed in pieces. All the surprise, suspense, confusion and sunk hope mingled with their puzzlement and they struggled to produce a repulsive result that cannot be qualified. He feared an imaginary keeper of the café. What of wild animals or reptiles?

The inside of the café was vast. Its atmosphere resembled a midnight of total darkness, of horrors, when the moon and the stars conspired against humanity and they registered their unqualified absence from the sky. Like the depressing darkness, a grave-yard-silence overwhelmed everywhere inside the café. The only favourable condition therein was circulation of oxygen. Else, the lad would have soon died of suffocation. Yet, inside the surprisingly well-oxygenated café, he sweated like a goat tied down inside a native shrine and surely destined to be sacrificed to a god.

Benlilo started to regret and to lament, plentifully, his odious mistake of ever running inside the café. *How will I ever get out of here? What hope? Is this how, with my two eyes wide opened, I have run into my grave so prematurely?* He thus mourned his *unacceptable presence* inside the mysteriously earthen bunker. He soon resigned himself to fate. Whatever condition cannot be escaped needs to be endured. The definition of life is in suspense and concluded impossibilities. Its itinerary is worked out by time to manifest at the appointed time of the season or era. But, oh fate, this was the junction of predicament!

Benlilo□s terrified mind flashed backward to the now-cut-off evil power pursuers and all his body frames quaked. He remembered the troubled fate that life had apportioned his destiny and he became sadder. Life was the unfair trade of light and darkness. It was the market of dilemma and confusion. His mother Suiggaria said so times without number, that, □Life is the unfair umpire!□

The trapped son sank deeper into an interlude of meditation, all unsupportive. Then, in the midst of this, he heard a very loud trumpet sound - shaking the whole café to its roots. Again, the loud trumpet sound roared, this time around, accompanied by some big rush. The rush resembled the type usually being made by a mob speedily hasting to somewhere of great interest. It bore a resemblance to the rush of feet to the execution ground of the late grandmother witch.

The lad did not know which step next to take. He stole a quick glance roundabout his stand to discover matter-of-fact evidences of those two happenings. He saw nothing. He stood at attention, as a subordinate police officer would do before his unseen superior officers. He was the low-grade policeman and his now-unseen pursuers were the bigger officers.

Involuntarily, he opened wide his eyes again but, still, they could see nothing. Either he was mad or blind or something! He was wholly lost into the new world of mental distress. The darkness was as thick and foldable as the one in the legend. A thought occurred to him and he quickly took an action.

He moved slowly rightward and there he stood still, expecting what fate would befall him inside the thick darkness of the café. He could move a step no further. Unbelievably, the darkness grew thicker and he could feel it. A total grip of incomprehension seized his person. Unqualified irritation became his lot.

Without notification, the boy discovered that his environment had changed. This discovery he made by gut feeling and he was accurate. Instead of remaining inside the café, he now met himself inside a thick forest - whether it was the earlier forest in which the café had appeared, he could not tell.

Yet, again, he remembered his unexpected transplantation from the City of Marpolio into the fearful mystery forest of wild mysteries. *What is impossible in this life?* In spite of his new transplantation, the deeply wicked darkness remained a paramount feature and this baffled him greatly.

A rain of dry leaves started to fall rapidly on him. By this, he could confirm and reconfirm that the environment actually had a transformation. The situation was as if a silent whirlwind was raging through the forest during the dry season and yellow and dry leaves were dropping down in their thousands every flash. Since it was all darkness, he could not see trees or greens but he knew that they were present around him. He knew that he was surrounded by conglomerated nature.

Benlilo reminded himself of how he had run into the café and how its opening closed against him, he sank deeper into the realm of an aggravated uneasiness. The lad closed tighter his two eyes and bowed his head. He could not move his legs forward, backward or sideways - or the idea did not suggest itself to him. Neither did he bear, in his mind, the thought of sitting nor lying down on the ground now cushioned by layers of speedily falling dry leaves.

He remained standing □ half swallowed by a fat heap of the dried out leaves. His dread mounted wilder; it graduated louder into horror. The revulsion could not be spelt out. *Is this how to pass through the University of Life? The valley of the shadow of death?*

Later, he heard the out-of-the-ordinary rain of dry leaves stop. For the umpteenth time, he opened his eyes but the whole place remained in the unusual total darkness. He quickly closed them again, as unplumbed silence ruled over the atmosphere. The two eyes had seen nothing but horror, hungry and boldly pronounced. His mind was now calculating many things unprintable.

As Benlilo wallowed away in this state of improbability, yet again, he heard the ear-splitting trumpet sound. The musical instrument□s blare roared again □ this time louder than before. For the fifth time, the trumpet boom roared □ followed by the earlier great rush that died down soon after. The openly caged teenager imagined that unseen claws of tigers, lions or crocodiles would clamp on him and tear his person into shreds. *Who the crazy person is trumpeting inside this forest?* he wondered.

Yet, again, all his body features pulsated to no stop □ he remembered the eulogies for the beasts, especially the lion-like monster. He trembled. The stark truth flowed into his mind and it got stuck therein that he had several enemies in the forest - the mystery forest of wild enmities.

The thought also infected his distraught heart and he saw himself standing under a huge object hanging inexplicably somewhere in the sky, with fork-like-sharps, and rolling down furiously to pierce and to crush him to the ground. It was this state so imagined, negatively, that led him, unconsciously, to go down dashing his person onto the ground, crying:

□*Yeah!* Please! Please!! Save me! Save me!!□

Either the boy was already crazy or somewhat! For sure, he did not know what he was doing, neither the person nor persons to whom he was making those fervent pleas for mercy. The combined spell of indistinctness and perplexity was now multiplying at work.

Tormenting!

CHAPTER 026

*Two Opposing Angels, The Ghommid Giant *

Battle cries in the field of battle
Demonstrations of light and darkness
Lost and won the fierce encounter of the angels.
The forest□s invasion by weird ghosts and ghommids,
Life never again the same for the baby adventurer.

LIFE IS JOY and sorrow. Life is battle and battle is life. Warriors fight the battle; warriors win the battle and warriors lose the battle. It is a game of life and death; it is the matter of victory and defeat □ unwrapped attendance of joy and sorrow, celebration and lamentation. Now, an *angel of light* flew across the forestry region. As he was flying, in a loud voice, he shouted again and again:

□Woe! Woe!! Woe and death everlastingly unto darkness!!!□

The heavenly battle crier had a torch of glowingly extra-bright white light in his left hand and a two-edged blazing sword in the right one. The torch of light marked his path clearly through the forbidding darkness; the mighty sword was for war. The whole forest submerged into a scratchy quietness, as the angel of light relayed his message largely and authoritatively. The powers could envisage, in advance, another threatening happening and it might not be favourable.

As soon as his voice had thinned off, another angel appeared on the scene. Armed also with an extraordinary two-edged sword, he was a particular *angel of darkness.* A thousand hosts of the dark world were greatly relieved. They hailed him for his starling initiative, courage and boldness to challenge the *angel of light:*

Well-done, warrior of life
The great challenger born for conflict
Sword of your judgement working the axe
We are rest assured that the battle you□ve won!

These three sizeable credentials - starling initiative, courage and boldness had established the angel of darkness, well in advance, as a war hero in the Army of President Satan, Commander-in-Chief of the Armed Forces of the Universal Republic of Darkness □ URD. The *challenger* countered the pronouncements of the light-bearer with a serial shout, also on top of his voice:

□Blessed are we! Blessed are we!! Blessing and life are ours forevermore in darkness!!!□ Hearing this, though he was far away, the first angel was furiously mad. He boiled with wrath, as his extraordinary two-edged sword thirsted for blood. He turned back on his flight to meet and to challenge, face-to-face, the second angel. Roars of thunder and scares of lightening-flashes across the sky heralded the angel of light□s return. Hosts of darkness watched, as forces of light were not asleep.

Later on, the dark angel, along with the watching hosts of darkness, was sorely troubled. The angel and the hosts were filled with wild anxiety; they could envisage an intimidating doom already. They therefore calculated their loss or tragedy in advance furthermore but the challenging angel refused to swallow his words of confrontation. He rejected the option to put the gods to shame. Like the true warrior of the divinities, he stood his ground to damn the consequence, whatever end result.

He decided to give the opponent a *good* fight, believing that darkness would eventually overcome light. For this, both angels had their swords, hungrily thirsty for blood, fully drawn for an open battle - their powers having now shifted from voices into hands. At the meeting point in the thickly darkened sky, the battle line was obviously drawn.

And, in a short while, the angel of light beheaded the demon of darkness - even as, earlier on, the sword of the defeated one had melted away like a piece of candle thrown into the midst of a Nebuchadnezzar□s fiery furnace. The victorious warrior, who was the angel of light, flew away in honourable dexterousness, his tongue filled with a song of victory:

Darkness shall never overcome light
Victory is master to defeat every twilight,
The coward will not stand before the valiant
The wise is ever lord to the fool,

As falsehood is vanquished by truth
But before then, the battle must be fought,
Fought, won and lost forever and ever,
Won by light and lost by darkness.

Then, amazingly, four of his six wings clapped more often than not to his body. As they were doing this delightfully many times and echoingly, still in his marvellous flying, a hymn was produced:

Tact and act as warfare methodologies
Yesterday, today and tomorrow □
The farthest and the nearest,
Joy, love, peace and victory -
The person of life beautifully decked

A difficult-to-qualify measure of silence perforated the decorated air. The dead silence ran wilder in some outrageous circles. It ruled all shadowy dungeons tyrannically. The fire of their once vociferous voices became extinguished, as their minds got wounded and pierced with pointed arrows of poison. The powers had expected their angel of darkness to slaughter the angel of light but what an infatuation!

The dead angel□s head and body tumbled down onto the ground. The dry leaves were all terrified; they gave way. On its own, the ground beneath memorialised in victory, as it happened in the lesson-laden story of Laala. It opened wide its mouth, as if it had for long been expecting the windfall, and swallowed them □ both his head and body.

A great deal of lamentations filled the air. Once again, the powers were defeated and it was too painful a defeat for them! But their throttleholds swore not to surrender. They grew stronger in rigidity. But for the lad, he was so pleased with the outcome of the two warriors□ fight. He exulted in the spirit extremely. However, it did not touch him that the fight of the angel and the demon was staged in his behalf. But even so, he sang:

Brave angel of light, congratulations!
The battle you□ve won; you□re the winner -
Oh glory, the battle you□ve fought and won!

Yet, this was just too much for Benlilo! The atmosphere became choked for the song. In his presence, happiness ran a race of defeat by hastily renewed apprehension and surprises. Sadness and tears wooed him into their ignominious bosoms. Glory was almost fainting but he struggled onward in order to hold on. Faith became troubled at heart. Hope and despair scrambled to possess his organism.

He longed for a place inside the temple of resurrection but he was shut out. Freedom warned him to beware of loss in transit. Bondage invited him to come, wine, and dine. He fell in-between the regions of living and dying. Life was half the living and half the dying. It meant existence and depression.

An evil deity by name *god of affliction* thundered angrily across the forest. Another idol called *god of shame* echoed its own cry like a thundering leopard. An image by name *image altar alternative* supported the boisterous echoes. The fourth personality by name *god of photograph* blew a whistle madly, *frooooohoooooh!* Other uncountable *gods* joined in the celebration and they laughed heartily. The wicked laughed the lad to scorn. He was fully oblivious of the reason for their disrespectful celebrations.

Some earthly people were beating drums of eternity - who would dance to their beats? A life was about to be plucked down like an unripe pawpaw fruit, from the tree of era, who would save it? The season cried for want of equity - who should comfort it? The era wailed in loss, who could restore its glory? Around the wanderer, the air of horror grew thicker, the suspense greater.

Strange and unfriendly voices cried against this lad, Benlilo. Dissolute roars thundered across the region. A raging flood quenched fire of love. A barrage of witchcraft arrows flew here and there. An indistinguishable bird of darkness hovered joyously but timidly in the sky. The wind became stiff and stubborn an invader and an intruder. A sick river of hope, close by, cried for rescue, as its inn was insufferably troubled. Joy became a flying bird in the sky and out of sight.

The night loomed to extinguish the light of the day and possess the atmosphere against every rule of logicality. Yet, ravening clouds threatened to conquer the sky permanently. Soon, a rainbow appeared in the same sky. The lazy rainbow struggled for relevance. Later, it gained the desired comportment and gleamed glowingly.

The peace of the tree is the peace of the bird! Atop a *Mount Transfiguration,* far away, a holy personality called *Courage* ministered unto the lad□s soul. He was alone and full of confidence. In next to no time, he was joined by some other like-minded beings.

These other friendly personalities numbered four. By names, they were *Joy, Hope, Faith* and *Victory*. Harmoniously, they all burst into a soothing song to pacify and to fortify the lad□s bothered spirit. Their beautifully rendered *Song of Consolation* ran for his well-being in this way:

Onward soldier, do not faint or weary
The night soon will be survived by day.
Only be brave! Be strong and faithful
For without the battle there is no victory

Without the cross there is no crown
The war soon will give birth to victory,
Victory long-lasting for you on the mount
Treasured love for you on Mount Success.

However, against the message of the song, the war continued to record extension □ why? The night became longer and more fearful □ why? Darkness appeared to be overcoming light □ why? The new morning refused to break □ why? Though strong and faithful, the *onward marching soldier* was beclouded by weariness □ why? Both patience and strength were running out with him □ why? His hope had sustained deep wounds □ why?

Benlilo was the wayfarer, the onward soldier! He was now prostrate on the ground. His two sets of teeth gnashed, *krekekeke!* His eyes opened and closed rapidly □ without ability to see anything, still. Peace eluded his heart, as his hope was fading away. His iron faith had become melted. His present became undecided, his future jeopardised.

After that, the boy noticed a little light up, far away. *Ray of hope?* he muttered in a thoughtful silence of a revived meditation. The light looked very much like a shy star in the sky. Up in a sloppy position, he raised his neck to fix his eyes on the lone star. He shivered and gasped for breath.

What fate held for him next the son of man did not know. He could not also cook up any acceptable reason for the hasty appearance of the little star up there in the sky. *Daybreak coming? A traditional hunter□s lamp can never be so high into the sky. Neither can a star come down this low. What kind of light can this be then?* the openly imprisoned slave wondered soundlessly in a succinct session of an interrogative soliloquy.

Still, Benlilo had his eyes fixed on the light. Later, he noticed that the little brightness was drawing nearer and graduating into a big and bigger one. The more the glow moved near, the brighter it turned into, and tighter the lad got bonded, spiritually and physically, in his perplexed state of the phenomenal imprisonment.

The light kept on graduating into brighter maturity, while the deep darkness was vanishing. The boy□s new meditation centred on what could come out of it all in the end! He had never trusted the mystery forest of mysteries. He had regained his wakefulness of the fact that he was still physically present inside the woodland of innumerable possibilities.

In a little while, daybreak dawned on the forest, courtesy of the light □ and, alas! Benlilo□s eyes caught hold of a giant ghomid. Standing at a little over nine feet atop the ground, the ghomid boasted of some features of a human being and others of animals. An untold measure of higher horrors invaded his heart with the undertaking to conquering his person.

The giant figure had two fat heavily hairy and incredibly lengthy arms. The two arms bore two hands, which were without fingers but equipped with scathing claws, all in a frightful blood colour. It had two eyes that were positioned differently: one on its forehead and the other slightly below the neck, right on the outward position of the human heart.

It also had three long and bristly shooting horns. The horns were all rooted inside a big and permanent calabash on its head that was all the while turning. The head itself was fully barren of anything hair - it reflected like a dirt-free mirror.

On the horns were innumerable flies and small sparrow-like birds and bats – swapping positions there and clapping their wings, lazily or lousily, against their bodies. Its light was rooted into the middle area of the tallest of the three pointing horns. It was with this light that the giant ghomid had illuminated the forest.

The two legs of the enormously huge ghomid were hairy like those of an aged chimpanzee. They were white, brown, and extraordinarily long and none of the legs resembled those of human beings. What could be called its nose was a pit covering the position of the nose, mouth and eyes altogether in a normal human being, while a small stream flowed sickly out of there. In short, the eye of the giant ghomid was the radiating and rotating light.

Benlilo contemplated calmly, and then agitatedly, on what the result of this encounter would turn out to be for him in the end, eventually. At this crossroads of predicament, he could not decide whether to continue to watch the strangest being or to flee. But flee to where? Against his will, he remained the feeble captive to the spot.

Now, he could not tell where he was, not to talk of finding his way out of the forest. Farther to the land of contentment, puzzlement became his closest companion. He was no longer thinking of his father's house. Now his topmost priority cantered on how he would escape from the envisaged wrath of the forest dragon upon which he had set his eyes. He prayed history to favour him. He begged the court of time not to convict him for posterity's sake.

'If your eyes are not blinded and they are opened to true realities of life in this forest, you'll weep more than the weeping ghost' – the distasteful words of the talkative ghostly creature reverberated deepest his spirit. Apologetically, he now agreed unreservedly with the departed ghostly being on most of its points.

Again, he begged posterity to vindicate him in the court of the powers. Only time could tell whether he was favoured and vindicated or tried and convicted by the court of the gods - it is the true story of his life!

CHAPTER 027

Straight Into A New Captivity

Just like a daydream, a phantasm,
A virgin scene rolls in applauded by the nature.
New methodologies never cease with the powers
By implementations their agents and nets everywhere
For the captive slip into a brand new imprisonment.

SURROUNDING THIS GIANT creature, horrified Benlilo discovered, was a battalion of guards in its entourage. They were all ghosts and ghomids as eccentric figures: snakes with human legs, birds with animal limbs, human bodies with fish or fowls' heads, etc., and other frightening creatures that were difficult to categorise or to describe. Some members of the giant's entourage were holding sticks. While some were armed with spears, others carried pots painted in many colours, either on their heads or shoulders or atop mighty hunchbacks.

Many armed themselves with daggers, others with swords, machetes, staves, darks, javelins and spears of various sizes and other lethal weapons. Some had bows and arrows. And, laughable enough, some were equipped with drums, flutes, guitars, tambourines and several musical instruments, as others□ were flying scarves of single, double or mottled colours.

Yet, some of the giant ghomid□s followers looked exactly like masquerades, native hunters, radically crazy African magicians, Rastafarians of Ethiopia and demonic chiefs. Benlilo remained lost in his confounding state. He could not tell his fate but he started to shed tears profusely.

Suddenly, he saw the weird crowd of ghosts and ghomids, led by the giant, stop drastically. They all started to hiss and to sneeze irritatingly. The whole forest was, in next to no time, filled with agitating noises of their murmuring, sneezing and hissing, and the teenager was further frightened. They had smelled the *little creature*, an abomination, around. Later, an edgy calm took over. To survive the lopsided level-headedness, the captivated boy discovered that the drummers started to beat their drums.

A group of the giant ghomid□s disciples started to sing to match the drummers□ beats, while the whole lot of the remaining members of the entourage began to dance lithely: some shooting high into the sky, others flying, jumping or hopping. All greens, seen and elemental with environmental forces unseen, continued to watch the exceedingly interesting set-up. Like Benlilo, they too were entertained exceedingly.

Hence, the spot was immediately turned into a carnival ground by these bewildering beings. But, yet suddenly again, Benlilo saw the eerie crowd of the festive creatures halt all their activities dramatically. They acted as if they were reciting a unanimous role in a Hollywood film. At once, they turned backward and rightward. No sooner had they done this than they resumed all their web of festive activities □ ploughing their way through the thickness of the forest. With this, the forestry region started to wear its previous look, as the light with which it was once brightly lit was disappearing little by little.

Benlilo remained motionless, as dead on the ground, wishing that the earth□s bowels would open up and swallow him but in utter vain. Confusion □ he started to regret why he had not remained inside the café □ yet, it had not at all been his doing. The more the illumination was dying, as the huge crowd of these ghosts and ghomids continued to distance itself away from the lad□s stand. The same thing happened to their beats and songs as well as their acrobatic displays. A charged silence invisibly obscene possessed the air absolutely.

It did not occur to Benlilo to stand up and run. In any way, this was unreasonable because the darkness had now returned and it overwhelmed everywhere maximally. All of a sudden, the Marpolian student discovered, to his greatest horror in life, that two unknown people, or four hands, but with cold and warm fingers seized, from behind, his right and left hands harshly and simultaneously. His life nearly flew out, as all his body parts and frames shook disgustingly.

He cried, □Yheaeeheeeee!□ with tears streaming fast down his cheeks. At last, he had been captured by his enemies, the wicked powers □ *oh, what a pity!* To his conclusion, he was experiencing his last minute on the surface of earth and the variegated ghosts and ghomids, on whom he had earlier set his eyes, would soon slaughter him to the gods and goddesses of the forest. Then, it would be celebration galore in the camp of his adversaries. Thence would it be recorded that darkness had prevailed over his light!

He struggled hard to free himself without success. His captors pulled him up by his two hands. It was then that he looked round to discover, also shivering, the owners of those cold and warm, yet harsh grips on him. In glorification of another startling instance, the boy set his eyes not on human beings really but two figures made up of human and animal features □ a ghost and a ghomid? Yes! Benlilo noticed that none of them resembled the weeping ghost.

The holder of his left hand was the ghost. It was a very short creature □ shorter than the shortest dwarf that the adolescent could remember in Marpolio. This particular ghost stood at nearly two and a half feet above the ground. It was ridiculously labelled with three long arms, each, both that were much longer than its height. Two of these arms shot out from the positions of the human left and right arms, while the third one was rooted into its chest. It had a thick and curved nose that resembled the beak of a forest parrot of the Bight of Biafra.

Its three legs were those of three different animals □ gorilla, antelope and rhino, all decorated with multicolour feathers of birds of many species and scales of varied kinds of reptiles. Like the human being, it had two eyes, two ears and one flat mouth □ all on a head positioned downwards and which faced the opposite direction. On its toes were impiously looking claws. The claws all appeared like a hyena□s while, upon all, this very short figure was clothed in an apparel of rawhide. The garb issued out an odour of indifference.

The second creature was a ghomid. It was comparably opposite to its colleague the ghostly captor. Yet, it had some features along with its companion subjugator □ in respect of its toes□ claws and legs. It had only one but a long arm having a set of twelve fingers. It came into sight in a pair of shorts of raw crocodile skin, while its head was in the typical position of the human being□s. The head carried three long and four short, yet, all-pointing horns.

On the apex of the tallest of these horns was a light □ rotating and radiating blue and red colours infrequently □ like those atop a patrolling New Zealander police vehicle on the roads of Wellington. It had a mighty nose with two branches, which were both flat and emitting infinitesimal smokes. Its eyes were also two like its comrade□s. But unlike the colleague□s eyes, they looked exactly like subsisting coals of fire.

Above all, it had a good height at five feet six inches. Benlilo remained openly incarcerated by the domineering condition in which he had suddenly found himself. He was sweating like a dog destined to be slaughtered in a sacrifice to *ogun,* the Yoruba mythological demon god of iron.

These two captors pulled up their captive Benlilo by his hands and they started to lead him away towards the opposite direction of where the giant ghomid and its entourage had gone. He remained guarded on both sides, as they continued to lead him away into an unknown destination, while the oscillating light on the head of the ghomid did not stop to light up their path through the forest.

Not quite long after their journey had commenced that Benlilo discovered lavish multicolour dots on leaves and the forest□s unmarked path. They remained going in silence with the two slaveholders guarding him on both sides. By now, his mind existed in-between the regions of chaos and peace and sorrow mixed with suspense. He did not know where he was not to talk of where he was being led.

Soon after discovering those splashed marks, Benlilo, still sandwiched in-between the two ghost and ghomid captors, the three walkers met themselves on a dusty road. The dusty road had bountiful decorations. This road ran through the forest, which provided it with overhead shades.

The road was lined left and right with tall poles painted in many colours □ red, yellow, black, white, blue, purple, pink, black and brown. The hostage lad would not know what these had meant. He remained the awfully ignorant sightseer on a journey into the unknown.

The teenager could not set his eyes on more ghomids or ghosts, neither on other living things such as animals nor birds. He was more than baffled to have discovered such a dusty highway inside the virgin forest. It was not a small mystery to him. And so it would remain for quite a very long time to come.

Not long after they had set their feet on the sumptuously decorated dusty road that they reached a point where it seemed closed. There was an immaculately bluish board of cotton across the road. When they arrived this particular point, Benlilo could see the ghomid and ghost bend down to pick the great cotton□s edges that were almost getting in touch with the road. They pulled them up so that they could pass onto a broader road highlighted in completely different manners.

The sky was now aglow with the setting sun. Benlilo was far from being sure if they were still in the human world or in the land of demons. He had been effusively oblivious of when the night exchanged position with the day. Meanwhile, the captors continued to hold his two hands tightly. The group took a bend and, soon, the hostage boy saw an extremely broad and wide billboard suspended in the sky miraculously. The billboard bore an inscription, which read:

□Welcome into the Kingdom of Ghosts and Ghomids,□ written in fifteen international languages: English, French, German, Portuguese, Chinese, Russian, Dutch, Latin, Yoruba, Swahili, Fulfulde, Hausa,

Arabic, Bambara and Greek. When they passed the domineering billboard, they took a new bend, this time to the left. They soon met themselves on a fine-looking plain lawn with few shelters, also fifteen in number, scattered thereon. All those signs or symbols remained unexplained to the captured lad. He got himself better prepared for his eyes to record what they had never recorded before. After all, all these had been predicted but he did not regard the prophesies.

The fifteen shelters were not mud or thatch roofed like most houses in the remotest parts of the homeland of Marpolio. They were all built with something that resembled aluminium. In glorification of yet another shocking discovery, the lawns adjoining the shelters were not of green grasses and flowers but, instead, they were decorated, scrupulously, with multi-coloured plants of near-grass sizes so natural.

Still, Benlilo and his captors remained in silence, as their journey progressed. All along, the two bizarre beings continued to hold tight to his hands. Getting to the last shelter on the beautiful and plain field, the captive saw the second billboard, but not as big as the first one, painted black that bore another inscription, which went thus:

□Welcome into our Kingdom □ the abode of joy, unity, peace and wealth.□ The new billboard demarcated the rainbow plain field and a thick forest. The billboard looked like a gate into this thick forest. The prisoner boy reasoned mutely on what type of joy, unity, peace and wealth that these eerie creatures could boast of. His mind had been divided on whether to wish for more of the horrible experience or escape from the strange creatures into the freedom of the *blossom* of his father□s house.

As soon as they entered the new thick forest, Benlilo overheard his two captors mutter in a language from which he could pick not a molecule of interpretation. It was called *Ghoitd* - the language of ghosts and ghomids. For the very first time, since he was captured following the disappearance of that big light, the two creepy creatures halted their walk, eyed each other and, again, muttered. They smiled.

They continued on their journey into the unknown to the prisoner Benlilo, but known to his ghost and ghomid captors. Life is the journey into the known and into the unknown.

CHAPTER 028

Kingdom Of Ghosts And Ghomids

Come, man, learn some lessons
For beyond your planet lie treasures
Like human beings like weird creatures:
They maintain identities; they also have their king,
As ingenuously necessitated by will, obligation and history.

THE CAPTURED LAD heard a great noise, followed by another clamorous trumpet sound □ both succeeded by a sweet song. This song was heavenly. It was a sick-soul healer, a comforter in a state of loneliness, depression and captivity like this. The song had ministered to his battered soul, but not like those of the cat and the he-goat atop the hill.

Then, the hostage boy discovered that they were moving towards another perceptive forest demarcated from the one in which they were in presently by light □ the source of which he could not see. Up to this point, the journey had been notoriously crude a mystery and so it chose to remain...

There was no sun or moon in sight. The weather was typical of neither a regular day nor an irregular night□s. Behind them was the forest enclosed by the thick darkness, while in their immediate front was this lit one. The journey acquired more strength in complexities, abstractedly, as Benlilo remained the friendless captive of the feral beings.

The sweet song continued as, at once, scores of other ghomids and ghosts shot out of green herbs and woods, as they were running, jumping or flying towards them as soon as they had seen their two comrades with their teenage captive. This was the outcome of the clamorous clarion-calling trumpet sound that had gone off earlier on. In advance, they had heard the news of the boy□s captivity; now, they were parts of the live show and the witnessing crowd.

The youngster Benlilo was greatly terrified. The invaders would soon count in hundreds. Soon after, they had numbered in thousands. He became more appallingly scared. For the two slaveholders in the midst of their co-citizens, they felt apparently more proud as captors of a human being. The unhidden pride advertised itself in their looks as well as through their postures. They could not hide their boosted feelings.

Reaching them, those creatures of various statures and features exchanged brief greetings, for as it is with human beings of the world, so it was with ghosts and ghomids of the wild. All the peculiar creatures were over joyous. They were all overwhelmingly flabbergasted. They became more elated in their wild jubilation, ballooning inside an air pool of promotion, following their capture of a human being, their main rival on planet earth.

Thenceforth was Benlilo handed over to another set of two new guards who seized his two hands straight away, held them roughly and they started to drag him along, even as their electric festivity intensified unobstructed. The boy would not stop to ruminate on what would fall his lot in the hands of these creatures in the end! He could only perceive that future as bleak with his life solely at the mercy of these oddball beings.

Along the way, many of the spectacular beings never stopped to touch his body and to stare at his face in wild surprises. Some smiled to him, as others frowned their faces. Some facial postures terrified him, as others invited. They were so happy to have captured a human being alive. It was evident that majority of them had never seen a human being before. They ran up and down in all pleasure. They shouted their rowdy approvals! They lost their heads and rejoiced the best, as the classical beats to that song sounded better and louder.

They all, with the exception of the two new guards, danced and many of them joined in singing of the song. Ah! the boy-captive saw great wonders for those ghomids and ghosts were awe-inspiring dancers, marvellous drummers, expert trumpeters, expressive singers and amazing circus performers.

Benlilo would never, in his lifetime, forget! Some of those ghosts and ghomids walked with their heads under ordinary circumstances. But when the euphoria of their musical and culturally emergency celebration electrified them, they rolled on the ground like empty barrels danced by undetected forces of whirlwinds. Some danced on one leg each or on their toes □ be the legs those of birds, animals or human or a combination of two or all. Many chuckled. Others, as weird butterflies and owls, flew low and high, crash-landing and retaking off.

Some had their two, one or three legs, each, raised up into or flying low in the sky, while others did whirlwind on nearby greens and yellow shrubs crazily. Some danced coolly in the same manner of happy human beings on the ground even as, still, others manifested on their odd heads or fingers. None of them could contain its joy.

Truly terrific dancers were those ghosts and ghomids! Necks and heads up, down and sideways - rotating heads with horribly terrifying features □ horns, feathers, scary and intimidating eyes, big ears flapping and rolling, noses of different sizes, the mystifying creatures engaged themselves in multiplex acrobatic displays of horrific interests indescribable.

Some of these wild and cool beings used their immense or tiny clothing folds to catch make-believe winds and to disperse the winds in the exhilarating moment. Some of them rolled superbly on the ground, as others jumped and hopped about flexibly. Some danced with their legs only, while others displayed their own dance talents with their heads and hands.

Some crawled curvaceously on the ground, as others swarm inside a play-acting ocean of flowing breeze. The boy remained totally lost in the midst of the festive ghosts and ghomids. He could never have imagined finding himself in this type of wild and weird assembly of ghostly and ghomidly creatures. Words of inwardly interrogating voices in collaboration with those of the weeping, laughing and talkative ghost raced through his mind of circuitous remembrances.

□Yes, it is vindicated, the weeping and talkative ghost is vindicated,□ Benlilo meditated inwardly. Oh, how the conviction from the meditation burned like fire inmost his spirit being!

As the mobile carnival progressed, more and more ghosts and ghomids joined the shapeless train. They laughed. They cheered. Some crowd like cocks. Some whistled variant tunes and tones, while others engaged one another in brief conversations. Others sang their own individual songs of joyousness, victory or thanksgivings, which only they themselves knew, very loudly. All of them freely exercised their exultation of celebration! The happiness continued to run unendingly for the unchallenged big feat achieved over humanity this super-historic once.

Periodically, few of them would jump □ far above the ground and higher unbelievably, even up to touch the leaves of the tall trees around. Some crawled on the ground like reptiles. Others frog-jumped or jogged. All of them had had their ego seriously boosted. They wore bubbles and robes of arrogance for this laudable achievement against mankind, their principal opponents on earth. They were satisfied with their onward celebrations. It was the very first time that they were setting their eyes on a human being.

Every nook and cranny of the immediate environment was now as bright as a healthy daytime. The large crowd of ghosts and ghomids progressed still on their journey with this captive Benlilo dejectedly defenceless in their midst. All interests were contrary to his. Every one except him alone was happy. They arrived at a place that looked like a playground for these mythical creatures.

The new area of land was very clean and neat. There were no small plants there at all, only tall and mighty trees that covered the sky and lent coolness to the atmospheric condition of this portion of the forest. From all directions, healthy wind flowed peacefully.

All the stems of the trees were painted in one colour or the other and some in the mixture of various glittering and dull colours. They all bore self-praise singing inscriptions ranging from,

□Ghosts and Ghomids are loving and peaceful beings□, to, □The Creator has given us this territory, who can take it away from us?□ and, □We worship you our Father, King of Ghosts and Ghomids□ □ written each in over a score of human international languages.

With the first message, Benlilo□s mind got divided between the land of hope and that of despair. The hope was that, since the ghosts and ghomids, □are loving and peaceful beings□, it was likely that they would have mercy on him and spare his life. *But my freedom to connect with my father□s house!* Would these anomalous beings ever be so stupid or generous to the extent of releasing him? To release him into a re-fortified enmity against the *honourable* generations of ghosts and ghomids?

These ghomids and ghosts, all who are over joyous as captors of a human being, their enemy □ would they ever make such a silly mistake? Here was the despairing side. His body frames shook as if they would yank out of holds! Back to the same point of hopelessness, he cried inside of him, *Who will save me from these abnormal creatures?*

There were national flags of well over a hundred and fifty nations. They were flags of all countries of the human universe □ no matter how big or small. For examples, the flag of the Vatican City and other bigger or smaller islands were similarly represented there prominently. These flags each flew resplendently on their individual poles according to the dictates of the piercing wind. What this symbolised was the assemblage of all earthly ghomids and ghosts, of all nations, on this territory, which they now possessed totally.

Also, flying at full mast and above all the others, was the national flag of the ghosts and ghomids□ nation. What this meant was that the nation of ghosts and ghomids was superior to all the nations of the human universe put together □ according to the unfading belief of the weird beings of the wild. The flag was a beautiful one in glowing spotty colours with the portraits of a male ghomid and a female ghost facing each other in smiling standing positions of two creative actions. It also bore an appropriate inscription in:

□Ghosts and Ghomids of all Nations, Unite!
□You have nothing to lose than your chains.□

The journey continued. The mystic beings□ festivities intensified. Benlilo remained the prominent prisoner, without chains and exclusive of a reserved prison, in their midst. His frame of mind remained unstable like the wooden particle dancing on the surface of a river.

The mobile gathering of these uproarious creatures swelled by every minute. It came to a point that hardly could anyone notice the presence of a human being, a slave in person of Benlilo, in the bamboozling assembly. In head count, the invaders would be running into several thousands by now. All the festive activities magnified. To the lad, singers of those *heavenly* songs remained unidentified. The same thing applied to authors of the accompanying, matching musical and cultural beats.

As the vast entourage ploughed its way progressively through the lighted forest, so were new things and happenings invading the focus of the hostage Benlilo. There were now drastic changes in all the forest□s ostentatious decorations. Whether the mystic beings had caused these to happen of recent or the decorations had been permanent features of the forest the lad could not tell. The youngster believed that many more wonders would be possible with these creatures. He could not limit their capabilities but trust them on beyond-belief-magical exhibitions □ more so that their abode was the mystery forest of mysteries.

He looked up only to discover that unlike the usual green leaves, many of the trees had complete red or yellow leaves on their branches, which themselves appeared in several colours. The trees□ fruits become noticeable in white or black colours. These fruits could be foods for the ghosts and ghomids, Benlilo suspected.

On the branches of the trees were multitudes of different birds and fowls, animals of various species and fishes and other sea creatures with human, animals or birds□ heads, bodies or tails. How all these exhibitions had been made possible constituted the bleak mystery to Benlilo even until the end of the regimented voyage?

All these living creatures were soundless on the treetops. They never joined the ghomids and ghosts in their carnival exhibitions of multidimensional phases. They looked as if they were unconcerned. They appeared sickly or in a mourning mood sort of, but none of them, including those creatures in the forms of sea creatures, fell down from the treetops - what another questionable contradiction!

Up at the meeting point of four branches of a mighty tree called *mysterypoint* was hung a titanic figure. The figure was clothed in grim darkness - yet, its rotten glory shined forth intensely. Several standing showers of magical fire and ashes shot out from its mouth. There were also drops of an irritant liquid from its sides and hands.

It was a demon, a fallen angel. Its name was *Ghosmidio*, one of the formerly closest aids to Lucifer □ the morning star. *Ghosmidio* was the god to the generations of ghosts and ghomids. All along, it was to it that the mysterious beings were dedicatedly offering their services of praises and thanksgiving □ in the musically cultural celebration of barefaced egotism so paranormal.

At last, the large entourage arrived at its destination. This was a vast plain of land also swept clean and adorned with sculptures and ivories of various shapes and sizes. The lone observer Benlilo suspected that these wonderfully created treasures were, no doubt, stolen from several lands of human beings, especially African nations. The sculptures and ivories exhibited multifaceted kinds of continental cultures and languages across the globe.

They mirrored life so dense and delicate in the human world, as well as in spiritual realms of both righteousness and wickedness. It would be difficult, even impossible, for an ordinary mind to understand. This must be so because they were symbols and images of life in and beyond the secular life of humans.

All the trees there had fresh and dry palm fronds atop with white cloths tied round their stems, which made them to look like gods and goddesses in Marpolioland. They spoke the wide-ranging languages of the deities. Their ways were of dubious runs in sophisticated outplays. They released no tears of regret for their spiritual and physical leanings. They remained not stagnant in their faith. They grew, developed and multiplied therein.

CHAPTER 029

A World Bizarre Than Fiction

Figureless figures! Contradictions of bold manifestations!
Where□s the photographer of time? The narrator?
The cameraman? The fine artist? The sculptor? The writer?
But why has the powers led the boy into all these?
To prove that worldly life two faces has.

HERE THEY MET another set of these creatures □ about five hundred in number, sitting in a circular format. Earlier, they had been dancing in their own separate musical and cultural show when they approached them.

But as soon as they sighted them afar off, they all sat or stood on their feet, focusing their total attention on Benlilo, the lone outsider in their midst. They were all elders of these creatures□ congregation and they had earlier on received, with boundless joy, the first-class news of the captivity of the human being youngster with utmost euphoria and ecstasy.

Yes, the waiting gathering was made up of *aged people* of this population of ghosts and ghomids. From all outward looks, their ages would be ranging between one hundred and three hundred years. Benlilo tried to guess what sin or sins he had committed to qualify him for this kind of involvement!

In spite of all that he had seen and heard, his disturbed mind could not find a solution to why he was removed from city life to wander lost into the territory of these types of weird creatures. His hunger for evacuation from the forestry life into Marpolio City magnified. His thirst for home became larger-than-life.

The weird beings□ beats and dancing stopped and the boy was led to a corner, still in-between the two egotistical guards. More, these ghomids and ghosts exploded into sensational jubilation. The lad wondered endlessly when the jarring creatures would stop their festivity over his captivity.

They exchanged words and pleasantries. They patted friends and comrades happily at the backs. They hugged one another in jubilation. They rejoiced the more for the victory this time around achieved permanently over a part of humanity □ human beings against who they were filled with envy and jealousy for having denied them, as they believed, the excellent opportunity to inherit and to populate the earth. They never forgave man for this *greatest sin.*

Captive Benlilo looked round to re-discover, panicky, the midst of horrific living creatures, in multitudes, in which he was. It was a complete opposite of the outside world of human beings. What he set his eyes on could not be called a full-size gathering of human beings, neither that of animals and, unquestionably, nor of birds or fishes. Few were of the standard human in figure and stature but they looked hungry and pale □ impatience having deserted their bosoms.

One was a mighty python with two dissimilar heads. The first head was that of a snake and it was in the usual place, while the second head, of an animal that is difficult to classify, occupied the tail position like a colossus. Yet, those two different heads always placed side-by-side whenever this fear-provoking creature was either moving or resting. Two of them had the heads of average human beings, but bodies of other reptiles - the first one a mighty tortoise and the second an enormous house lizard.

Some of these ghosts and ghomids were ridiculously short, while others were of average statures and giants. Several of their legs were toeless, while those with toes had on them claws that pointed west and east, north and south, and up and down. One particular ghomid walked robustly tall, her feminine figure an embodiment of pretentiousness. Some wore remorse postures.

Some were soaked in sober reflections, while, still, others wore portraits of jesters. Some had smiling faces unlike others with grave or stone looks. Some looked sickly, while others bore different trademarks of dismal sights. Some recorded their appearances in immaculate white dresses, even as others were attired in regalia of green, red, blue and black, *etc*.

Several ones□ were multicolour. Some were symbols of nonsensical excessiveness, while others appeared naked or half-naked. Some were in bones, others as elephants and hippopotamuses □ full of flesh, muscles and hunches. Some bubbled like dropping spring water; others seemed as covered in blood, while one appeared like death with its set of teeth in the shape of unarranged bones murky. Others appeared in simple and casual dresses beyond description, as some were clothed in assorted kinds of raw animal skins.

Figureless figures! A world of contradictions this truly was! Many of the ghosts and ghomids, Benlilo could see clearly, were well figured beautiful *women* with finely plaited or woven hair, but nonconforming enough, with, what! long and thick beards.

The mind of Benlilo flashed back to horror films. How he wished that at least a video cameraman were around to record the mysterious beings□ activities and personality revelations for posterity! He was triple sure that such a movie would have fetched the fortunate professional cinematographer billions of Dutch Marks.

About three or four of these creatures resembled men but with earrings on and bumping breasts or tails to show off. Many had the faces of babies but bodies of elders. Others had bodies of babies but heads of aged people. Many were headless bodies but, still, another recorded sensation of darkness, they could easily find their ways through the huge crowd like majority of their headed counterparts.

Yet, a few of them were only heads without bodies. Some looked like witches. Some as familiar spirits. Others resembled wizards and sorcerers. Five of them appeared like lunatics. Many were with horns but only one ghomid could boast of a crown. Some were armed with bows and arrows and they all dressed like primeval warriors in the Greek mythology.

If there was anything uniform in the appearances of these beings, that thing was definitely their non-uniformity in all things physical. Sometimes, Benlilo forgot all about his captivity; he nearly burst into laughter unconsciously. At other moments, he would be very close to tears. Irritation found a suitable abode in and out of him. For many at times, it seemed as if his soul was about being terrified out of his body for his head to swell and every strand of hair thereon to stand on end endlessly. Almost every minute recorded a groundbreaking thing with the grisly multitude.

Of particular importance in this mystical gathering was a ghomid, about eleven feet in height. Its body was built in the format of a human being□s. It had a three-feet-long neck that was thinner than that of an Angolan ostrich. Surprisingly, the extremely skinny neck carried two big heads that faced two different directions.

Both heads were of a human being with, each: two eyes, one nose, two ears, one big mouth stuffed with crocodile-like teeth - but the heads were completely barren of hair. From these two hairless heads shot out each eight tiny snakes with their tail ends rooted firmly therein.

All the sixteen snakes danced here and there to some beats unheard by the ear. The ghomid□s three legs faced three different directions. They were as hairy and strong as those of a chimp of long age. And on the three different legs each were seven toes, all with non-uniformed claws measuring almost a foot apiece in length.

It had no arms. In the positions of arms were two big wings labelled with long feathers of myriad insignia, clapping up and down. It wore no clothe and no organ of reproduction was seen anywhere on or into its body. Still, Benlilo could not see the weeping and laughing ghost in the midst of the hugely strange get-together.

The boy looked left only to see the giant ghomid that had once offered the forest the grandest elucidation. It now sat on a majestic chair, which was golden in colour. Its body was decorated with all indescribable sorts from ankle to neck. How these creatures were able to achieve this singularly multifarious feat, so quickly, baffled the lad terrifically. Only its head, hands and the lower parts of its legs could now be seen clearly. It resembled an Indian god in a feral fable of pursuing horror.

In short, it was the king of these ghosts and ghomids and chair of a greatly unforgettable occasion. It had a small but gorgeous crown on its head. The crown was made of the combination of gold, diamond and silver - with some precious stones. It had a petite beaded staff of office held in its left hand, while its wrists and neck were prolifically bejewelled with costly droplets.

By the king□s left-hand side, there was another creature of a spectacular look. It appeared in spotless white regalia lined, beautifully, with delicately flowery blues. A supposedly *woman* ghomid, it had its body adorned in very artistically convoluted manners.

This particular ghomid was full of copious smiles and it had its hair, of deep green and pink in colours, plaited in super-complex manners. By all conclusion of Benlilo, no African woman hairdresser or professional weaver and plaiter could ever achieve this exploit of the female ghomid□s hair-do. This clearly demonstrated that ghosts and ghomids were highly talented creatures artistically. They were creatures with grand artistically cultural backgrounds and they were very proud of the budding heritage.

Tied to the variegated ends of the plaited hair were some decorations like gold rings and thin, long scarves flying coolly according to the orders of the blowing breeze. Its two hands were like harmless but restless green snakes and they were very long □ both also craftily decked in all sorts of conceivable and inconceivable jewelleries. It was the queen of the ghosts and ghomids. It also sat conspicuously on its own illustrious throne made with a combination of valued stones.

There was as well present in the gathering a distinguished *male* ghost. It was dressed in admirably flowing cassock attire made of something like dry leaves, pure red lined with white in colours. It held a long staff of white and golden brown in its right hand and a big book of golden hard cover in the left one. Its head, to which a tread that flew a short kite was tied, was that of a leopard.

Its two ridiculously short arms were those of a human being but they carried two moderate fins downward, each. The two fins were both sharp and beautiful and they were rooted into the arm□s socket. It looked peaceful and loving. Around this priest-like ghomid were others, about six of them in number. These ones looked like officiating ministers. They all radiated *love* and *gentleness* unlike some of the ghosts and ghomids who could fright to death. They seemed to be very reserved.

The fact was that these creatures were actually in a wedding ceremony. The bride was the imperial *woman*-ghomid. The bridegroom was the king of the ghosts and ghomids. The day recorded two outstanding achievements for the king of the ghost and ghomid□s populace according to the tradition of these beings. First, it was the day of its coronation as the new king of the ghosts and ghomids kingdom.

And, second, the moment marked its wedding ceremony. Not surprising therefore, both the *bride* and the *bridegroom* wore, on their hands, snow-white gloves dotted with blue spots □ as it is in the normal world of humans, so it was in the strange world of ghosts and ghomids. They were the happiest and most honoured and colourful *couple* in the gathering.

According to the highly cherished custom of the ghosts and ghomids, the heir apparent to the great throne must wed its wife on the very day of its coronation as the king. The two ceremonies □ the state coronation and wedding, must go together. Thereafter the husband became the crown-king and monarch, as its wife emerged the crown-queen and a member of the *Supreme Council* □ the highest ruling body of the ghost and ghomids□ kingdom.

Benlilo had his two eyes fixed on the real scene whereby the priest and its assistant ministers, and the queen with the king, were the foremost actors and an actress. A messenger came in with a big bowl containing not less than nine gallons of a coloured liquid.

The woman-like messenger knelt by the feet of the king. It handed over the big container to the new ruler who then guzzled its liquid contents. The zealously watching mammoth crowd roared in a thunderous ovation for the openly demonstrated ability of their new monarch. This was their stamp of approval for its Royal Majesty□s kingship, as it had openly demonstrated.

It was at this point in time that Benlilo remembered, yet again, the departed weeping ghost and its hurtful words of harrowing truth. The lad realised that he could not see this particular ghost □ a self appointed sympathizer of the human race, in the midst of the convocation of the unconventional beings.

At this junction, the lad became very unsure whether the talkative creature was actually a ghost. Or if it was a ghost, why had it been missing all along in a popular gathering of ghosts and ghomids like this? Maybe, at a later time, it would still come up to introduce itself to the boy, he would not know. Maybe it had changed form, who could tell? He left the matter for history, through time, to sort out by itself.

He also called to recollection the truthfully ingenuous words, in a fractional part, of the interrogative voice of whether he had passed through the valley of the shadow of death before. These pained him but his mind was soon off tracks with the two awkward issues. An uneasy addition came with the voice□s introduction, to him, the University of Life. He resigned himself to fate, the fate of the unknown.

The horrifying population□s happiness and celebration multiplied for the additional good omen that it was during the double-portion august occasion, of the king and queen□s wedding and their concurrent coronation, that a human being from the land of the living was captured. This had never happened in the history of the ghosts and ghomids kingdom. It was categorically a symbol of good things to come into the ghost and ghomids□ country during Their Royal Majesties□ amalgamated reign.

As soon as the messenger had departed, the king beckoned to one tall and *male* stout ghomid who could have been passed for man but for its head of a cock with a fairly long beak, yellow bright in colour like that of a large diurnal bird of prey, precisely a peculiar eagle of might, courage and bravery.

Reaching the king, it crowed like a cock, once! and knelt down by its Majesty□s feet. Cavernous silence reigned and all eyes were focused on the king and the messenger. All minds concluded that the king must have had an important directive to issue in respect of the lone intruder to their august gathering and they were right. It was highly forbidden for □loathed man□ from the □abominable land of humans□, to witness the most important ceremony of □dignified ghomids and ghosts□ inside their □decent kingdom.□ Benlilo was the only human being, in history, to have eye-witnessed part of a ghosts and ghomids□ ceremony like this.

The king pointed at the boy captive in the corner and gave the ghomid messenger an order. It was the first official order from the new monarch of the ghomids and ghosts kingdom on its illustrious throne. And for being royally selected for this assignment, this particular servant was considered by the ghomid and ghost□ populace to be □so lucky.□ How their eyes of envy were olive-green on him!

The servant ghomid too was saturated with gratitude and fulfilment. Involuntarily, its ego ballooned. It rose summarily on its feet analogous to a well-groomed soldier, crowed once again in its own fashioned traditional salutation, crowned with a gentle bow. It headed soldierly for where Benlilo was.

Getting to the captive, he rudely seized his right hand with its own left and started to pull him away as if he was a convicted criminal. The lad□s two former guards did not struggle to retain the boy. Its Majesty□s order had prevailed. Majority of these creatures eyed one another and they concurred pleasingly that the new guard was up to the task.

Benlilo followed his new arrester without any protest whatsoever. Thus was he led away from the scene of the tremendous celebration, down to what could be identified as the western side of the area, as all the strange creatures followed them briefly, in high-flying pride, with their eyes of egotism and of curiosity. Not quite long after they had departed from the crowded scene that a bell rang very loud, followed with a great shout and then the big trumpet sounded again.

The drumbeats roared, all over for a second time, into fabulous eminence and the goodly incomparable music blared. The hostage young man Benlilo stole a flashy look backward only to see those ghosts and ghomids dancing in very boisterous and convoluted manners. Having ridded their multi-coloured event of the intruder, the royally communal ceremony of their new king and queen□s combined coronation and wedding had resumed.

NOTE: Coninued in Volume Four

<u>Blurb – For Back Cover Only</u>

UNIVERSALLY SATIRISING, THE mystery forest is alluringly beautiful and inordinately ugly. The uncommon experience is thrilling and horrifying an extraordinary adventure. Decorated culturally with high-class dramatic, musical and cinematographic outplays, this is, figuratively, the super-complex story of the student man□s struggles, battles and journeying through unwinding labyrinths of the *University of Life.* Time□s recorded observations and interpretations are coded heavy in abstract planes, racing scenes and flying acts. Boisterous and thunderous seasons run along paths of eras, as history for posterity pursues unendingly. Refluxes of retribution. Harvests. Testimonies. Bizarre even obscene deeds are meaningful messages to humankind. Rooted epically in the collective African Mythology, this is the narrative of Benlilo in a dead night yet virgin day of wonders and mysteries. Weighty words and active actions through lucid prose, singing poetries and striking dramas tell philosophies. Night and day, light surviving darkness. Symbols, images, allegories, metaphors, parables and proverbs - all represent multifaceted life and the earthly place belongs to both the living and the dead. Terror! Thunder and lightening! Horror! Fear! Bitterness and joy! Ultimate dynamics of power! Coal is for fire, as pearl is for beauty. A field of silver, diamond and gold. Vision flies, as mission runs. Messages relay, unlike ambitions in displays. Excellences compete with extreme cruelties. What of affiliations and diversifications? A fiesta of fast, lethargic and rolling events! This train of awe-inspiring revelations is the hot narrative of love and lust, war and peace, hope and despair, successes and failures plus tragedies, as juxtaposed with comedies through amoebic layers of wonderful surprises and action-packed suspense spots □Yes! this is *Operation QMC-UKDDC* the superstar account: galaxy of a thousand stars and a thousand thorns. Beauty and crown glory of the African storytelling culture, with its volume at well over two million words, *Midnight of Horrors!* is the biggest, most complex and longest storyline; largest, greatest(?) and richest(?) literature novel that has ever come out of Africa □ and you reserve the right to find out why □

MIDNIGHT

Of

HORRORS!

(Virgin Day Chain Revelations Explosive□)

****

SANMI-AJIKI

Volume Four

<u>*NOTE: Continued from Volume Three.*</u>

CHAPTER 030

The Ghosts And Ghommids□ Anthem

In possession of identity for bold manifestations
Beauty of culture in jolly good demonstrations:
All at attention, they rise in honour of their beloved land.
Now, tell, who says only human beings have etiquette?
Behold unimaginably weird creatures of the wild□!

BENLILO AND HIS new guard were soon distanced from the gathering by a space of about a hundred yards when, abruptly, all the melodically enriching festivities stopped and an introspective quietude reigned. Then, an additional broader, wilder and more beautiful *National Flag* of the *Ghosts and Ghommids Nation* was hoisted to fly at full mast right in the midst of the eminent social event, but high-tall to the sky. This had stamped official recognition to the binary royal ceremony and all the ghommids and ghosts roared in wildest jubilation.

After that, many trumpet blasts roared from the commands of the professional trumpeters. The talking drums rolled out their meaningful voices by the proficient handlings of the accomplished drummers. The angelic lead-singers took off in a magnificent style so formal and rhythmic.

It was truly a serious affair. Subsequently, the whole congregation, including the king and its queen, rose in attention. Thus, classically, the ghost and ghommids□ *National Anthem* entitled, *Arise All Ghosts and Ghommids* was marvellously rendered.

The *anthem* was a clarion call to all ghosts and ghommids of the universe to come together as one to dwell in their *own homeland*, and separate themselves from the □polluted world of human beings where you□re in hidings and love, peace and joy are abominations.□ Of course, rendered in *Ghoitd* their universal language, below is the translation of the eighteen-verse two-stanza *sacred* song into English Language:

Ghosts and Ghommids of all lands
Anointed, blessed and preserved □
Arise! Unite in love; unite in peace;
Unite in service; unite for progress □
Unite in voice, song and deed:
One nation! One destiny for better
Never to war! Never again to famine!
Ghommids and Ghosts of all lands, unite!
You□ve nothing to lose than your chains.

Ghost and Ghommids of all lands
Favoured, beautiful and reserved □
Arise! Unite in faith; unite in hope;
Unite in joy; unite in hospitality □
Unite in soul, spirit and body:
One identity! One goal for best
Never to slave! Never again to famish!
Ghommids and Ghost of all lands, unite!
You□ve nothing to lose than your chains.

After this followed the rendition of the *Liberty Creed* of this congregation of ghosts and ghommids. Every one of them remained standing unshakable on its feet. They threw away their faces like no-nonsense Adolph Hitler□s soldiers on a warpath to recite the ten line one stanza *LC* that goes:

Liberty is freedom honey-sweet
Joy is rest ever fresh, oh sure!
Peace is the glory of life holy
Beauty is our rainbow of age
Unity is love duly exercised
By Hope sustained for Victory

Benlilo was not opportune to study the situation for long. His new arrester pulled him by the right hand; it gave him a flashy but deadly slap with its left. It, by this, proved itself to the enslaved boy, so soon, that it was a no-nonsense taskmaster. Task mastering was the first order of oppression and the unhidden repression had started already. The oppressor could not hide it.

The angst-ridden teenager did not speak a word or indicate any sign of resistance whatever. He knew that if he resisted the slaveholder in any way, it was trouble for him. That would simply mean he was dangerous for only one ghommid to keep. A greater measure of keeping him would then be designed and that would crown his future freedom from the land of reality more of an illusion.

Some of the ghosts and ghommids who had watched the one sided drama of how the bombastic ghommid had pulled him and awarded him its dirty slap became reassured that the king had made the right choice, that the guard was competently up to the task. They nodded their heads jubilantly. They became happier that their superiority over humankind had been established once and for all.

The overconfident self-satisfied slaveholder led its *sheep* Benlilo on and they continued with their walk down into the forest, which was now completely devoid of decorations but normal in outlook. The identity of the forest was at the present wholly lost to the boy hostage. His journey into the unknown strengthened. He could nil guess where the journey of his life, as defined by the mystery forest, was heading and ending.

They reached a point where they turned left, climbed a small embankment handsomely carpeted with wooing green grass. They descended it and continued in their walk until they arrived at the foot of a mighty cottonseed tree. They walked leisurely round it and staring them directly at the face was a small mud hut with thatch roof. Still holding him by the right hand with its left, Benlilo□s guard bent down. It pulled the gate of the hut with its right hand and led its detainee inside.

Contrary to the hostage□s thought, they did not meet any creature, be it ghost or ghommid, inside the small hut. The hut was furnished with three different wooden chairs. One was in the figure of letter six. The other took after the pattern of a canoe, while the third chair resembled the junction of two branches of a tree.

Exhibiting a good measure of confidence as a capable slave keeper, the ghommid guard sat on one. It crossed its legs arrogantly, while the lad sat sorrowfully on another chair. Now, the cock-headed ghommid had left the boy□s hand but its mind and eyes would not depart from the slave. Benlilo could see that the guard was all attention, exactly in the manner of a competent slave keeper.

Now and then, the ghommid looked up the rafters. At irregular intervals, it returned the probing eyes and inconclusive mind on the slave who remained speechless and befuddled beyond gage. Benlilo meditated, negatively, on whether his end was actually near in the hands of those ghosts and ghommids. He got more anxious on whether he had been kept away from them so as to be slaughtered later as a sacrificial goat to their deity.

He remembered that the baffling beings were in the midst of a greatly memorable carnival. What in particular if they desired a special feast to memorialise the coronation of their new royalty and their collective mind went straight to him? For sure, these spine-chilling and crazy creatures would be happy, contented and fulfilled to make history by slaughtering a human being, their archrival, for a special feast on the occasion of an unsurpassed festival like this! All histories would record it for posterity to treasure forever more. A great honour to the ghosts and ghommids□ world and a mighty dishonour to the humanity fold!

Benlilo was thus deeply concerned, in particular, on the possibility of these extra-wild creatures turning out to be carnivorous beings. The boy remained lost in his lone world besieged by abject ignorance and, but the tragedy that was soon to befall him □ how pitiable!

The film of how the weird creatures had captured and treated him so far ran rapidly through the eye of his mind. Their curiosity, happiness and eyeing □ all had pointed at the conclusive realism that the ghosts and ghommids were self-appointed unpretentious haters and egotistical enemies of human beings. He concluded, persuasively, that all the vituperations of the weeping ghost had bordered on nothing else but envy of the human race. After all, the ghost was a true representative of these ghosts and ghommids kingdom!

The idea crossed his mind of the probability of his rushing at and seizing the guard by the head and throat and strangulating it right inside the hut but the consequence of failure would unquestionably be dire □ nothing short of on the spot death! What about the idea of throwing a nearby strong rope around its neck and falling it to the ground strangulated?

But, again, the possible failure and its aftermath! The guard looked mature and battle-ready. It was gigantic and terrifying! For it to be chosen by the king to take charge of his detention, all alone, it must have been a war hero in the past or in the present □ somehow! On the other hand, Benlilo was only a lad of sixteen years and he looked worn-out at the present.

The ghommid guard appeared domineeringly dangerous! Visibly, it looked like a devoted hunter after and hater of humanity, which really it was. It could luckily escape any of the strangulation attempts to quickly alert its fellow ghosts and ghommids. All by itself, it could be up to the task, as the king and the generality of the ghosts and ghommids had trusted. The wicked slap that it gave the boy at their departure from their gathering demonstrated, forcefully, that this was a practical slave keeper. Benlilo could only see in it a visual rendering of death and nothing of life.

Flying, running or crawling, many of those scary creatures would abandon the royal ceremony immediately. They would then be set loose in an enthusiastic competition to capture him, all at once into a renewed more brutal bondage. As they could elect, one of them could be ordered to swallow him up or he would serve as meat shreds for just a few of them.

Benlilo seemed to have sunk deep into a pit of loss. What of if, as he had earlier thought, they chose to keep him forever inside their zoo as a permanent and living exhibit of disgrace to abhorred humanity? He believed strongly that there was no experiment that these creatures would not want to perform with him as the living human object of ridicule and disgrace.

Meanwhile, the royal celebration of the ghommid and ghosts□ population had resumed and it intensified beautifully. The mysterious ones□ musical and cultural song□s rendition flowed thinly into the boy□s ears. At the same time, a lot of positive and negative thoughts furthermore crossed his mind. Majority of them bothered on the possibility of securing his escape, miraculously, from the open gulag of the wild creatures. But how? Like a timed bomb quietly and successfully diffused, the stupefaction spot had left him now.

Not long after they had taken their seats inside this small hut, the ghommid guard stood up. It stared at the rafters all round about it like a busy human building examiner. Irregularly, its monitoring eyes did not cease to re-connect onto Benlilo its prisoner. It headed towards the small gate made of palm fronds and ropes; it removed it. It passed through to the outside but left the entrance open.

Soon after that, the lad also stood up from his seat inaudibly. He tiptoed near the gate and peeped through it to see and to study the outside world and, in particular, know what the ghommid was engaged in. There he saw it looking up and down, admiring the trees and their green and yellow leaves? It would also look right and left, enjoying the pleasantly natural atmosphere? It seemed to be fully engaged in the natural pleasures of its observation.

Peeping further, Benlilo saw a big river running its natural course down the forest. In distance, the river was just less than seventy yards to the hut. The river flow did not rush; it did not cone or crow. It appeared peaceful and reserved. The boy peeped boldly and he was caught by the bodyguard ghommid. The guard shivered badly. It had thought that the slave was scheming for an escape from its prison.

The ghommid guard hurried to the captive's side but before it could reach the entrance of the hut and push him inside after some ruthless slaps, Benlilo had stepped out gingerly □ but not to engage it in a wrestling or a fight. As they met, the lad quickly gesticulated to it, very respectfully, that he was thirsty and wanted to drink water □ on his knees. The youngster had learnt the lesson from the ghosts and ghommids, the way they respected their king, that they were lovers of reverence, honour and culture.

The ghommid guard got his message right but it was ignorant of how its captive's problem could be solved. *Deep silence.* The ghommid raised its both hands to support its waist. It seemed all lost in a tangle of how the problem of its unusual hostage could be resolved. The boy's inner eye surveyed the mind of the ghommid. He could discern some thoughts going through and scrambling for settlement inside the captor's intelligence.

The slaveholder folded its hands across its chest, as it glanced through the treetops, still thinking. Knowing fully that his keeper was lost in this sticky situation, a good actor, Benlilo sneaked a look down and he drew its attention and pointed at the river flowing down the sloppy side of the forest. As a response, the slave keeper also stole a brief look and it caught sight of the river. It smiled broadly for the first time since it took over the sole guardianship of the lad. Its mind secured a relief but for how long?

It nodded its big cock-like head satisfactorily and then demonstrated to the captive to let them go to the riverside so that he could quench his thirst thereby. What a kind gesture on the part of the guard! Again, Benlilo went down in a gentle bow and kneeling to appreciate its kindness. A feudalist like their king, the honoured ghommid was well pleased. Ghommids and ghosts too cherish honour by gratitude. It smiled flourishingly. It did not know that it was having its very last laugh, that it would soon weep and howl bitterly...

It walked up to Benlilo and, self-importantly, signalled to him and both of them wadded, quietly and pleasantly, through the chunky layers of the dry leaves in-between green plants and trees, down to the riverside. Now, it no longer held the hostage's hand. The lad followed it very closely and freely without hurry. As they arrived at the bank of the big river, the ghommid stepped aside, pointed at the water and gesticulated to him to satisfy himself.

Again, Benlilo bowed gently in gratitude to the kind-hearted slave master. The ghommid guard stayed about four yards to the river, on the dry sandy area, as the slave had knelt to thank him dearly more for its love. The lad moved to get nearer to the river so that he could drink the water. He got there, did not look backward but bent down and formed his two hands into the shape of a cup to drink the water with. In the state of doing this, he stole a flashy glance at the ghommid who was now busy looking up the treetops. Benlilo smiled.

The fool in its game of foolishness does not know anything! It will soon learn the saddest lesson of its life and it shall never survive the tragedy - the thought rang its knell against the guard. Benlilo's mind did some beautiful and tedious but fast calculations. His heartbeat jumped.

Tool of kindness fated for blunder
Candidate of boo-boo in the season of joy
Getting lost and never to be found

Beware of slippery son of man, beware!
Life is never smooth to the traitor!
Beware! No leper is beautiful in the society.

Thus would an anonymous voice sing, proverbially, from the keenly watching wind for the ghommid but it did not hear and it did not heed the repetitive warning. Benlilo would later understand, much to his delight, why the warned ghommid guard did not hear and why it did not heed the warning.

Like a spark, the hostage lad remembered a mythical fable once told at a moonlight gathering of women and children around some men elders in a Marpolian farm, after dinner, to tell stories of the land. In the tale, it was a taboo for ghommids and ghosts to enter rivers, especially big and deep ones. Some conclusions of positivism settled inside the loaded soil of his hope. Again, he smiled flowerily.

According to the weird beings□ traditional belief, great and mighty spirits, hungry and carnivorous, inhabited inns of the rivers and seas. To compound their tough stance, as hinged on this strong mythical credence, many of their ancestors they had lost to rivers before they became wiser and the sad experience taught them never again to have anything whatsoever to do with rivers, which they now regarded as death traps □ truly like gallows!

Hence, in permitting its captive to come to the river□s side at all, the ghommid guard only shunned traditional sentiments to wear a garb of a wholehearted hospitality. However, whether the ghommid was ignorant of the traditional taboo or it did not remember it or something! It had thought and believed that it was its duty, as a host, to take good care of its guest. It never suspected that there was limit to everything in life, including showing kindness. A ghommid of the wild, how could it have known that life had two diametrically enemy faces? That it existed in-between joy and sorrow, victory and defeat, tragedy and comedy?

It never knew that its hospitality would land it inside a furiously burning trouble. It did not sense that, armed with the combined digger and shovel of kindness and hospitality, accordingly, it was digging its own grave with its own hands. That it was on its way to becoming the greatest enemy of fellow ghosts and ghomids in the *beloved* kingdom. An outcaste to the *decent* society in the making. The unbeautiful leper as the proverbial song had predicted.

It did not know that its appointment by Its Royal Majesty to take guardianship of the internee Benlilo could mean life or death. The story turned out to be funny and boring, so interesting, even thrilling a master piece□

CHAPTER 031

Amusing Tragedy Of Kindness

Life and death! Blocking post along the journey of time
The forestry venture climaxing into drama of the unforgotten:
Wisdom speaks in the assembly of loss, wisdom mightier than strength.
Proverb is lost wholly to the powerful fool in the season of kindness,
As first-class joy willingly transfigures into sorrow unlimited.

BENLILO HAD BEEN thirsty for long and this was a fair opportunity. He got the first cup full of the river□s water and drank. He also drew up the second filled cup and drank it off. Then, dipping the third into the water, he stole another flashy look at the ghommid.

The kind and brutal custodian was still admiring excellent nature, as the forest had offered. His head, eyes and mind back in place, all of a sudden, the lad frog-jumped neatly far into the near middle of the river and he started to swim, very speedily and eagerly, across it.

For the rowdy bubbling of the water, the ghommid immediately turned backward, saw the saddest happening to its disaster-prone life □ the most *beautiful dream* actualised by its slave, and it raised an outcry. It ran madly and sadly very close to the river, desperately wanting to stop the fleeing boy, but it could not enter it. It now remembered the mythical taboo? Oh, how its exercised kind-heartedness pained it like fire burning mercilessly within its flesh! It remembered the ageless enmity between ghommids and ghosts and human beings. Children of man, ever untrustworthy! Forever and ever dangerous!

Instantly, it became over-worried. Continuously, it stamped its feet on the wet sand at the thin edge of the water. Anxiously, it moved as if it would dash inside the river to bring back its escaping slave into its detention but it dared not commit the greatest blunder of its life and it never did. It surged forward and backward, up and down, like a drunken masquerade upon which hot water had been poured. How it wished that history could be reversed □ but no!

At this point, Benlilo received the sure confirmation, in his spirit, that the ghommid had now remembered the taboo. How pitiable! What had happened could not be made not to happen. History had recorded the mystic creature□s disastrous blunder and that was it. Posterity had treasured it for partial and impartial time against its person. The escaping lad, on his part, was seized by greater optimistic demonstrations in and across the river.

The foolish ghommid thus got drowned inside the sea of regrets. It danced and ran like a wild lunatic of a ghommid freshly baptised by an overbearing spirit of rampage. It made a dying cry like a captive who was under a serial persecution with a hot piercing iron deeper into its flesh. It ran some short circuits of the madness. It held its cock-looking head with its two hands and wailed like a shot big bird. The campaign of swimming Benlilo augmented for the fear of the wailing and weeping ghomid□s colleagues appearing and gunning for him.

Besides, the ghommidly once overconfident creature tried to stop the lad but it was too damned late! Still dancing about crazily the riverbank, it suddenly rushed downward, bent down and filled its two hands with sands. Standing up with its eyes as red as an evil fire, it showered the swimming boy with the tiny pebbles but the swimmer escaped unhurt by diving deeply covered with the water only to reappear farther to this dream side of the river and nearer to the other side. This aborted effort pained the ghommid guard harder. It also got hold of a piece of wood, which it hurled at the escaping lad but the weak arrow missed the target as well.

The anguished one whistled some odd tunes broadly irritating and appalling, and topped it with another cry of running grief. It roared like an amputated young lion encircled by a gigantic bush fire inside an enclosure with no chance at all for escape. It gnashed its two sets of long teeth to produce different kinds of a new round of funny sounds. Atypical of some radio martial jingles when an African village despot has been overthrown in a dawn and bloody military coup d'état, the odd sounds magnified and waned off randomly.

The trapped ghommid crowed like a dying cock; it hooted like a captured and angst-ridden owl. Falling and rising, thus it met itself in not a little trouble. Thus it was wildly confronted with a problem that had no solution. Its body was soon covered all over with filthy sweats. Avid restlessness became its fortune. Groaning in the severest pain of non-forgiveness for itself, it emerged the almighty loser of all time in the kingdom of ghosts and ghommids.

In full force, Benlilo increased his speed on the river like a good swimmer that he was. Poor ghommid! no wings with which to fly after him, its erstwhile prey. Moreover, if at all it had got or suddenly developed one, the lad was resolutely determined to engage the slaveholder in a tough and rough battle right inside the river.

Determined resolutely never to allow this more-than-golden opportunity to be lost, the boy had sworn to overpower and drown it therein for a feast for wild and carnivorous spirits that believably inhabited the river□s deep. The swimming boy grew fiercer in desperation. Within the next ninety-five seconds, he had swum across the big river to the other side successfully.

Fast, Benlilo climbed up the muddy steep and looked backward again to see the ghommid running helter-skelter like an anguished lunatic. It ceaselessly stamped its feet angrily on the thick layers of the dry leaves and on the sand, still wailing and weeping, howling and hooting □ it was more than true that a fire of life was burning inside its skin. It stuck a finger of bitter regret in-between its two set of teeth and bite it for blood to rush there out.

It was now that the boy realised, to his crowning pleasure, that the ghommid creature was a deaf and dumb one - this was the reason why it did not hear or heed the windily proverbial message of warning. It was a member of the weird beings□ deaf and dumb family. It longed to shout for help but its voice would not reach anywhere. This pathetic disability and its attendant frustration pained it to no end but it pleased Benlilo abundantly. It aided greatly his evolving process of escape. He sincerely wished that the ex-slaveholder would remain inside the captivity of its natural dumbness and deafness.

The severely agonising ghommid had actually lost its senses. It fell down again but it speedily stood up and resumed its soulful lamentations its weepy eyes still focussing at the escapee. Again, it rushed to the slim edge of the water for Benlilo on the other side of the river far away. The boy faced its direction, made sure that it saw him, and waved to it jubilantly atop the mound rise before he dashed behind a tree and raced down a slope into joyful disappearance. Oh, this was certainly the bitterest point of the story for the devastated ghommid! The agonising guard intensified on its painful exercises of bitter regrets and expressions of grief.

A typical slaveholder, how it avidly wished that a miracle of the unexplainable would bring back the ex-slave into its slavehood! Watching greens, the wind and other environmental and elemental forces applauded the escapee for the wisdom egg that hatched his fast freedom. Their open ovations seemed as additional thorns into the flesh of the swaggering ghommid. He wailed and wept the more; its hammered head ached as if it would fly off the neck carrying it.

Idiotic ghommid! Isn□t it a truism that every act, including showing kindness, has its limit? No ghost or ghommid appeared in sight. Thank goodness! the ghommid remained its dumb self. It certainly was stuck in the dilemma of whether or not to run and report the tragic incident to the congregation of fellow ghosts and ghommids. It leaned to the side of disagreement than that of agreement. Benlilo continued to widen the gap between him and the ex-guard at the other bank of the river. *Freedom is honey-sweet* - he could not heave a sigh of relief yet.

Immediately after his miraculous escape, the fright that invaded the heart of the lucky boy was the possibility of some of the mystic ghosts and ghommids, who had wings, flying over in a frantic bid to re-capture and re-enslave or kill him gruesomely. He could never tell whether the broken-hearted ghommid, in its mixture of panic and madness, had been courageous enough to run back to its colleague ghosts and ghommids to report what tragedy its person had run into. For this, Benlilo swore never to rest until his hard-won victory was safely ensured and his liberty ground properly consolidated.

But now, by dint of imagination, the variegated lamentations, weeping, wailing and crying of the *stupid ghommid* the youngster could faintly hear in his mind in the distance, as he continued to find his way inopportunely through the forest, directly opposite to the forsaken river, his route of escape. As he was running, it now seemed as if the trees and plants were afraid of him. They appeared to be giving way to his passage.

Having covered a presumably good distance to the riverside, the lad halted his race and he began to walk fast. Still, remembering all he had shortly gone through, he would break loose sometime, racing like a mad sprinter while, at times, he looked backward and sideways in glances of curious survey, now by stroke of the imagination.

The night was drawing near - yet, Benlilo intensified on his efforts. He was avidly hungry. He sighted a pawpaw tree with two ripe fruits but for the fear of the injured ghosts and ghommids, he could not wait. By now, he was totally lost to the roars and howling of the guard ghommid. Having committed the heinous disaster of its life, and knowing full well that there was no remedy whatsoever in sight, maybe it had been ghommidly enough and had hanged itself with the rope inside the hut or jumped inside the river to commit suicide! *In any case, that is its fated funeral to celebrate! Its own catastrophic business to oversee!*

On the other hand, how would it go back to the ghost and ghommids' kingdom, Their Royal Majesties the King and its Queen, to tell them that the goldenly uncommon slave trusted into its care had escaped, courtesy of its foolishness in the art and act of kind-heartedness? Surely, everybody in the weird kingdom would see him as a spoiler, the greatest rebel ever. All would henceforth picture him as nobody but a disgrace, more of a bastard - a rebel to the ghosts and ghommids□ kingdom.

Surely, before the king would voice out its punishment, its first ever judgement in the exaltedly imperial seat of authority, the communal traitor must have been torn into shreds and eaten up by angry and hungry fellow ghommids and ghosts, just a few of them, in revenge for its bald-faced stupidity! Benlilo was all the more self-assured that the guard would never return into the kingdom of ghommids and ghosts alive. Not a sign of human existence was visible around. The forest remained in its naturalness.

Yet, the spontaneity of the forest was all fraudulent innocence! The deceptive naturalness conjured nothing but composed disgust. Nonetheless, Benlilo could also observe a rich river of hope flowing smoothly through the newest sphere. Additionally, the beauty of the forest transmitted no fear or anxiety. The cooling wind continued to pierce charmingly - invoking the love for his newfound freedom, and manifesting the supposedly stainless hope. Life was amoeba inside the anonymous forest.

At the present, the lad had forgotten all about the lion-like monster, the he-goat, the cat and the ghommid with the head of a cock. His total focus, the goal, was finding his way through and out of the forest to the backyard of his family□s house in Marpolio. Therein, inside the father□s house, he hoped to find his desired long-lasting love and peace together with rest. Therein also, he sincerely believed that all his juicy dreams and visions of life would begin to see realities. However, he could not imagine how this would happen, having been lost completely to compass.

The night suddenly submerged into a silence of furry. Dawn dew baptised greens. Happy cocks sounded their well-heeled crows to herald the new morning. The lad Benlilo prayed, silently, that the looming morning would be beautiful. His heart burdened with longing for the peace and future expectations of success in life. His goal was success and never failure. The broadest joy of life is success. The infinite sorrow of it is failure.

The weather came on edge with sharp slashes. The harmattan season, African version of winter in Europe, Asia or America, with its winds and whirlwinds, beat angrily about the forest. Its voices sounded harmless but its touch was harsh and offensive. Cold is not a friend of the body. The wayfaring teen would not know how the forest□s weather had so dramatic a transformation! Oh, how he longed for an emergency rescue! He suddenly broke loose and ran like a mad boy but to where? Where was the place of safety for his weather-beaten soul? The way out of the mystery forest, where was it?

Without delay appeared a footpath running through the forest upward. The path was smooth and glowing like virgin snow in Finland. The path spoke of love and of hope. It also typified the cherished peace and rest. However, where was the hope? Where was to be the practical reality of the love? The rest and the peace, where were they?

The forest, immediately above the running path, remained insolent against all the hope and the love, the peace and the rest. Fear ruled the atmosphere extremely. Nervousness whistled tunes of heard and unheard. Emotions struggled to burst, alike smokes struggling for freedom from the prison of the bottle. Then, the hope became fragile in danger of extinction. The faith ran wounded sore. The glory of the forest maximised to level zero.

The beauty of the greens became fear. Benlilo remained lost deep into an abstract situation further than portrayal. He transfigured into a prisoner of the new environment. The dread attained greater height. The boy captive refused to step onto the smooth and glowing footpath. He continued to play the lonely observer. How was life a theatre of the incongruous in an age kind and unkind! How was this life so difficult to define!

A dove appeared atop a tree. The dove was truly a symbol of the peace and the desired love, rest and hope. It was brightly beautiful and tidy in its shimmering white so dirt-free. Not quite long after it had landed inside the greens of the tree that the fine-looking bird started to dance and to sing in a human voice:

Benlilo, the rain may drench you
The sun your head scorch
Keep your cool. Keep your peace!
The Heavens are watching
They are watching
For your hopes betray or upheld.

They are watching
The Heavens are watching,
Only be firm and courageous
Just be bold and firm terrific
Your glorious morning is approaching
The night soon will pass into history.

Nevertheless, converse to the song of the dove, Benlilo the adventuring lad did not see any new dawn to herald whichever glorious morning. The night refused to pass into history. The journeying remained masked in both broader surprises and deeper suspense strokes. Life was the adventure; the adventure was his storyline. He grew avidly intolerant but what could he do at this instant? What solution to his problem of continuing incarceration inside the endless mystery forest of mysteries?

Whirlwind of a number of thoughts encroached against the embattled schoolchild□s person to overthrowing his spirit. He prayed, silently, for his survival of the forestry experience. The life, in chameleonic manifold, remained unrelentingly watched. Again, he remembered the prayer of the weeping ghost that he died not inside the forest. He could now see clearly that the *loving being* was sincere after all with its prayer.

He said so, that I would regret. How had I been blind but it had the eye that could see? Benlilo queried himself honestly.

CHAPTER 032

The Dove And The Path

Where is victory
Along the highway of history?
Battle calls for courage
Life atop or below a barrage of testimony
Beyond the tell of man□s language.

THE SONG OF the dove overtly and covertly tickled Benlilo. He was better entertained by the fact that he was hearing a bird call his name for the first time and assuring him to relax. Confidence found its honourable inroad into his being, alike the trio of joy, peace and assurance - for success and victory in life as a sojourner in the human world.

The lad avidly longed to domesticate the dove for its meaningful songs and its elegant beauty in modest simplicity. He had hoped that when he survived the forestry experience and arrived back in his family compound, the pet would remain his best friend *forever kept*. He did not know that the dove singing in the tone of man was not an ordinary bird but a supernatural being. This was part of the weeping ghost□s messages of raw philosophy. How is ignorance a part of life!

Benlilo continued to stare at the little bird in bewilderment as it, time after time, rendered its *Hymn of Invigoration*. When it was exactly the third occasion that the dove would sing its song, contradictory to all the background benefits from the bird□s meaningful song, the lad was expressively carried away. He burst into loud tears. The dove noticed this. It therefore changed its song and sang even more beautifully:

Benlilo, what have you seen?
Life is a battle, a merchandise,
The only profit of it is victory.

Life is the fiery battle, oh yes!
Continual warring of far end,
Only the daring is victorious.

Be resolutely bold and courageous
Be steady and firm with no fear:
Boy, the battle of life is the fair for you!

Thus the nightingale rendered its new song but instead of being comforted, Benlilo could now -feel a greater pinch and pang of the pains. *The singing bird has not said that the battle would be over soon. It does not prophesy that I would regain my lost freedom from this forest of evil. Oh pity, it has not even mentioned my father□s house!*

The tears flowing across the boy□s cheeks ran more smoothly and they dropped rapidly onto the ground. He surveyed the singing bird closer with his eyes at the same time. The bird also eyed him studiously. It then changed its song, challenging him to the inevitable battle of life and, thereby, charging him more psychologically:

Benlilo, much-loved giant,
Tears contradict manhood.

Benlilo, the golden vessel,
Fear is opposite of courage.

Benlilo, the victorious warrior,
Shedding tears means defeat.

Benlilo, if you cannot fight,
You must need be fought.

If you are not the victor,
You sure will be the victim □

Regain fast your manhood,
Possess firm your courage -

The sun shall shine on the morrow
In the land of your new morning.

Benlilo heard the third segment of the dove□s message and he received it with abundance of joy. His river of hope resurrected; it resumed its flow. He regained the lost portion of his rest, his fainting faith having secured the necessary refuelling. In terse summation, comfort seemed to have re-possessed his being spirit, soul and body.

The stressed boy wiped off the tears with the edge of his short-sleeved shirt - patched here and there by the aid of needle works - a bold testimony to anomalous time in prominently pronounced poverty. The nightingale clapped its wings against its body gently and offered to render the third stanza of the song one more time. Immediately thereafter, it flew away.

The lad returned into the consuming loneliness at the departure of the super-beautiful nightingale. How he had cherished the short-lived company of the singing dove! It was too painful that the friendly nightingale could abandon him so early, just like that! Nevertheless, he was all gratitude. How powerful - communication and positive messages of life! How encouraging song is realistic resurrection for his wearied soul! He was now truly invigorated, as he resumed his lonely journey through the mystery forest - heading for nowhere really but for somewhere. Somewhere unknown but yet known.

A beautiful footpath ran left and right. Its straightness was like a computer drawn line. Benlilo stood still. He continued to observe the path in an admixture of love and dismay. Life had counselled him to beware; the forest had taught him to be cautious. He longed, still, not to raise a foot to cross it. He could fathom no main reason for this. His body frames was becoming cold. The blowing wind of inactivity seemed to have paralysed all his body parts.

Standing there gazing into the lone path, the lad heard a loud cry. The cries of the jilted ghommid invaded his ears. Still, the cries were nothing but a product of pessimistic meditation through his fabrications of an imagination. The reality was that the ghommid guard's wailings were dead and forever gone? The certainty was that history had recorded his successful escape from the hideous kingdom of ghosts and ghommids and posterity had endorsed it.

The teenager stood still like a rock, still! He suddenly woke from the sleep of perception. He looked back to see the ghommid or its colleague flying after him but he saw none. The gentle flow of peace ran notably felt in his spirit. A renewed river of joy flowed in his soul but it was not yet freedom. He soon faced the lone path and he maintained his constant gaze at it.

Not long after this, he met himself inside a purely transparent cubic glass. *A glass cabin inside this thick forest?* He remembered Igbokoda Glass FACTORY. All the six sides of the cube were glass - in fact, the whole structure. He stood still inside the square glass, gazing into the outside world in downright amazement.

How the four-sided glass had come to be he could not tell. How he got inside it remained a mystery to him. Both had superficially turned out to be a combination of mysteries like the forest. The lad could not explain how, again, he had become a captive so soon. The powers continued to run his person through the school of mystery. The mysteries defiled decoding. The student Benlilo passed through the discipline and the discipline through him.

Inside the crystal clear glass, the boy continued to observe the outside world. The long bush path was still in its position but, soon, a thin smoke oozed out of it. The lean smoke changed into a fat one but it could not go up straight into the sky. A new agent of the powers, it tried to locate the boy inside the translucent glass. This it frantically did by flowing towards his side but this was impossible. Then, suddenly, the smoke vamoosed and Benlilo saw it no more. Subsequently, his ears recorded grumblings, murmurings and hissings from a section of the powers, the gods and their agents. In particular, they had been angry that the poisonous smoke could not locate him inside the glassy cage.

At speed, the path regained its natural posture. It became smoother and more gaily sparkly than before. It soon appropriated a better transformation, blistering like a polished golden ring of South African origin. The lad was attracted more to it. He continued to gaze constantly at it. A voice roared out of the path. It was an unapologetic voice of bluntness and exhibition of haughtiness and it ran angrily:

□Away with your cover, this mindless boy called Benlilo! The day would not for long serve as your shelter! The light is no light! The nighttime is here! Your night of sleep is nigh!□

Benlilo heard his name from the undiscovered voice and he shivered. The voice sounded like that of a marijuana-smoking hooligan, its owner could never have been his friend. For the voice was decorated with fear and horror interchangeably. The entirety of the forestry region vibrated to its uttermost roots at the latest roaring voice. He remembered the just departed singing dove, an exact opposite to this.

Joy and hope scrambled, yet again in ostentatious unity, against the conspiracy of sadness and despair for the occupation of his spirit. Did this mean then that both the positive and the negative powers knew him well, even by his name? He would not understand the happenings around him. The vision and the mission were beyond his scope and above his knowledge, wisdom and understanding. However, he remained the protected captive inside the transparent glass. He had no choice.

All of a sudden, the boy, in his new state of positive captivity, discovered that the path had turned into a tiny stream. The minuscule stream started to whistle repulsive tunes. In actuality, the melodies were obituaries. They reminded him of loss and of vanity. They mirrored life in the market of death and sorrow in a completely hijacked morrow of profit and loss.

They conjured dread and consternation. They sent fevers and shivers through his human spines and veins. They invaded his manly body, soul and spirit with mess dosages. They announced a tragedy looming to fall on somebody. They hungered to rob him of all hope against hope.

They fiendishly longed to pluck him down earth like the unlucky ripe fruit from the tree of life. They transmitted hate and lust, intense dislike and spitefulness. They were tears of the aggrieved that refused to be pacified. They sounded like aborted efforts of an aggressive fighter of fortune uncomforted. They were disgusting lamentations of stuck oppressors. They were curses of hate and abuses of abomination. They represented the groaning of wounded lions and roaring of wronged lionesses.

The odd and even voices soon died down. In their place was a session of hissing. The hisses were of misgivings along a highway of sordid mourning. They tarried for long; they roared loud and clear. They changed to the chorus hymn of a thousand insects. But, then, the creepy-crawly living things□ hissing session came to an abrupt end - for a brief period of laughter to take over. This lasted for a few minutes before a new round of quietness befell the environment. The boy Benlilo became more entangled in the beating.

The thin stream flowed eastward. Benlilo discovered, surprisingly, that it was one of the gods of the east. The stream□s destination was unknown. It was pointedly in the straight line and it was called *Straight of No Return*. In other words, it was the pathway of the gods and goddesses, the door of higher powers and the harbour of spirits. Several fishes and crabs appeared inside the water of the stream. They rejoiced. Some of them drummed, as others rendered hymns of spirituality. A quantity of them danced gleefully, as others demonstrated athletically.

It was a festival of hope fulfilled in religious grubbiness. It was a carnival of madness in a calming moment of far-fetched relaxation. It was a crusade of darkness broad and yet costly. It was a high-class celebration of vanity whereby life was forever lost. It was a jocular manifestation of faith like the iron but solely in the harmful. A real testimony of hope in contradiction of the desired hope. Concisely speaking, it was the peak of a gala season in severally shady kingdoms.

It was a brand new morning. But, alas! the new morning was no morning. In plainer words, it was not the one foreseen by Benlilo. It spoke of hatred and of lust misrepresented as love. The pure and impure new morning was both splendid and ignominious. It heralded sensation and malfunction. It was the imbalance of loss and profitability. It smoked unpredictability and mobility. It was the new morning of the deities and the divinities when the spirits walked naked unashamed.

In their celebration, the crabs and the fishes of the miniature stream hailed the coming sun. They mourned the gone night. They thus rendered hymns of good luck and ill fortune. They bemoaned the good and the bad. They accredited the vile and the fine looking. But how far the darkness? The sun could burn in its stead. Joy might run away for sorrow's invasion. Beauty of life had, for bad testimony, turned to the ugliness of fate.

Then, the unlucky one could be lost deep contained by the valley of wretchedness. That simply meant the night, again, had come according to the last direct prophesy of the powers by their representative tone of voice.

Yet another extermination of daylight that was no daylight.

CHAPTER 033

The Seven Shadows...

Seven is symbol of perfection
But where is the round perfection?
There is joy of leisure in the land of the unknown
When thorny memories are relayed in possibilities,
As weakness looms wilder in the bewitched atmosphere.

QUIETNESS BEFELL THE water of the stream again. The tranquillity was short lived however. For, suddenly, a little lizard crawled out of the water. The lizard was long. It was fierce in look and hungry in posture. It made its appearance in dark grey colour and it looked responsive - restless. The lizard shockingly grew two tiny wings, took off and it flew away happily. Benlilo did not know what its source of the joy was. It was yet another mystery layer for him in the adventure.

After this, a water toad appeared at the bank of the stream. The fat toad crowed, exactly like a cock, seven symbolic times. Unlike the lizard, the toad was butter white in colour. It was fat and sluggish. It hopped around happily. Like the bony lizard, amazingly, it also grew wings, took off and flew away to the land of the unknown.

There was an outburst of sweet rejoicings inside the belly of the water of the stream, as the last demonstrator, the toad, did its exquisitely magic flying happily out of sight. The celebration knew no bounds □ all in glorification of the powers and their diplomats in their expositions of diplomacies by might.

The water of the stream regained its quietness for the third successive time. As before, it flowed straight and smooth to the unknown - the unknown remained unknown. Yet, the quietness also lived a very short life. One, two, three, four, five, six □ seven!

Seven shadows jumped out of the water of the stream in quick progression. The seven shadows became seven figures. The seven figures metamorphosed into seven spirits. The seven spirits transmogrified into seven ghosts. The seven ghosts bore seven different identities. Yet, the seven identities were one. They symbolised *perfection* according to the definition and rendition of darkness.

The seven ghosts walked in seven assorted ways; they danced in seven different manners. They ran seven altered paths and jumped in seven wide-ranging patterns. They smiled untypical sevenfold and danced seven dance styles on experimentation and they were not for satisfaction. They were of seven shaded ambitions laden with seven exceptional strategies to fulfil seven missions. They were seven messengers to seven seen and unseen deities - four gods and three goddesses.

The appearance of the first ghost was complete nakedness. It was neither male nor female. Stone black in colour, it looked pitiless and untamed. It walked like a robot and, so, its steps were well premeditated. On its forehead was an eye, which was protected by a large eyelid. Its nose was like that of a buffalo. Its legs were those of a rampaging elephant, while its general expression read danger.

Like the other ghosts, it could not see Benlilo where he was hidden inside the lucent glass. It would not bother itself about the lad either - maybe it was not aware that an 'intruder from the human world of abominations' had encroached on their 'sacred territory'.

The second ghost was in the figure of a woman by manifestation. Its mouth was like that of a toad in rich loamy mud. Its head was extra-big and it was wavering up and down. It appeared sluggish but stable. It looked like a lone suicider. In other words, it appeared rigidly determined. Its countenance was immorally vicious.

It had the hair on its head plaited in a very convoluted manner. The hair was pasturing two tiny snakes. The serpents rose up and they fell. They hissed annoyingly and danced merrily. They became overjoyed at a particular end. They soon flew down onto the ground and ran into the water of the stream, which admitted them without grudge but with adoring appreciation. The water later burst into a *Song of Welcome* for the two swallowed messengers:

Honour so sweet in the morning of peaceable sunshine
Labour so great in the afternoon of booming sunray,
Welcome home into the bosom of your loving mother
Honey love of glory - smelling hopes of fervour age
Messengers of hope and doom, welcome! Welcome!!
Your places no one shall take, as life never dies.

The woman-like ghost looked back into the stream; it smiled. Soon after, it turned round, looked straight and roared like a bleeding lioness. Its growl shook the forest to its roots. It seemed as if the earth would wobble and swallow up the forest at once. The earth and the greens were all scared taut. It was a moment of horror for them! Yet, they could not desert their positions because this was impracticable.

The beastly ghost's roaring was further long lasting. It thundered and boomed through the forest. By it, a group of birds were scared beyond measure. They flew furiously through the forest and speedily out of sight. But for a band of bats, it was sweetened rejoicing.

For, hearing the wild roaring of the beastly ghost, they flew round and about amenably. They cried and laughed. They, too, soon winged across the forest and out of sight - for an unprecedented air quake of arousing laughter to take over. The gods were honoured; they were fulfilled. The harvest of mischievous laughters was one of the heartening signs.

The womanly ghost transmogrified wilder. Its skin colour turned from black to red. The redness took on the dye of white. The white tint became dirty and fetid. The ghost started to vomit maggots and the ground was filled with its vomits of numberless maggots. Benlilo quivered inside his glassy cage. He looked bewildered. He was helpless and wretched as a captive of time in a completely fairy-tale version.

The wind blew hot and cold. The wind's hotness became hotter. Its coldness turned colder. They craved to meet at a point, cold and hot, and fight? The youngster Benlilo was further terrorised by the two opposing atmospheric conditions. He wanted to jump out of the transparent glass cage but there was no way out of it. He wanted to shout for help but to whom? He resigned himself to fate. Earthly life itself is a cage; the world is the transparent prison and human beings are its prisoners!

The boy remembered the core-messages of the departed dove□s songs. In particular, the exceptionally challenging theme of the third and last stanza rang loud and unambiguous in his ears. Again, it flowed rapidly within his mind of memory:

Tears contradict manhood
Fear is opposite of courage
Shedding tears means defeat
Regain fast your manhood
Possess firm your courage.

The third ghost was charcoal black in colour. It was tall to ten feet and thin like an electric round pole on the street of *Isiewu Village* in the eastern part of Nigeria. His two arms were skinny too, and they were long like tiny snakes of the Sahara Desert □ a perfect place of consistent drought and victorious famine. The two arms were restless; they roved here and there ambitiously in the sky. The piercing wind worked and danced them inappropriately.

They became more exasperated, as they remained busy, plucking leaves from the treetops. The robbed trees groaned in the spirit but the ghostly being rejoiced in its. The trees wailed in the physical. They grieved for life so provoking and unfair. They lamented their bad fate in the hands of the ghost. They regretted their existence and why they were so callously treated. They pitied their helpless condition but the more heartbreaking they became the better happiness for the ghost.

As the plucked leaves landed on the ground, there were outbursts of unadulterated weeping and wailing from them and their trees from which they had been compellingly detached. It amounted to a severe moment for all greens and their mother trees inside the troubled section of the forest.

The mother trees struggled to recover their detached leaves but this turned out to be unfeasibility! They tried to hold back the two demoniacally long hands from their atrocious operation of robbery but, on this, they also failed woefully. Their fates at the mercy of the charcoal black ghost turned that of waterleaves against two extra-sharp knives. Their hope of re-union with the leaves failed. The two long hands became violently active. The tragedy of the trees and their leaves grew more intense; it was the tragedy of life. The life was affliction and oppression!

In spite of the continuous weeping and wailing of the trees and their leaves, both plucked and yet to be plucked, the charcoal black ghost did not pity them a bit. Yet it was not its fault: pity was nowhere found in the dark sphere because this was plainly impossible. Mercy too was therein forever lost for the sake of the normalcy that good could never have proceeded out of evil. Darkness does not give birth to light.As their enduring culture, spirits related to spirits strictly on the basis of business□ fairness and not on feelings.

Instead, the ghost□s two long and slim but tough-strong arms became more agile and avidly active. The ground was soon filled with green leaves. But while the two hands were still working, a conspiracy of vengeance was conceived, incubated and hatched by the detached leaves. How?

They came together as one and formed a big heap of green leaves. The ghost watched bemusedly. Instead of thinning down, the green leaves□ weeping and wailing became more rowdily pronounced in their assemblage. They sobbed and howled for pressing revenge against the ghost, their oppressor. They swore to avenge themselves of its heartlessness. They hailed such the time that had come.

How they hoped to achieve this goal was mysterious to all watching environmental forces. They continued to watch. But on its part, the tall ghost laughed them to scorn, for it was confident that the congregated leaves□ conspiracy would come to nought.

As the self-assured charcoal black ghost had judged, the leaves set themselves afire for the sake of exercising their settling of scores. Smokes gushed out of the apex cone of the heap of leaves. The oozing smokes grew wild and wilder and thick and thicker, metamorphosing into a big ball of mad flame. The flame became appallingly black and it grew tall and taller. It soon turned scarlet red.

The red fire graduated into a bonfire passed for an inferno. The inferno magnified into a conflagration. The conflagration soon became gigantic. It roared and boomed within and without. In conspiracy of strategy, like a roaring destroyer bullet, its target was the standing charcoal black ghost to shatter him into pieces by the streamside. Patchy flashes of lightening and thundering across the sky heralded the looming death to the soulless oppressor.

But that was not to be! Survival in life, even among greens and wicked creatures, was by might - not just in the physical but better in the spiritual. The roaring bullet thundered back into its team of senders. The watching trees burst into an additional edition of justifiable expressions of grief. The silent air became chill and charged. The earth, on which the conspiracy of the ghost and the leaves was conceived and executed, groaned helplessly in a serial torment.

Meanwhile, the two long hands never minded the happening; they rested not from their works. They continued to pluck, now very rapidly, the green leaves down to earth. At the work, they had graduated into a tireless machine of woes exercised for a deeper tragedy assured.

What concerned them? They never minded, as their sharpest and unkindest cuts went deeper into the flesh and bones of their casualties. They never saw the severed ones☐ pains. They never heard their cries. They remained rigidly stubborn, deaf and dumb ☐ pity or mercy having no place at all within them.

They typified darkness in its absolutism. Cruelty!

CHAPTER 034

The Ghosts And The Woods

Of course, cruelty is the ruler of darkness
In the region so cruelly elderly and unmindful,
Brutal expressions exist side-by-side with kind glorifications
For, across the forest of life, events remain knotty in abstracts
Like actors and actresses on the stage of time mobile and passive.

A NEW SET of plucked green leaves continued to carpet the ground. Unlike their colleagues that had elected to sacrifice themselves by forming the failed inferno, they stood aloof. They remained uneasily calm on the ground where they had landed, having rescinded themselves to fate. The success, glory, or joy of oppression is when no voice of objection by the oppressed.

They were wholeheartedly on the side of their burning colleagues however. They cautiously watched the tragic scene, as it progressively unfolded. Inside the forest, leaves, too, had brain. They had eyes. They were fully-developed organic creatures.

On its part, the standing ghost had burst into another phase of derisive laughter when the gigantic conflagration roared and burst out towards it as its prime target. It had blinked its three eyes concurrently for the fired destroyer bullet to backfire. It so to its joy and boosting of confidence and recharged faith in its power. Its mouth started to conjure actively. Its head rolled round. Its body frames began to emit water and smokes like dew. Its complexion changed from charcoal black to blood red. This meant that its cruelty gravity had acquired a graduation, a level boiling absorption.

So rapidly, it transfigured into a portrait of more horrifying fear. It graduated into the monstrous terror and oppressor of the entire surroundings. Beholding the happening, the trees groaned and wailed more noisily. The atmospheric condition graduated terribly charged. Both the tortured and yet-to-be-plucked leaves did not keep their silence.

They mourned loudly and cursed their torturer generously. They did this for the possibility of a saviour materialising from nowhere to rescue their lost glories from the merciless hold of the ghost, but no such saviour appeared in sight. Benlilo remained inside the cubic glass cage, his committed eyes beholding all the happenings. He had never imagined that greens could suffer such cruelty in the hands of a ghost.

The new blood red ghost started to vomit venomous incantations. It shortly slipped into the realm of invocation. It invoked higher powers to come to its side with tougher fortifications and they granted its request without hesitation. After that, it was overshadowed in the plane of pure conjuration. The spiritual stratum appropriated higher into bewitchment and enchantment for further spiritual and physical buttresses.

It conjured with the same higher powers more actively. It turned its face downward and commanded the earth beneath its feet to obey it without argument and devoid of any delay. The earth beneath heard its voice and heeded it; it opened its mouth and swallowed the once raging but now dying inferno □ remnants of the once-upon-a-time green leaves.

That was how the mother trees and their detached leaves finally lost the battle? The bowel of the earth was terribly troubled, as intense wailing and weeping; loudest mourning and lamentation possessed it and the bewitched atmospheric condition. Injustice is never a breeder of peace or love but a generator of curses and bedlam!

Seeing the miracle that it had additionally wrought, the ghost was well satisfied. It smiled and laughed broadly. Furthermore, the phantom looked up to the winds and it conjured vigorously but briefly. The winds laughed, hypocritically, in acknowledgement of its power for the whole environment to be alarmed and the ghost became happier.

The ghostly giant grew more ambitious? No! Again, it laughed more heartily and hissed rowdily. It recalled its two working hands and they obeyed it like loyal soldiers of a typical African military tyrant. By now, all the adjoining trees had been robbed miserable of their once beautifully green leaves. They now looked pitiably barren and helpless. A kind of desolation! They remained standing logs and branches robbed of their natural glory. They swore never to forgive their oppressor. They continued to rain abuses and curses upon it.

The time had changed, it was now afternoon. The sun burned with antipathy. All his chequered sixteen years in the earthly planet, wristwatch had been a luxury to Benlilo. For this reason, since the beginning of the adventure, he had not been able to confirm time. The trees and their remaining leaves still groaned in anguish. Both of them had no place to hide.

Flying birds of the sky above them fled at their humiliating sights. Greens form beauty and glory of trees and the birds were horrified to have discovered the trees in such irregular nakedness. But it was not so in reaction to the situation by the sun and the sky. The seen and unseen phenomena laughed them to scorn. The invisible wind too. On its own, it whistled cynicism in passage, issuing a song and an advice:

Beauty lost never regained
Glory once forever detained,
Helpless tree, pray for rain
New clothes for you by Heaven.

The robbed trees received the wind□s sarcastic song and message with displeasure. Instead of heeding the phenomenon□s advice, that is pray Heaven for rain for new clothes acquired, they cursed the singer without restraint. But on its part, the unseen vocalist was unmindful of the trees□ negative reaction. Dramatically, it changed its song□s tune and picked its second stanza:

Once elements of beauty, pity!
The sun will smite you by day
And merciless moon by night
Your nakedness seasonal shame!

And the trees shrank into a shameful silence. The thinly tall blood-red ghost roared the more and ran out of sight. Its destination was inside the woods.

The woods received it with rejoicings. They clapped jubilantly to welcome it, as rowdiness conquered the air. It had been a mere sojourner inside the water of the stream and a worker by its bank. Now, it was back and free amidst its own kin and kith. How sweet the re-union! They sang delightedly to welcome home the exile:

Ageless glory tall and beautiful
A new noon wonderfully bountiful
Harvest of hope and faith renewed
In the season of sweats and wealth
With the hero coming home to rest
Amidst its own kith and kin attest.

Silence re-possessed the atmosphere, while the fourth ghost stood by the streamside. It looked more of a Caribbean ape but its legs were those of an antelope inside Bambidu Games Reserve of Kenya. Its buttock was only one, flat and restively boogying.

Its full body was covered with little feathers of multitudinous colours. Its stepping was fast and unpredictable. It was an outstanding illustration typical of some beautiful, prostituting half-naked corporate and shameless girls at the University of Lagossia. Yet, it had agility boldly written on its face. It was much anxious to fulfil a mission and it could not hide it. It boasted of these qualities, tall to frame. It had a goal.

Standing at three feet, its complexion was dark and dirty brown. It had two large eyes, two long tails and a forehead like a small clay pot of Maiduguri. It stood at akimbo □ preoccupied. Its overall posture was noticeably arrogant. It conveyed an inflexible strength of mind to overcome all conflicts of life.

The aping ghost posed like an ancient Roman war conqueror. It fumed all over. Later, its eyes were soaked in tears. Benlilo did not stop to watch it from within his glassy cover. He would not understand the mission of the latest ghost by the streamside - like its forerunners□ at their first appearances. The air smelled of re-invigorated suspense and silence. It gathered fear and re-distributed the same ingredients nastily.

The dwarfish ghost did not see the lad. It did not mind him where he was hiding inside the see-through glass. Instead of climbing a tree, the ape-ghost ran gingerly forward and it stopped. It looked here and there like the self-confessed and confused Ajuiba □ the witch caught in a public glare. It bleated like a lamb. It grew more impious, looking there and here the more nervously. It turned back to the stream. Getting there, it did not stop.

It jumped over the water and landed on the other side of it. There, it did not also look back. It ran wrathfully into the other portion of the woods. The woods received it with effusive cheeriness. Too, they clapped to welcome home one of their own. Thus was the ghost seen no more. Silence lined the environment. Benlilo kept intact his persistence as the helpless watchman for the environment from his hideout inside the cubic glass.

The fifth ghost became more visible, its shadow having vanished. It was now beaming green in complexion and it walked on its head and two arms, positioned downward, to support it without any hindrance. It had a tiny head like a one-penny walnut of Ifaki-Ekiti. It had a large belly like a big plastic bowl made in Malaysia. Its nose was boisterously bogus and equipped with three holes. Water dispensed out of the first gap. Flame leaked out of the second outlet. Smoke poured out of the third opening.

The fifth ghost was a great dancer of a gymnast. Who argued that music was not a transmitter of peace, an unmatched healer of wounds? Let the person come and see. Let him or her learn the vital lesson that music is the food of love, as love is the food of life.

Its own mission was peace and entertainment, and not to scare or to terrorise the environment. It branded its music, *Macadabraica* □ whatever that meant. Therefore, some beautiful beats oozed out of the wild woods and it engaged itself in the dance of the drunkard whose all earthly problems had vamoosed without any reason, as it danced in an enviable nimbleness.

Life was contrast, a rich house of contradictions. Darkness was the house and the contradictions were components of amoebic compositions. The dancing ghost was all hope beyond hope, its senses having deserted it? It was all joy in the region of sorrow. It was crammed with elevated optimism of zero, as against a pessimistic state. The lost refused to be lost.

Music was truly a powerful tool of resurrection, even with darkness. The joyfulness of the robbed trees regained life. Their hope came on board, as rescued from the gorge of despair. Their love for life was renewed. For with the cooling musical beats on, coupled with the ghost□s acrobatic display of tumult, the earth was saturated with happiness. It willingly opened its mouth large, whereby all the once-buried leaves gained not only their naturalness but redemption as well, and they flew joyfully to their rightful positions on their mother trees.

Come and see diverse brands of rejoicings, as Benlilo had not witnessed before inside the mystery forest! The trees regained their lost leaves and glories. Fresh and green as when they were once on the treetops □ oh, how healing to wounds is music of life! They rejoiced more as the melodic beats intensified. They were profusely grateful to the ghostly entertainer. They rolled out their acknowledgments for all ears to hear:

Wisdom pool of rescuer giant
Proving that might is small.

Mighty warrior ever victorious
Music dance its weapon of victory.

Restorer of huge losses in their places
In blessed evening of restoration of no price.

The breeze heard the readout of the greens□ appreciation in honour of the dancing ghost and it transformed into wind. The wind pierced powerfully, dancing the willing trees and their greens fabulously. By this, all the trees of the forest excluded by the charcoal black ghost joined in the dance and the entire environment turned into a vast carnival ground. Just then did the second and last stanza of their esteem boom and it flowed sensitively:

Mystery plane art and act unravelled
By the stream of death watching stupid.

You the charcoal ghost of profitless labour
Blood-red creature senselessly joy-mad

The trees and their reunited leaves were good laughers and so they burst into a provocative spell of contemptuous laughter against their tormenter, the gone charcoal black ghost. Supplementary to this, the trees and their leaves joined the dancing ghost to boogie away the time and to celebrate the victory of re-possessing their lost possessions. As they did this, unwounded submissiveness was the portion of the woods. During its callous operation, the woods had sided with the ghost against the greens. The trees, their leaves and the ghostly musician danced and sang:

The trees, with their leaves and the dancing ghost, were celebrating a life of re-possession in good belonging. They celebrated their victory over their archenemy the charcoal black or blood thin and tall ghost, as well as over their robbery and burial. Benlilo kept up his look at the spectacle in amazement, as the attention-grabbing show lasted.

It was another moment of magical manifestations: darkness fell and the cultural music fiesta was no more. When light eventually re-appeared, the dancing ghost was also nowhere to be seen. The once dancing trees were now standing confidently in their places. Along with their recovered green leaves, their joy knew no bounds.

Deliverance from subjugation is victory in life. Permanence of it is its insurance. Yet, that was the typology of revolving life, as it had been: nothing new and nothing old. Nothing lost and nothing gained. Thus would Benlilo receive yet an additional confirmation that the forest was truly a forest of cool, wild and implicit mysteries.

The sixth ghost made its appearance. It was tall to six feet and corpulent. Yet, it looked frail in health. Dark grey in complexion, it bent and bowed down towards the east and six sparrows flew out of its mouth. The first sparrow was yellow. The second sparrow was white. The third sparrow was green. The fourth sparrow was pink. The fifth sparrow was blue, while the sixth sparrow appeared in the colour of black.

The six sparrows formed a circle. They danced round the ghost, as if they had been drunk from the intoxicating wine of jocularly mental illness. In short, their dance styles were confusion and excellence rolled into one - extremely difficult to define and impossible to classify.

The ghost rejoiced in their midst like a fulfilled aggressor of an olden emperor whose soldiers had just conquered the land of a powerful archenemy. It was all a portrait of self-assurance and bubbles of self-fulfilment. It felt to the highest degree honoured. It later ran like crazy out of sight, as the birds pursued it hotly, freely hailing it all along. There were outbursts of variable laughters to greet its disappearance into the woods.

Benlilo remembered the assurances of the weeping and laughing ghost, the toughest chastiser of the human race ever. His recollection also stumbled on another voice that what his eyes would see and his person would experience inside the mystery forest, his mouth would not be able to tell. On an equivalent note, he called to his mind the ingenuous voice of interrogation of the seen present by the unseen future. He succumbed. He got broken down.

He prayed that, without postponement, he be removed out of the open incarceration of the powers for a quick relocation inside his family compound in Marpolio. How he missed the home!

CHAPTER 035

Season Of Sevenfold Events

Beauty of pleasure unashamed
Glorification of retribution actualised, oh,
How torture abounds in the land of torturers
Unhidden injustice typology of the intact incident
Entertainment by the dead for the living and the dead!

THE LAST BUT not the least and seventh ghost was awesome indeed! Like the first phantom, he was wholly naked. From its toes upward, its body was covered with soiled scales. Its legs were short and they looked as those of a patient afflicted with elephantiasis. It came into view as a feral beast that could never be pacified. Gushing out some dreadfully hideous sounds that beyond definition, it stood not far away from Benlilo□s stand inside the crystal-clear square glass. It steadily gazed into the still glass as if it could see the lad therein.

It had a lamp on its forehead and its light was in every respect red in colour. The light struggled hard to chase away the darkness of the forest but this became shameful impracticality. Darkness cannot extinguish darkness □ this was and is the lesson.

In thought-out steps, the ghost moved to the streamside to do what no visitor there before it had done, and, of course, to see or experience what no one had seen or experienced. It bent down and drank of the water to quench its thirst. However, for doing this, the stream became terribly angry. The stream had considered the act of the ghost, in the drinking of its water, to be a daylight robbery. Or did it take any permission from it before drinking its water? This was so for among hosts of darkness, orderliness reigned side-by-side with disorderliness, as protocol amounted to the rule of life.

For that *heinous sin* so-committed by the ghost, some water bubbles covered the surface of the stream and the spine-chilling creature suspected nothing. The steam□s mild roars were soon survived with fire smokes. The fire smoulders rolled into bunches and then into a fireball. The fireball burst directly into the only eye of the ghost and it was blinded instantaneously. The smoke□s ball burst also quenched its reddish and once radiating light. The belief of the watching lad got concretised that darkness could castigate darkness inside the mystery forest.

The tortured ghost was dazed! It burst out in a severe suffering, and imprecision in no mean measure, possessed its being. Behold, it raged around the muddy bank of the stream in its thorough blindness. It ran forward stupidly and backward witlessly. It stopped. It could no longer determine where it was. It hooted like a tormented owl. It whistled like an antique Assyrian flute.

It stood fumingly straight, raised up its single arm and rolled like the whirlwind on its two legs in an acrobatic display of complications in the straight and curvaceous insanity. It wept and wailed uncontrollably; it□s pain was away from comfort. Afterwards, it ran blindly out of sight with no help at hand for it.

Its destination was inside the woods but it missed its way. It staggered further like a possessed drunkard before crashing violently into a brook at the entrance of a small groove that bordered with the woods. For the first time in the expedition, a harvest of laughters, as of scornful lamentations, exploded out of a section of darkness. Thus, for the rare time in the adventure, darkness was sharply divided against darkness. Thus darkness made jests of darkness as a part of the same darkness. The woods maintained a position of indifference.

The water of the stream rejoiced for its victory over, and the retributive calamity that had befallen the unfortunate ghost. The greens, on their part, sympathised with it. The earth mourned for its forsaken fate. They both pleaded with it to seek asylum inside of them. It did as the earth opened its mouth and received not only it but a larger portion of the brooks☐ water as well. A charged non-violence fell as the lot of the forest. Life was nothing but a theatre of the incongruous. The tortured ghost entered into its perturbed rest and it was no longer seen. Life was conquest and expulsion by admission.

Observing Benlilo☐s eyes were soon back on the stream in fullest attentiveness. Behold, its water sang a song of indifference and an unhidden revelation. Its beats to the song were ear splitting and mind numbing. Its tune was personalised for the lone lad human spectator:

Watching wayfaring lad of fortune
Recorder of histories and of stories
Through the forest of wild mysteries
Beautifully entertained and hunted
Soul sought much after by the powers.

The air of the forest became charged. Unseen flowers of obsequies decorated, luxuriously, the air. They were all, also, meant to honour the passage of the lad's soul from earthly life into a fail-safe eternity. Yet, the boy would not understand and who dare apportion to him a smidgen of guilt? Life was filled with ignorance. It was a hamper of nought. Both the ignorance and the naught were yields from conscious and unconscious investments of seasons and eras. The profitable or unprofitable harvests were safely stored in barns, silos, or warehouses of time.

When Benlilo☐s attention concerted again on the snaky stream, seven other events, negligible in nature though, happened one after another in rapid evolution. There was a roar of thunder and some sizzling lights of lightening fumed. The forest shook fervidly but the lad was not moved where he remained inside the lucent glass.

Plenty of wild expectations raced through his mind. Pregnant therefore with the hope for more squalid happenstances, he expected the rolling time to give birth to more and it actually did. The fair of nought was never tired of manifestations. It was by no means exhausted of rolling out mysteries.

Second, an eagle flew down from the top of a mahogany tree. The eagle was skilful in flying. It circled round in the low sky of the area. When it had rounded the area seven cool and fashionable times, it shot straight in the flight and took a plunge into the water rowdily. Straight away, the stream swallowed the desperate eagle and there were some noticeable bubbles again on the surface of its water.

The water bubbles soon gave birth to a fire blast out of the stream. The fire rolled out in a conical shape and it whistled devastatingly. The whistling later changed to weeping. Not long thereafter, the weeping ceased for a graveyard quietness to take over. As afore times, the calmness was quenched in no sooner a time.

A mighty arrow danced acrobatically down from nowhere in the sky and it rumbled into the water of the stream. The water groaned at the unwilling receipt of the violent weapon of war. Long-standing publications of lamentations ensued out of the bowel of the stream. The troubled water discharged aggressive bubbles of hot smokes. For the third time, this would give birth to some evident fire blows. The fire blows shrilled different tunes of detestations. Glories helplessly perished as captives therein and honours remained in bondage.

Fourth, a lame ghost came to the side of the stream. Standing at almost three feet, it stretched forth its two short hands and invoked calmness to baptise the stream within and without and it was immediately so. Seeing the *miracle* that it had presently wrought, the dwarfish lame ghost relaxed in its standing position and laughed riotously. It was legitimately happy that its power remained intact. It laughed more to celebrate this.

The short lame ghost then conjured, in a wild language, and its band of musicians and drummers appeared physically in sight by the right-hand-side bank of the stream. These musicians were all shorter than the lame ghost their bandleader. They all had large mouths and a lone eye, each, on their foreheads. They appeared in cerise red of a skin texture and every one of them looked nasty and stern.

Each of them was branded with a fairly long and sharp horn, red in colour, on their heads. There was a discharge of fire from a hole in the apex of each horn. With this, the environment was terrorised by those strange beings. Apprehension possessed everywhere maximally in negation of the reality that these ghost and ghommid people had come to entertain. Benlilo wondered, sombrely, whether the other word for entertainment, inside the mystery forest of mysteries, was either horror or terror.

Landing therein, their musical beats rolled into eminent boldness and this crew of singers started to render the stream□s praise worship fantastically. All the outlandish beings cast away their unfriendly looks and they wore costumes of bona fide entertainers. Life was consequently injected into the area, as those ghommids and ghosts □ all of the same stature and height, except their master the lame ghost, started to dance with dynamisms.

The little table of the stream had since been transformed into a rock-hard podium for the master to actualise its own dance exercise thereon so expertly. It was a testimony for the watching Benlilo to observe that at the start of the show, the lame ghost had been perfectly healed of its deformity. This *big favour* time showed it so that its performance on the stage would be perfect as desired. The powers worked in collaborations with the time and they fashioned out the best in the interest of darkness.

At end of the musical show, it regained its original position disability ungrudgingly and the gods were thereby glorified. Unlike in light, life in darkness is stable and permanent. Yet, like the others before it, the fourth phase of the seven-fold exhibition rolled away. Life, even with ghosts and ghommids in the woodland of time, was a stage. The stage rolled round and about in the theatre of unpredictability. The unpredictability was a precious trait belonging to the powers. Yet, the amoebic powers promised more□

The tiny stream again regained its original form. Its water was at peace with itself, as it continued to flow southward without any obstruction. Any unacquainted observer would believe that it was a natural stream flow. It was so cool in look and delightfully wooing. No new bystander would suspect that it was a demonic stream - life was the now-wooing stream, truly deceitful. A band of yellow leaves soon covered the surface of the stream.

As numberless as they were, amazingly, each of the leaves, by its apex, started to issue out candlelight to illuminate its respective area. Again, darkness was encroaching fast on the forestry part. There was no beam of the sun or light anywhere. The day was already aged.

Benlilo remained standing inside the cubic glass cage. His two eyes sustained their focus, untiringly, on the stream. A yellow duck, very big, appeared thereon and it swam up and down to trace the length of the stream. Sporadically, it would bury deep its head to drink of its water, as its swimming exercise lasted. The boy remembered that this was the second time that he would be seeing a water duck in the adventure. The first duck he saw was inside the beautiful spherical brook early in the exploration.

Suddenly, the fat yellow duck jumped out of the water and it flew cheerfully into the woods. The woods were pleased a good deal at the entry of the duck. In its honour, they rendered an acclamation resonantly. They would not stop chanting the wooing duck□s flattering remarks until the scene had rolled away and another event overtook it. Life, in the wacky world, was a rising and falling stage.

Seventh and finally, Benlilo saw a group of seven elephants invade the tiny stream. The seven elephants were made up of four lean ones and three fat others. They, however, all had two things in common: one - they were hoary in colour and, two - they compulsively thirsted and, so, their mission to the streamside was to quench their hurting thirst with its water.

In the process of doing this, however, they drank off, thoroughly, the water of the stream. The stream, now an emaciated rope of lowered mud, murmured and groaned. It wept uncontrollably for its irreparable loss. Its place was soon taken over by the original owner, the long and unbending path. But the stream did not keep quite □ it did not accept its fate as it had come. It took its place and battle of revenge to inside the bellies of the individual of the gluttonous elephants. Therefore, the seven elephants were sorely troubled inside their stomachs.

Behold, a posse of typecast avid fire cooked within their tummies! They could not endure the pain of the internal fire. They danced fiendishly like possessed and confused priests of *sango* the god of thunder. They danced to unheard tunes and unkind beats of the fire burns. They fell. They stood up, tortured sore by their bellyaches. They cried and wailed. For sure, internal fire is the worst burning type of combustion.

They all ran amuck, jumping up and down in the forest. Benlilo laughed loudly in his post. Nature and its conglomerated members also had a supplementary show to watch from their multidimensional duty posts for free. They all could also not help themselves but exploded into rowdy sessions of laughter. Life, like the seven elephants, was a humorist. The humorist of danger and death.

Like crashing caterpillars, the seven elephants ploughed their ways into the woods and therein they all perished. The woods were very reluctant to receive the beasts but now, they could not resist their forceful entries. They groaned audibly and agonisingly □ in glorification of the time-honoured fact that even in the land of the dead, deadlier ones were outcastes, as no one justified failure from whatever angle.

At their discomfiting death, the bodies of the seven elephants swelled triple their original sizes each. The ballooning corpses soon burst out in flesh, innumerable maggots and stinking water. Disgusting odour was the lot of the atmosphere, while their carcasses became feasts for hosts of birds of the air and fowls of the bush of the forest.

Thus would the dead stream avenge itself of its overwhelming adversaries the seven invading elephants. Inside the forest of anonymity, life was reward and revenge. It also therein meant sowing and reaping. From the woods, it was then calmness of sordid mourning and lamentations for the fatalities of the two agents at war. The sombre celebration of the woods' mourning and lamentation lasted for a season.

CHAPTER 036

Amalgam Mysteries Of Darkness

The Prince of Africa is fallen!
Oh, the Prince of Persia is fallen!
Yet, the wind blows; the sun shines; the rain falls
Night after night - myths following one another
And the stuck passenger remains at the square of life.

BENLILO REMAINED COMFORTABLE inside the quadrilateral glass as clear as a semiprecious stone. He reasoned distractedly what mythological scene would roll in next. He remembered that with the powers, both imaginable and undreamt of magics were possible. He reminisced that their off-putting manifestations seemed to have had no end. His focus shot back at the footpath; it glowed better than before.

The path appeared so natural, meek, beloved and loving. A new onlooker would never have suspected how it had been transforming itself in multifarious manifestations quite unbelievable in the ordinary sense. In particular, such an observer would never know that it was once a stream.

But, abruptly, the path betrayed, again, its own composition unashamedly. Darkness could invest in pretences for some time but the role-plays would only be ephemeral. Evil could masquerade as good but evil would never cease to be evil. Inside the mystery forest of mysteries, the evil could not legitimately change to good, as the good was ever sacrosanct. The latter□s holiness could not be contaminated, as the former would never be converted.

The vividly lustrous path turned into a very long and mighty python. The python moved and the lad was frightened beyond what the mouth of man could tell. All his body frames shook as if they would break into pieces. His container, the cubic glass also shook to its underpinning. The python was so enormous and horrendous! Benlilo had guessed right that the python would have something to do with him in due course. His besieging fear got puffed up. He could not run away □ no place to hide from the fright.

Behold, the mighty snake was unmindful of the boy□s presence, at least for now. The python moved round and coiled around itself. Within a very short time, it had formed a unit of many fat heaps of live flesh, radiantly brown with butter-white splashes in colour, all over its body. Its tail was at the middle point of the huge flesh layers of the circle, for its head to make the end of the whole coil.

The python raised its head tenderly. After that, it vomited a bird and a hare - both of them live. The bird was spotlessly white in colour, whereas the hare was dark red. The bird skated sickly and it stumbled a couple of times. It stood up urgently, turned round to face the python, and bowed to the ground for the master seven mild times.

After this, it raged whirl-winding about seven other hot times before bursting into an extended chapter of whistling. When the squeal subsided, the snow-white bird started to hop around cheerfully. Its source of joy was unknown to Benlilo. Demonic beings could be so funny and happy. The droll side and the happiness were parts and parcels of networking and strategic mysteries of darkness.

The vague red hare, on its part, ran forward like its type stormily pursued by a serpent. At stop, it also faced the mighty python and bowed to the ground seven times in obeisance. Thereafter, it stood on its two hind limbs, rolled about lithely seven other times before it, as well, burst into a long-standing session of whistle. The screech roared finely into the ear to touch the soul, spirit and body of man. No power in the forest could hamper it. The trees, their greens and all seen and unseen environmental and elemental forces watched unrelentingly.

When it would stop the whistling, the red hare was face-to-face with the spick and span white bird. The bird challenged the hare to battle, as the hare also confronted the bird. The hare raised its head and front limbs against the bird to pounce on it sadistically. The bird also moved angrily to descend on the hare by shooting up its wings. Likewise, it aimed at the hare with its beak.

The hare struck at the bird with a quick bite, while the bird hit at the diminutive hare with its beak. Their fight thus began and continued and the two fighters were soon dead on the ground at the same time. Benlilo was scared. The python that had all long been watching the two messengers-turned fighters raised its head again. It looked here and there and smiled. The enormous reptile moved near and swallowed up the lifeless bird and the dead hare. It returned to its normal place well satisfied.

A fever mounted its barricade against Benlilo. The boy could not deduce what the unexpected action of the master python had meant. He did not suspect that darkness was demonstrating before him its act of no-nonsense. That if the darkness could swallow darkness dead, it could swallow and devour anything. A lad, how could he have known that he was being warned by the powers not only to beware but also to be ready?

A new morning was impending. A couple of cocks□ crows heralded the most up-to-date crack of dawn. Some birds sang interestingly and uninterestedly in greens and they would not be stopped. The flowing wind whispered in odd and fascinating tunes. The trees grumbled for the cold because there were no coverlets for their bodies, their stems. An owl hooted within the woods.

The mighty python moved and, surprisingly, it roared like a starving and angry lion. It rose and it soon coiled round the glass in which Benlilo was, as, at the same time, dark clouds would cover the sky. Both the python and the clouds were faithful envoys of the powers. The sky groaned audibly for the terrorism of the invading clouds; the soil remained dumb as a spectator. All environmental hosts and elemental forces watched what was about to happen in arrested nosiness.

The lad was greatly scared. Tremor of cold jumbled through his veins. His mind was invaded with the possibility of the cubic glass being uprooted at once and destroyed harshly by the enormous python. In that case, what would be his fate inside the open space glass? Where would he run to or hide in safety from the evil reptile? His mind burned with a raging fear as of incineration!

Just immediately, a man flew down from the sky and landed near the spot. The man had six big wings □ all which disappeared at once at his landing with his feet touching the ground. His head with beard were completely covered in silvery white. He was a giant whose look resembled that of a battle crier and an executor. His eyes transmitted bright rays of hope and brighter evidences of victory. He was smart and fast. Robed in long white and purple apparel, he was armed with a two-edged sword flaming like an afternoon sun of an arid land in the season of summer. With his military look, Benlilo was surprised that the man was not arrayed in warfare attire.

The silver-haired man was truly a gallant and tactical warrior. Immediately he landed, the lad□s grade of amazement augmented and the clothing of the man transformed into that of a combatant soldier complete with the sword. His look had also malformed from that of a gentleman to that of a no-nonsense fighter. How his face showered visible flames! These sudden transformations made Benlilo to be assured of his safety inside the glassy cage. He was cock sure that the winged man was out to do something extraordinary. Now, he could give out his word on it that his appearance on the scene, whereby his life was on the line, would not be for nothing.

The emerged warrior moved drastically to attack the enormous python, as the reptile also geared up to assault and swallow him up. It had sensed the ominous danger, unwounded itself from the glass box speedily and rushed aggressively at the man with the intention to knocking him down sadistically with its head to the ground at once. The first approach of conquest by the powers was attack, as preceded by aggression.

The forestry feeling became immensely charged. Suspense flew in the wind and all could feel it decidedly. Breath seemed to have ceased, as cold silence drenched the idiosyncratic condition. Wild tension mounted on the wings of suspense on behalf of all the watchers concealed and revealed. The viewers were all enthusiastic and apprehensive eyes and ears. They were believers in yesterday by today to shape tomorrow. Their beliefs trusted in history to record the pending event for posterity.

The man too was very crafty. In a second, he had regained two of his disappeared wings. He flew lowly into the vacuum of the sky but the python was also steady. It shot up and pursued him into the air most flexibly. The man dodged the python□s attack in the air cunningly and their game began as it should be but not like the eagerly watching lad had seen before. The crowd of spectators continued to watch. Like Benlilo, they sharpened better their eyes and ears.

The enormous snake crashed onto the ground. Before it could regain consciousness and recoup for a re-launched attack, the man had landed back on the ground. He moved radically like an electric current and, at a go, cut off the python□s head with his sword. It was certain that the enormous python had never expected what had just happened to it. The severed head jumped over and above again apart from the body and farther away, rolling confusedly in pools of irreversible anguish. A troubled passivity befell the forest□s air. A leaf dropping onto the ground would be heard without any problem.

Endless gush of blood built up from the two separated parts. The longer part of the python stood straight and tall into the mournful air. It rushed wobbly and crashed sadistically into the woods. The woods made a great deal of grimy requiem over the dishonourable defeat of the python by the winged man. Life, really, was a battle in the woodland of history

With the victory of the man over the python in his behalf, Benlilo heaved a secure sigh of soporific relief. He remained inside the lucid glass however. He was sincerely grateful to the warrior for his out-and-out victory over the enemy. He rejoiced over the mourning and lamentations of the once-again-defeated powers in the wild woods, which the slaughtered python represented. But, now, how he wished that the glassy prison would release him into his much desired freedom - the unknown liberation!

The warrior man knew better. With his two big wings, he flew back in another glorious re-appearance □ and all the hosts of the forest watched for what was about to happen. Landing directly in front of the cubic cage, he repossessed his sword from the wind. He pointed the long and still searing two-edged instrument at the oblong glass and its two edges were ripped open. Its front side fell flat onto the ground without more ado.

Power surpasses power! Or in a Nigerian colloquialism, □power pass power, as man pass man.□ The greens and their trees, with all elemental forces and ecological powers of the forest, all watched awe-struck. They trembled at the ghostlike demonstration of the militaristic power. The winged man took off. Midway his flight into the sky, he disappeared. Silence would have trailed his disappearance but for a seven-versed victory song that sprang out of the blues, relayed to earth, that is the forest□s environment:

Beauty of beauty, victory
Glory above glory, victory!

The Prince of Africa is fallen
The Prince of Marpolio is fallen
The Prince of Persia is fallen

Beautiful victory for the heir
Daybreak of victory smooth roll.

□The Prince of Africa is fallen! The Prince of Marpolio is fallen! The Prince of Persia is fallen!□ The victory song was a rusty six inches nail lost into the flesh and brain of the powers! The singers had reduced them to *nothing,* but were they now ready to surrender? Time promised to answer that question.

Moreover, with the victory falling flat in favour of Benlilo over the python *Prince of Africa, Prince of Marpolio* and *Prince of Persia,* according to the song, the lad thought that the battle against his life was over. How wrong, yet again, was he! He did not know that the authentic battle was gearing up for him to engage in inside the mystery forest of mysteries.

The lad□s mouth echoed the word, *Grateful! Grateful!!* over and over repeatedly in excesses. He jumped out of the glassy cage and started to run, running to nowhere in particular but to somewhere... Now would he relocate into his beloved family house in Marpolio.

The sky appeared in reddish yellow glows of wiry and bulky plasters. Love transmitted through the sky□s splendour. It also mirrored hate. Some crews of butter-whitish heaps of clean and tidy wool struggled frenetically to overthrow the stainless beauty of the sky. The reddish yellow radiance survived the attack. But not all.

At the same time, the Heavens testified to the goodness and badness of man. The earth bore witness to them. Soon after, there were terrific roars of thunder across the forestry sky. Still, the woodland refused to be petrified. Escaping Benlilo never looked backward.

He continued to run for his dearest life. Wisdom of action is the preserver of life. The victor from the battle of life is its survivor. The vanquished is the conquered. Earthly life, for man, is singular and there is no alternative to it. A one-time opportunity! No heroism within the grave□s territory. No gallantry or brightness when life is lost □ at what time the mystery forest of mysteries swallows up man.

The lad ran to the edge of a dodgy dungeon. A voice roared across the severity of the dungeon, □Look!□ The boy leaped forward to look. He was fussily dazed at what his eyes caught. He could never, in life, have imagined them. Life for him was a pack full of surprises. Like the mystery forest, the exploration was yet a reservoir of unfolding wonders.

For Benlilo□s escape from the defeated python, the powers□ revulsion for the boy multiplied fourfold. They improved on their oath; this meant a fourfold of their indignation looming to fall at once on the sought one□s head or life or destiny. They increased their combat stratagems. Their traps were numerous and they had no problem whatsoever in choosing which to deploy along his routes in order for them to capture the prey. They repeated their declaration never to be discouraged or to faint, never to wane, weary, or fail. Their hope boosted greatly in the vein of their confidence as broadly equipped militarily.

A weedy pasture overgrew the deepness of the dungeon. Multitudes of two generations populated the notorious bush. The first generation was that of several scores of thousands of scorpions, all in unsmiling sickly colour. The second generation was made up of heaving scores of thousands of serpents, everyone in yawning russet colour.

The latter spoke the language of vengeance and confrontation. The former communicated in the dialect of blood. The scorpions were the most poisonous of all the scorpion family's species. All the serpents were fiery in nature. They accommodated no sympathy or clemency. This was monopolistically so for the crude level-headedness that their riches and glories were all licentiousness. However, who would the two set of warriors, the serpents and the scorpions, fight+?

□You wait and see,□ an inconsiderate voice reverberated in the haunted wind. Benlilo waited to see□

Numberless battalions of locusts soon descended from nowhere to feed on the well-heeled greens. But instead of them to enjoy their ready-made feast on the greens, the serpents and the scorpions combined. They attacked, conquered and devoured the locusts.

Only a scantily few of the greedy grasshoppers escaped being munched through. The lucky few ones would never forget the experience. They flew cowardly away singing *songs of unexpected wonders and irreversible losses.* From that time onward, their lineages would flee at the sight of the generations of the masters □ the serpents and the scorpions. Life was an experience. Surviving therein was a story, a testimony and the history.

Again, Benlilo was lost to the interpretation of what he had just seen. He did not know that the serpents and the scorpions were the powers; the grasshoppers were human stars, virtues, glories, treasures and destinies in the earthly place.

Again, the young man heard the voice say, □Look!□ Over again, he made the move to look and he discovered that the serpents and the scorpions had disappeared totally out of the plain of the dungeon altogether with the green pasture □ implausible! In their places were now graves. The graves were angry and hungry. They hungered night-to-night in all seasons and eras for more inmates to swallow.

They, for the same cause, thirsted for blood, human blood. Their appetites grew larger and hungrier for more admittances of invading inmates from the earthly planet. The graves were never satisfied. The normal standard, they were never to be contented but ever to be famished.

As far as they were into the far deepness of the valley, some of the graves started to fire evil arrows at stars in the firmament of time and many of the targets were precisely hit. Benlilo was intolerably annoyed and nauseated at this. The causalities tumbled down earth in turmoil. There were shedding of tears and renditions of wailing by souls of men, women and children.

Yet, the downed stars were in the firmament of heaven - what a great mystery! The anonymity became complex when voices out of space yelled to the hearing of all:

From age yore of battle

Genesis of warring portions
Kingdom divine suffers violence
Kingdoms of men volcanic eruptions!

No response to contradict or corroborate the voice. The entire vicinity was swallowed up by motionlessness. The silence acquired superior depth and broadness. It coroneted into horror. The terror coveted to kill, to destroy and to devour.

The lad Benlilo ran. He renewed his resolve not to lose hope, not to stop running until he had relocated into the place of protection, which was his father's house.

CHAPTER 037

The Rescue Operation

Flight of life! Rescue for living!
Again, life blares it beautiful teeth. Benlilo is
The talent the parable of the wealthy palm tree
Openly and avidly envied by weak plants of the forest:
Storms, winds and whirlwinds plus earthquakes all attack.

FOR THE THIRD time, the youngster Benlilo heard the massage relayed: 'Look!' He was about to do so again when he noticed, to his uttermost horror, a huge figure standing behind him. The figure was about the most fearful and gigantic he had stumbled upon so far. His corporal and mental frames vibrated as unseen before, while all powers watched with an overriding interest.

It was that of a funeral shadow, full of disquiet bones an unpretentious courier of death. It, in all its strength and with both its astonishingly large and rough hands, pushed the lad from his back into the cavernous dungeon. The ultra-violent push made sounds of pathetic conquest, as the pusher did it.

The boy tumbled headlong. The waiting hosts of the graves cheered the pusher outstandingly. They were impatient to receive the latest victim and swallow his body wholly or in bits. The huge figure burst into laughter to celebrate its unchallenged victory over the arch foe, Benlilo. To its credit, it had recorded, in a flash, a supersonic achievement, which none of its contemporaries had made in history. Then, overblown by an air of consuming self-importance, how interesting it watched its victim tumbling down into a final destruction!

It was not to be, still! A flash of radiant light roared across the surface of the dungeon. A different kind of silence reigned over the region. The funeral shadow pusher watched the changing scenario with overwhelming interest. The powers too. All forces and hosts of darkness. They were all dumbfounded because something unforeseen had just happened. They kept their minds, ears and eyes wide opened. Confirmation mattered most to the powers similar to conquest. What naturally followed was celebration galore in their gloomily dark sovereignty. This was, nonetheless, if the event had favoured them.

There were some euphoric clouds raging down the dungeon, as, miraculously, Benlilo floated mid the air. The man with six wings surprisingly re-appeared; he dived unbelievably down below. He mounted the lad on his back and flew him cleanly to safety. This was incontestably Benlilo's closest shave with death to date. He too was pleasantly embarrassed in respect of the manner of his rescue by a greater power beyond his human comprehension. With the successful hostile push of the ghostly funeral shadow into the dungeon, the lad had already believed that the end to his earthly life had come.

Instantaneously, the rejoicing of the hosts of the graves turned instantly into mourning. The latest defeat beat flat their imaginative conclusion. The laughter of the figure funeral shadow involuntarily twisted into weeping. It found it painfully impossible to believe what had just happened. As tall and huge as it was, it dashed itself onto the ground in a fêted instance of grief, mourning the abortion of its evil project. The sound of its fall itself shook the soil as if it would cave in; its crying and sobbing that followed scared stiff the forest. In addition, many members of host of darkness joined the loser in its grieving celebration.

That was not all that befell the pusher. The rule was, □An eye for an eye, a tooth for a tooth and life for life! If, as a professional hunter, you cannot provide, you must be presented; if you cannot conquer, you must be conquered! It is a taboo - graves do not open their mouths for nothing; they must swallow something; they must need to be propitiated!□ all the hungry graves of the dungeon demanded chorally. They would not be pacified in the absence of nothing. They knew their rights.

An east wind blew and the funeral shadowy personality suddenly met itself tumbling down as feast for the embittered and hungry graves. A grand deal of sorrowing broke out, concurrently, in and around several enclaves of the gods and goddesses and the powers. This was all because, for the very first time in the adventure, darkness consumed darkness instead of the hunted foe Benlilo. There was no sympathiser on their side beside their own. Still, they were determined not to give up the struggle and the battle.

Accordingly, the six-winged man flew Benlilo into safety and both of them landed coolly together on the other side of the dungeon. Upon landing, the man faced him. He smiled and said:

□Boy, your journey continues – bon voyage!□

□Bon voyage! but why? Where? How? What are you saying?□ Benlilo looked straight into the face of his rescuer in bewilderment □ he cried out disappointedly and asked. He quickly added, □How dare you do this wickedness to me, man? Complete your favour! Fly me straight to my father□s compound where there is safety, peace, and joy for my soul. I bet you will surely do this for me, kind-hearted man, or won□t you?□ he said smilingly.

The boy had enjoyed the breezy comfort of the momentary flight. He had therefore sincerely expected the rescuer to continue to fly him at his back out of the frightful forest into an ideal safety, far away from the forest and close to his father□s house in Marpolio □ at least. After all, the man had the ability and the opportunity freely at his disposal. He knew the way. Thence he was disillusioned at the latter end actions of the flying man. He surveyed the lad briefly. He smiled coolly and responded:

□Benlilo, I cannot fly you to your father□s house. □

□But why, man?□ the lad asked again in amazement.

□Because you are still in the forestry zone, boy,□ the man had not yet finished his statement but Benlilo was intolerant. He shouted at him:

□But why?□ and the man replied:

□Lad, the time is not yet,□ he revealed. He knew and understood Benlilo inside out. He did not give the baffled boy his needed opportunity to bombard him with further questions before he disappeared out of sight. Benlilo looked round sadly. How bitterly disappointed! He at least had expected the rescuer to show him the way to his family□s compound but nothing of that nature. *Oh shame, the half-kind-hearted man evaporated!*

The saddened boy could sense that the malevolent dungeon was not far away by what he could now call the southern compass. He took to his heels northward. The lesson of life was bound to transmit action. Either positive or negative action. He had since forgotten about help from the vanished *saviour of a man*. His hope to relocate to his father□s house boomed. His faith strengthened; his brain strategised □ but where was the direction?

The weather had turned ice-cold. A new moon appeared in sight. Some cock□s crows heralded a virgin dawn. The lad continued to run. He would not even dare to look back; to be forewarned is to be forearmed. Life is a tale of two warriors: the victor and the vanquished. It is the storyline of the success and the failure.

Though the battle had been tough, he longed, straightforwardly, to be the victor and never the victim. His positive hope boosted for no reason justifiable. The fire of his faith, in living and not in dying, refused being quenched. The mixture of consistence and persistence was the power for survival in life. He persevered in his running□

A pregnant rat ran for an escape into an overcrowded big hole of ants. It, in next to no time, perished irredeemably inside the captivity of the countless ants. Yet, the rat had its ambition and distinctive mission, alike the busy ants. As its spiritual cycle ran, so was its physical dream. The rat, though a small animal, was pregnant with rosy ideas about life as concerning it. *Life is only worth weighed in gold if it is preserved,* Benlilo meditated conclusively. If unpreserved, it is counted in coals or ashes. He quickly reasoned out an irrefutable plus: *There is no mission or ambition inside the grave.*

A lion roared incessantly in a jungle northward. A group of miscellaneous kinds of birds hailed the carnivorous animal in its imposing prominence. The opposite experience was the fortune of all lesser animals that had heard the lion□s roar □ they scampered for safety □ history told stories; memories recounted events and experience was the principal tutor. Benlilo's heart was invaded by a blazing fear. *The lion is a carnivorous animal. It is not a friend of man but his enemy.* The adolescent changed his course and he ran westward. The lion□s roaring thinned off as he moved on.

He got to the foot of a wealthy palm tree where he rested his back, standing, on the palm tree□s stem. He breathed heavily like an alligator that had luckily made its escape from a bush firestorm. While still standing and resting under the cool shade of the wealthy palm tree, the cut off student heard a voice, which said:

□Benlilo, you are a palm tree.

□You are the wealthy palm tree. □

□Inside this forest of terrors and horrors?□ a thoroughly irritated Benlilo asked lackadaisically.

□Life is the shadow of life, Benlilo. It is an irony. A proverb. The palm tree□s flower flourishes best in the midst of thorns □ there is no human being in the history of humankind who lived a trouble-free life of pleasure who is worth remembering by either history or posterity. Season tortures and era lambastes but time is the master of both season and era,□ the imperceptible voice offered some proverbial explanations. For this, Benlilo was angry. He shouted:

□But why, for God□s sake, are you faceless people speaking to me in proverbs and by parables? By the way, why are you hiding your faces? Are you all cowards? If you are men, tell me, why are you afraid to show your faces freely? Why can□t you just be plain and straightforward?□ Yet, instead of an immediate and an expected straightforward answer, there was an echo of mild laughter. Thereafter,

□Life is the proverb, boy □ the proverb of coming and going. Yesterday, you were in the city; today, you are inside the forest. Life is deeper than the ocean; it is shallower than the clouds. Life is wicked than darkness; it is more kind than light. Life is the parable - the fool cannot understand it, only the wise can. Benlilo, you□re the wealthy palm tree,□ the voice went more proverbial in spite of the boy□s objection. It had not finished but the lad argued:

□How impossible!□ and the faceless voice replied:

□That is the reason for all these strangeness and displeasures, lad. Birds of the same plumage flock together, but you are different. You are not part of them, Benlilo. The very moment that you made up your mind to succeed in life, you have already had plenty of enemies. The enemies increased but they will still multiply,□ it explained and Benlilo was better startled and worse saddened. He burst:

□*Hnhen,* what do you say, voice?□ As an answer to his latest question, the invisible voice went further:

□But, alas and, oh, pity! he blessed with life does not know the full-blown value of life. He who gifted with freedom lacks the knowledge of freedom. Neither life nor freedom and their meanings are sold in the market; they are all celestial gifts to man. Now, the owner of the brightest star is, as a rule, the most pursued by the powers. Envious agents swear never to leave him alone.

□He is eminent in their record. He remains on their priority list but both the powers and their agents have no time at all to waste on unenviable or desolate talents. See the lunatic naked on the street; behold the doomed drunkard who has lost the sense faculty of his destiny to manipulative time. Learn a good lesson from the parable of the cemetery richly populated with graves housing talents and geniuses. The gold has no place to hide in the market of time. The gold is the desire of all eyes and every mind but not so with the coal, the exact opposite of gold. You are the wealthy palm tree. Benlilo, you are the brightest star. You are never a coal; you are the gold.

□The enemy of human goodness has no time whatsoever for worthless life. Therefore, remember, or have you forgotten, before the gold ever becomes gold to emerge the darling desire of everybody, it must have passed through the fire? Passing through the fire is not a pleasure. The gold that has not yet passed through the fire is not yet the gold; it is the dross.□

□True saying but, and thanks!□ a hesitant Benlilo did not know when his mouth issued loud the positive response of reservation. He did not see anybody around or the speaker of those plainspoken words. He was however sure that the voice was that of a friend. A truth bearer. To be candid, it was about the best compliments that the boy had received since the beginning of the forestry adventure. The lad stood straight, looked round to see who was talking to him in a sequence of parables but he saw no one. He looked up to see the fronds of the palm tree and its beauty of wealth thrilled him proverbially. Then, he received the substantiation and he meditated loudly:

□Yes, the palm tree is the portrait of life par excellence. No part of it is wasted. Palm oil comes from its fleshy fruits, as well as another brand of oil, especially for soap making, from its kernel. The hard shell of the kernel too is never wasted; it is a good worker of fire □ either inside the blacksmith□s smithy or for the homemaker for cooking. The broom comes from its leaves, as a roofing material. Finally, the stem is useful for many things.□

Behold, the fronds of the palm tree were all in beautifully radiant greens, while about five bunches of ripe fruits graced its top. Before the boy could bring down his head, ten ripe fruits, big and fleshy - two each from a bunch, dropped in rapid succession onto the ground.

However, they disappeared into the soil as soon as they had landed thereon. Benlilo was not happy that the soil was *competing* with him for the *manna from above*. He was much sad that he had fallen a victim of the earth□s oppression inside the forest. He was very hungry. He would not understand that the ten released fruits meant ten little or big unalike misfortunes for his life. A little mind, how could he? His thinking faculty did not stumble on the reality that the soil was only obeying an order from a *higher* authority.

Yes! for the divinely appointed intervention, the first fruit was designed to earn the lad tuberculosis in the physical realm. The second palm fruit was to translate into a raging fear in his heart after he had eaten it. The fear would have pushed him to commit suicide at the noon of an allotted date and an appointed time. The third fruit was failure for the boy.

The fourth one stood for sorrow brewing chronically in his heart. In other words, he would never again be a happy person in life. The fifth fruit symbolised lies. This simply meant that the youngster would not be liberated from telling and treasuring lies. He would have been outgrowing one-step of lies and be graduating into a higher degree of them.

The sixth one meant amputated victory □ meaning that full-fulfilment would never have been his lot. The seventh one would have germinated inside of him to grow into a prosperous tree of hate and envy. And since envy usually mothers murder, he would have ended his life tragically one afternoon as a murderer. The seventh one was a harbinger of minor misfortunes very problematic in nature.

The eighth palm fruit was programmed to serve as a source of vanity-based anxiety for him. This meant that he would have been worrying endlessly for nothing, specifically on vanities of this world. The ninth fruit stockpiled a large sore for one of his armpits, while the tenth and last fruit meant arrows targeting his handiworks. Those evil arrows were to render all his efforts unprofitable and thereby crowning him the highly talented but profitless hard worker, an amputated victor □ a rich human vineyard where limitations, embargoes and evil family patterns flourished victoriously as fruitful trees without barriers.

In a scheme, all the ten palm fruits were evil - incongruent enemy bullets for his star, glory and destiny. They were arrows or products of marine witchcraft powers acting their parts as virulent and serpentine pursuers of the lad□s life, specifically his first class glory. They were designated wasters of his life, talents and resources. They were all meant to destroy his glorious treasure of life.

The powers were very clever and calculative. For as soon as the wayfaring boy had paused along his journey and he rested his back on the palm tree□s stem, the evil powers had seen a new opportunity and they quickly seized it most subtly. Members of the generation of the old serpent, they knew that he was hungry; hence the miraculous express dropping of its ripe but now poisoned fruits onto the ground directly in front of him. Then, going by their conclusion, they expected and believed that he would pick at least some of the fruits and eat.

The powers had no mind to give up. They were soon back, from that land of what they had tagged □minor defeat□, better armed onto the battlefield. Benlilo was still occupied with the thought of his losses in the buried ten beautifully ripe palm fruits when, out of the greens, a strangely white monkey jumped onto the ground. The monkey made for his side aggressively.

□Rush him!□ a silent but very cruel voice roared in the terrorised wind.

Though scared, Benlilo resisted the monkey□s aggression. He gave it a muscular kick in its left ear. The monkey was shocked at the jagged reaction of the boy. The powers, its masters, too. The animal rolled on the ground frontward. Yet, it meant business. It soon stood up and followed the boy, as he continued to find his way farther westward.

As the singing dove had rightly prophesied, life was a challenge and the lad, at present, knew it off hand. Life was a race, he knew this too. He gathered more speed against the efforts of the monkey.

The monkey was greatly disadvantaged by virtue of the fact that it had only three imbalanced limbs. It had once jumped into a hunter□s trap, which cut off its fourth limb. Yet, to its conclusion, that disability would not matter a whit. It was an epitome of rigid determination. It believed, strongly, that nothing would hinder it from achieving its goal against the person of the lad. This was to demonstrate how indomitable the powers could be.

At a particular point, Benlilo changed his mind. He remembered the tough challenge of the singing dove; he asked himself whether he was really a man or a woman. In the morning of creation, he was created by the Creator to be man and not a woman, no doubt. How could a monkey, an animal, be terrorising him in the forest if he was really a man? Untenable! Indefensible! He concluded flat that the time had come for him to be courageous more than ever before.

And there is time for everything in life, he reasoned out further. There was time to play the gentle teen wayfarer and the time to be the uncompromising fighter. There must be time to play a lamb and the time to act the lion. For the straight conclusion that he must be a man, the man - the lad Benlilo resolved that he would fight back. *The time is now - action!*

He gathered all audacity within and without him. He waited for the three-legged monkey *for a fight to death!* For this, he looked for a piece of hard wood that resembled a rod. Armed with the wood, he waited in hiding at the back of a tree. Soon, the monkey appeared running zigzag like a big crab. The warring lad was battle ready.

In ultra-aggressiveness plus a designed move, Benlilo appeared from his ambush and with all his strength, smashed the head of the animal with the durable wood and the pursuer was down unconscious on the ground in a few seconds. The lad had never imagined that victory over an enemy could be so cheap.

Now equipped with greater degree of confidence, he paced nearer, knocked the dying monkey□s head three deadlier times and the aggressor breathed its last. That marked the direct victory number one for the lad in the expedition. The vindicated boy burst into the smiles of a victor. His good hopes in life received very great fortifications.

Obstinacy with the powers was indefinite by amoebic expressions to achieve a goal. As Benlilo stood, still armed with the long wood and watching the animalistic thing on the ground, a series of reprehensible wonders tried to manifest. The dead monkey wanted to change into a viper but it could not. It tried to transform into a huge scorpion but this too turned out to be a failure.

The deceased monkey made a frenzied effort to convert to fire to pursue the boy but its hope also received wounds. As its butchered mouth was igniting the fire, so it was going off. Had the victorious lad not smashed the head piteously lifeless, at least one of the repellent wonders would have been possible for the monkey to resume its fight against him in an unanticipated style.

Darkness was that magically wonderful but the genuine revelations were just coming the way of the adventurous lad. This was part of the primary reason for his miraculous transplantation into the mystery forest. A student in the *Department of Adventure,* he was by now a second year undergraduate in the *University of Life.*

Who could tell the number of years he had more to spend in the higher institution?

Who are you? What are you? Why are you?
Where are you coming from and where are you going?

PART THREE (B):
THE ADVENTURE

He who loves life, let him fear death
He who loves death, let him treasure life.
Labour is vanity when hope is fast lost,
Harvest is lost when faith is broken
Joy is wounded when life is the valley
The valley is life for the defeated

CHAPTER 038

The Flower Garden And Its Keeper

Life is a challenge, the toughest challenge
By argument of wits and physical battle
Beyond the realm of power and might.
Yet, cowardice reigns within the same life
Had man his weapons of war gallantly employed.

OH! HOW MIGHTY stars and glories fall on surface earth! How love is lost and could not be regained! Behold the battlefield of life as red as the sweltering blacksmith□s fire. Several flowery lives were magnetised thereat and they burnt to ashes. Consider their falls like the sand back onto the soil of time. How the electrifying stars had gone into the dust for emergency burials!

Behold several hidden but wealthy treasures - up in flames like hay fields of the dry season! Earthly life, truly, is the fiercest of all battles. Therefore, only the lucky survivor can render songs of victory therein or thereafter. The vanquished warrior is lost and cannot be found. His place becomes uninhabited, no more an asset, unto all generations - what a misfortune! How a big, unrecoverable loss □ the cataclysm!

Having clubbed to death the monkey, Benlilo eyed it on the ground once more. He threw his head backward and laughed. *Yes, victory is sweet - I am truly a man,* he soliloquised a self-congratulation! He threw a fist and beat his chest to celebrate his victory over the latest enemy. He threw up his two arms and congratulated himself the best. Victory, by manhood, generates from the fountain of valour dramatised; the victory lays waste in man if he refuses to act.

In the vein of plants, heroism sprouts from the loamy soil of bravery put into action. The boy□s action and voice provoked a serial reaction from his enemies: the powers, the gods and their agents □ more so that the defeat and the tragedy of the monkey was another painful thing to them:

□See him!□

□See him!□

□See the idiot!□

The youth smiled and laughed. He relaxed a little before he started to walk away leisurely, albeit gallantly, the true champion. He felt like changing his course and he did. He turned southward and examined the trees of the forest. Another time, he could notice the axe man□s marks, as he had seen them in the inauguration of the adventure, firmly fixed on the trees. The so-branded trees groaned visibly for the evil marks with death just around the corner.

They were conspicuously marked in blood red ink of various shapes and sizes. All the marks were coded. For only the unidentified markers, and none of the marked trees, could decode the signs. They could only feel and experience the fevers and the looming tragedies to befall them nearer or later.

By simple interpretations, while some were fixed with the mark of premature death, others had that of one deadly sickness or the other on them. While some were marked out to be felled by one evil destiny or another, the others were re-destined to be rooted out of living by hailstorms and whirlwinds. In unity of laid up fate, all the trees, largely those carrying identifications, already had their days on earth numbered.

All the tags manifestly spoke of passing away in the end unto the marked trees, which were in the overriding majority. The unmarked ones were few. As the uniform identity of the trees was in that beginning, so it was still. The forest was life personified. All the trees, marked or unmarked, represented human beings on earth - along with their beautiful destinies.

The florid destinies were stars, glories, or hidden treasures of sons and daughters of man. Encased inside these, in each individual human, were the triplets of mission, vision and ambition. They formed the prosperity triangle of objective, focus and goal of the individual human being on planet earth. They were the reason or reasons for his coming here as a sojourner. The divine package had covered his yesterday, today and tomorrow.

The marked trees soon started to fall even though no detectable axe was seen laid on them as of yet. Those ones served as examples to how human beings could fall victims to the powers. They were a message to the wayfaring boy that earthly life, for man, was that of challenges, attacks and woes. They typified unpredictable death striking at defenceless man.

Benlilo increased his strides, as the marked trees started to fall down one after another or in groups, left and right. He looked here and there like a fear-possessed lad alone in the wilderness of hateful time. He narrowly escaped being struck on the head by a falling tree, as another one targeted his left shoulder.

He slipped into the pattern of the weeping ghost. He prayed earnestly that he would not die in the forest. He prayed that divine mercy would find him out of the mystery forest of mysteries. He looked backward □ forward, and ran! Life was a gamble. Truly a venture, the highest risk. Comparable to his journey all the way through the forest, it was an adventure.

The marked trees□ session of falls stopped for a while. Benlilo felt relieved but he was flat wrong for where was the relief? Terrifically, the immediate sky of this part of the forest started to cast stones of flames down at the standing trees except, however, the unmarked ones. The unmarked ones bore, also, unhidden identifications. They were trademarked with the mercy, favour and beauty of the Maker of all living things. They all carried marks of victory and success in variable grades.

The unlucky ones that were struck by the stones moaned. Many of them fell. They cursed the sky and the forest rowdily and endlessly. However, their curses only multiplied the falling stones because the powers throwing the stones were more maddened. Mercy had no place in them. Their principle of operation was totalitarianism, no half-measure.

As Benlilo□s grandmother Ajuiba had publicly confessed, they rejoiced more in deeper exercises of their wickedness. The more they meted out their naughty portions, the better satisfied they became. To them, life was all about cruelty and callousness - and the generations of man were their targets, their soon-to-be fatalities at the receiving ends. The graves were waiting; the coffin builders were ready too. They cherished tears, from the eyes of men, to wet the soil of time like the rain of June.

Benlilo was dismayed. He picked yet another race and ran watchfully out of the danger zone. He arrived in a new area. The falling stones did not pursue him there; neither did he hear of the groaning and curses of the hit trees, nor those of their perforated or destroyed greens any longer. He felt a little bit pleased now, but it was not yet *uhuru!*

Again, he started to walk fast through the forest but he was actively conscious of any accidental happening. He still looked here and there like a thief who had just escaped an irate mob□s lynching bid. Rest deserted his person. Peace could have no abode in his heart. Torture!

He arrived at the edge of a garden of flowers. Arrested by their extreme beauty, being a passionate lover of flowers, he started to admire the beautiful flowers but not for long. A baby figure of a ghost appeared unto him. The fright assaulting his reins swelled. The stronghold of fears seemed to be consolidating its hold.

At the abrupt appearance of the latest frightening creature, his body frames vibrated like a wearing-out locomotive engine. Life was a tale of the odd. The teller of the tale was the other side of time; its operator was life itself. Its hearer and receiver was man.

Even so, the wayfaring lad rushed at the ghostly figure, armed with the woody rod with which he had killed the monkey. The tough-strong-fighter raised the tool up confidently to descend fatally on the babyish creature and destroy it all at once but, to his greatest bewilderment, the rod turned into a piece of rag before his hand came down coldly. Hurriedly, surprised Benlilo threw away the filthy rag in biting disgust; he was deluded of the negative miracle that had just happened in his hand and right before his eyes.

For the dwarfish ghost, he threw his head backward and laughed most heartily. He clapped his two hands rowdily. Then, some sarcastically phrasal voices roared inside the wind:

□Excellent!□

□Beautiful!□

□Marvellous!□

□Demonstrate more your power, boy!□

□We want more!□

□Give us more of the stupid manifestation!□

A rejoicing team of some enemies□ voices roared across the hemispheric air chorally thus:

□Oh, ah! it has happened. Darkness is terror to day and it is much! The beauty of darkness is in wickedness and it has started to manifest so soon and we are witnesses. We are the champions! Light is quenched by night, as justice is done! The anger is vanquished by the demon of war and all can see. It is won □ the battle is fought and won and who the fool can reverse it?□ it was yet another loud sound of battle cry and no contrary voice was raised anywhere inside the forest.

In respect of what had just happened with Benlilo appropriately on the losing side, he was shocked and dazed. His two eyes seemed to be seeing stars falling down from the firmament of heaven, his brain calculating in the ugly expanse. Nevertheless, for the raw death staring him at the face, the boy regained himself fast unbelievably. As the dwarfish ghostly warrior was still boiling with anger too awful for words, and preparing to strike, many rowdily agitating voices from the turbulent space boomed:

□Rush him!□

□The bloodthirsty fool must die and it is now!□

□Yes, he has been sentenced to death! He has lived long enough!□

□Strike at him!□

□Knock him down at once!□

□Punch him out forever and let him become history!□

□Hit him the hardest; destroy him!□

□Crush the fool out of life! Kick him battered onto the ground!□

□Master destroyer, fall him □ make a direct collision against him □ let his living expire!□

□Blow out his candle light, his sinful heart! I say extinguish the ray of his awkward hope!□

□Dispatch his soul straight into where it belongs, the hellish conflagration! Show him no atom of clemency!□

□Let him experience the world of maggots! Let him be fed full of the cruelest side of life! Let him know the most callous punishments that he deserves!□

□Blow his heart out; let his faith become useless as the dirty water!□

□Master teacher, teach the boy bastard the capital lesson of death!□

□And with your conquest of his wretched person, let him become the past forever! He must not have a grave!□

□Yes, Champion of evils, attack him most sadistically! Conquer him! Devour him □ he is not anything but a bit of meat for you!□

□Let his greedy star fall from the firmament of heaven to rise no more and let us Princes rejoice at his extermination!□

□He has dared tragedy □ so, let the most gruesome tragedy befall him and forevermore - now!□

□Conquer the greediest sadist □ fall him! March him! Let the earth have a taste of his beautiful feast!□

□Eminent annihilator, it is time we celebrate his obituary □ he has lived long enough!□

□Adage of history singing disastrous prosperity for the unwise lame □ slaughter him with your unseen tack hammer of death!□

□Master destroyer beauty of flat impiety, this is a challenge from the cheapest prey! Crush him bones and flesh □ drink off his blood as of sweet wine; eat his flesh □ it is free for you from the Lord of the Forest!□

□Oh tactically strategic fighter, let his place in the land of the living become vacant and let another star be established. Let his shameful glory be obliterated now! Let his treasure house of woes become ashes to him but gold in the possession of others!□

□Pride of darkness the bravest warrior, stardom of soullessness, treasure mine of indignation, why are you wasting time on the damned? Let your boiling wrath fall upon the ignoramus! He deserves to be treated like the truly condemned criminal!□

□Saddest epoch of revenge □ soldiering soldier of the gods, teach him the other side of life □ red means danger! It symbolizes fire! Hottest death - pluck the life out of him! □

□Master dispatcher - enough has got to be enough! Enough of his insults and assaults! Let his father Amaldia celebrate his obituary. The gods have spoken; they have willed him out for rebelling against their wish and command. Let the Commander do his own bidding! □

□Powerful ambassador of the grave, give him no opportunity to survive! It is taboo; he must not survive! It has been decreed that he must die and he must have to die the death! □

□Desperately deadly slaughterer □ slaughter the trespasser with the axe of your teeth and then devour him along with his talents and stars! □

□Epitome of gushing cruelty, prove to the goat that it is an animal for ritual, and that you are the custodian of death! Tell him that death is the cheapest ware in your bosom! □

□Mobile messenger of the gods, courier of urgent calamity, show him the only way into the grave! Show him the gate into most up-to-date death and let his ingenuity be celebrated in the world beyond, sure! □

□Emergency sword into the belly of man □ show him a fraction of your power! Let him have the galling ration of your brutality! The wild goat has no alternative but to die! □

□Reservoir of boiling indignation, give the fool just a cup of your violent gift of death and let him be lost forevermore! □

□Direct opposite of life, you harbour no mercy □ therefore, exhibit to the son of enemy your iniquitous ware, that you are truly the pit of mercilessness, depth of demise! □

□Let death rejoice over him! Let his bones serve as chewing sticks for the goddesses! It is settled □ the sacrificial animal must face the dagger at the abattoir! □

□Maximum power the first-begotten of the Devil □ collide against him like the solid rock of the bottomless pit! Help the deities and the divinities to carry out their sentence! Strike the hardest at him! Tear him into insignificant bits! Feast on his delicious flesh for the joy of your soul! □

□Most wicked of all spirits the most violent attacker and destroyer □ prove to him that you are not his equal! Shatter his head; dispatch his soul! Blow out his heart! This is the moment of judgment, the hour of reckoning! Knock him down at once and let us write the last chapter of his life□s story! □

□Stable rock of destruction, pour on it a mere portion of your wrath and he is finished for evermore! At once, let his star be blackened and blotted out of the firmament of time □ into the grave! He deserves no pity or an atom of mercy and he must have none, yes!

□Author of brutality, ocean of plentiful sorrows □ silence him; give him the crudest knock into his good-for-nothing head! Kick him! Batter him! Destroy his animalistic being! He is the worthless dog for the gods! □ thus would the conclusive roar of the ghost□s last encourager sound. The entirety of the inhuman voices□ outburst was survived with a prolonged offensive laughter session of,

□ *Yeaahaaaaaaaahaaaaahaaahaaheh!* □

From all indications, the dwarfish ghost was happy and enjoying the eulogistic outpouring of his colleagues□ words of encouragement. He smiled victory-in-sadism already, as it seemed that it received high-invigoration and fortification by the eulogies and instructions. It was now extra-charged. It raised up its head and roared like a wounded lion, □*Ugbuaaaaaarrrarahah!*□

Its depth of wrath exaggerated within and without. The boiling anger of its indignation gushed and jumbled. Repeatedly and hurriedly, its two eyeballs rolled and blinked. Its thin lips shook and beat some drumbeats. It sounded:

□*Gbi-bes-gbe!*□ etc. Furthermore, a tambourine of darkness sounded his raging heart, as another musical instrument roared inmost his brain.

□So this Benlilo, you are the greatest coward! You are seriously afraid to die but death is cheap, so economical. Son of the bitch son of man, beauty jungles for manifestation inside the forest of taboo and I am the heartless devourer! Age of wickedness counts its toll and I am the death carrier! The belly of the gods is hungry;

it will rejoice at your feast - the powers and the gods will rejoice. Farewell, son of the swine, I say adieu! Its acidic wrath magnified and multiplied.

The strange personality later appeared, surprisingly, inside a long winter coat that was almost touching the ground □ and, no doubt, the dressing added to his ultra-wicked outlook.

In another second, the diminutive figure had removed the winter coat and the real frightening posture of its personality manifested. It had two bowlegs and, unbelievably, the hair on its body, especially the legs, arms and chest, all were now like shooting-out tiny thorns. Its two sets of teeth were deep scarlet red, noiselessly singing song of blood.

Seeing the babyish personality, for its unhidden cruelty, Benlilo fled eastward. He had discovered a narrow path through the forest and thereon he ran and ran. He was running and sweating uncontrollably □ believing that he had escaped from the wicked creature when, suddenly, the same evil being appeared directly in his front, facing him.

□*Aaahaaaahaaaahahahaa!*□ it laughed reverberatingly for the entirety of the forest to shake like never before. The laughter harvest of the evil creature was meant to alert all environmental, elemental and atmospheric forces. It was a clarion call to war.

□*Aaaaaahaaaahaaahaahah!*□ again, it was the vibrating laughter session of the smallish ghost and all concerned received the transmitted message. The gods and the goddesses too □ all stood on their toes on red alert! Oh, how they all eagerly looked forward to seeing the newest thing to happen, the already fashioned out tragedy to end the archenemy Benlilo.

□Benlilo, I am not your equal in any way □ physically and spiritually □ and I want you fool to understand this plain reality. I am your master; yes! the champion - your sworn and unrepentant enemy □ but why are you running away from me? They say you are the hero □ hero of a nonentity!□ it was the query of the dwarfish ghost, shaking from head to toes and boiling in indescribable anger. Benlilo turned rearward and ran. He arrived back at the edge of the beautiful garden of flowers. Again, the evil being appeared directly in his front with an outburst of great laughter as never before:

□*Aaahaahaaaahaahaaaahahahaahaa!*

□The battle is won before commencement. The gods are glorified, praise ye the gods!□

Thus, the seven voices exulted. Then, echoes of □*Hallelluijah!*□ roared across the fearful terrain, even as drumbeats of echoing □*Yaaaahah!*□ also boomed. The dwarfish being too enjoyed the artlessly phrasal exclamations of sarcasms. After the last voice, it laughed a little more before it frowned its face like a monstrous killer. The look soon acquired another horrific standardisation of uncontrolled bitterness.

□See yourself in a better viewpoint now? Funny, oh very humorous! You small boy, you call yourself a man and you are so bold! *Ehnen!* What do you rely upon? Where is your power? You are not afraid? You are meeting death face-to-face and you are not even afraid? The gods are hungry and they have got a free feast in you, *aaaaahaahaah!*□ boasted the strange face but the confronted lad did not know that the antagonist□s existent points of boasting were still coming.

Its face was like that of a famishing fowler. Its mouth twisted into the shape of a badly woven basket. It hissed noisily, agonisingly. It yawned like a wounded and hungry boar. Its eyeing turned more vinegary and bloodshot. Its outwardly fragile body fames vibrated rapidly and they stopped. It released some bitterest strokes of smiles. Thereafter, standing like an impostor, it addressed Benlilo in the tone of a brute:

□Who are you? What are you? Why are you? Where are you coming from and where are you going? What is your problem? Why are you wandering about stepping on sacred toes of sacrosanct territories? Troublesome orphan, why can□t you stay within your own boundary? Are you confused? What do you want here and there - all about? Did you miss your way?□ the speaker paused but the lad had no mind whatsoever of giving a reply to any of its flying acidic posers. It continued in a while:

□Redundant son of man, are you Apollo Eleven or is it Apollo Thirteen? Do you take this consecrated territory for the free zone, the moon or the space? What exactly do you mean by this your unholy encroachment? Do you mistake this place for the ever-mute sky at your mortal mercy, which you habitually terrorise with all sorts: jetliners, fighter jets, helicopters and all forms of carbon dioxide released from mechanical engines to deplete and to destroy its ozone layer?

□Poke-nosing thing, why are you here and what is your mission? Are you a nomad? A vagabond? Are you not the abominable son of man, a spy on our world? You have this day trespassed into a strange land, the strangest of all lands - the land of the gods! The territory of the goddesses. You shall not go unpunished! This is an affront, an insult, and the greatest assault! Nobody does it and goes scot-free, ask history! Consult with posterity □ ah, it is simply impossible! You will take the knock of cruel life on your head and your life will never be the same again! Foolish boy, I assure you, you can never survive it!

□You deserve the hardest hit, yes! You surely deserve the knock! I will make you a public example, an open disgrace □ now-now! You are in for the optimal trouble of your entrapped life and there is no escaping it. Boy, I sincerely hope that you have dug your grave and bought your coffin. I believe your mislaid soul is prepared for the journey of no return. Your time is up □ be prepared to sleep in your death!□ shockingly, the tiny ghost poured its more-than-vituperative words of indignation upon Benlilo.

No mistaking it, the wrath of the ambitious attacker had reached the condensing boiling point. Never in his life had Benlilo been aggressively confronted like this. The boy was more than astonished but he was not confused. Seen and unseen hosts of the mystery forest watched. The miracle of the woody rod turning into rag had fortified its power greatly. The lad was still watching the high-speed gutter-speaker when he broke the charged silence in-between them and spoke again:

□Jobless small boy, I am talking to you □ or do you say that my multitudes of words deserve no response? Do you call me a fool and say that silence is the best answer? What do you want near my garden of flowers?□ the violent baby figure challenged him further in a strictly pitiless voice. Benlilo could see that the challenger was now in aggravated rage. The lad was, to the highest degree, amused and annoyed by the challenge of the baby figure.

The sweet memory of his victory over the three-legged monkey was still green fresh in his memory □ the never-expected negative miracle notwithstanding. His bravery recouped; another feat was guaranteed. He was amused because the challenger, though a portrait of terror, was about two and a half feet tall with short legs and tiny arms. Its face was like sour milk.

Two teeth shot out of its mouth and they measured up to half a foot each. Blood dripped out of the mouth - exactly like that of the desperate witch on a suicide mission but who suddenly stumbled on a cheap prey. Its belly protruded and it carried an extra-large head that was decorated with a long horn. With no strand of hair thereon, the head seemed to be bumping, as the mystic being moved in all ambivalent ambition towards the direction of Benlilo.

Its lone eye, on the forehead, was large and it rolled in all directions like a restless basketball in the low sky of America during the championship season. It had an emaciated and long beard, dirty green in colour that was, interestingly, nearly touching the ground. The baby figure appeared in the complexion of radiant pink but it was freely decorated with visibly green incision marks in many strategic positions of its body: cheeks, neck, chest, ankles and hands.

Its right arm and hand bore two hammered incision marks, alike its left one □ while its body from head to toes were decorated generously with various types of fiendish marks. Majority of the incision marks bore close resemblance to those of Bornu culture in the northeastern upper region of Nigeria.

Its face bore testimony to a conglomeration of nearly sixty-six such tribal marks. The tribal marks were of various sizes, lengths and designs. They represented different but one interest. They routinely communicated in scores of languages. Life was a heavily coded message - only the deep could call to the deep, even in cynicism.

Benlilo did not bother himself to answer any of the numerous questions of his latest challenger. He surveyed the baby figure all over again and burst into a terrific session of laughter. For the sarcastic laughter, the challenger became terribly angry now. Supporting its waist with both hands, it looked dissolutely up to the boy and fumed all over.

Its countenance read threat and madness combined. It concluded that the contemptuous laughter of the boy was a no stunted insult to it, a direct slap across its unsmiling face. It had been austerely offended. It was touchily charged for battle. Life was the battle.

□What do you mean by your laughter and your arrogant posture, small boy?□ again, it looked up at Benlilo in all pomposity and asked.

□I, a small boy, you this shapeless tiny rabbit?□ angered-Benlilo responded with his own bombshell of an interrogative challenge. The baby figure never expected such a biting response from the lad. It had its dislike rapidly reproduced. It shook all parts of its body fervidly - in preparation for war with the intruder. Most bitterly, it surveyed the boy up and down and shouted at him:

□Tell me, who are you by the way? Who are you little but haughty maggot □ tell me who you are?□ it demanded harshly and determinedly. Benlilo exhibited another round of soldierly smiles of confidence, though still unarmed, the more as the babyish figure boiled with continuously brewing inward and outward fury. Then the boy talked:

□Hostile midget of an evil baby brain, I am the prince of royalty. I am the son of the Most High. I am the victor on the mountaintop. I am the star of my season. I am the joy and success of the royal household. I am the glory of the human age. I am the salt of the earth. I am □,□ the boy answered but he was yet to finish. He halted the flow of his rhythmic philosophical poetry, as that minute had offered him the inspiration, because the little figure shouted him down ferociously when it barked:

"*Heh!* stop there you mad-boy human earthly maggot and foolish ignoramus - *aaahaaaahaaah!*" it laughed, so heartily and bitterly, also Benlilo to derision and the whole forest shook badly. Thunderous roars of elated hosts in several dungeons greeted the creature□s valiant counter-challenge by its offensive words. The boy was greatly embarrassed but he composed himself.

Again, the baby figure acquired a more atrocious composure. Knowing fully that it was not alone in the ensuing fight against the lad, all over again, it ruptured into its extended fragment of laughter, as it yet watched Benlilo with a half mind of irresolution.

The only fear harboured by the ghost towards the boy was, of course, sourced to the open record of victories trailing his path against his enemies through the mystery forest of the gods, the latest of which was his destruction of the limping ape. What of the tragedy of the funeral figure? His running accounts of miraculous escapes from the powers□ abattoirs of stars had been open exhibitions. These had been pounding cold their *methodical imaginations* and *projected conclusions*. This was the toughest challenge to their warfare creativities, alike their wealth of experiences in murdering destinies and slaughtering stars.

Benlilo worried briefly on the possibility that other wicked creatures of the forest might have heard the noisy laughter of the dwarfish ghost and come, in scores, hundreds or thousands, to join him to attack him but there was no such occurrence. Then, the phantom threw its head aggressively presumptuous and laughed the more. As a survival to that, it shot its two rolling eyeballs at Benlilo's with its lips recounting:

□Who do you really think you are pitiless Benlilo and where do you think you are? You are inside our forest, our forest of heartlessness □ do you know that, lad?□ it asked, its voice encumbered with jocularity of scorn. Dead silence marked out honour for the dwarfish ghost for its doughty words. The lad would not, however, allow the perturbed silence to be long lasting before he too reacted to the challenge:

□And so what, rotten head?□ Benlilo hardly allowed it to land before he replied, also in an ultra discoloured tone. The wild ghost got more infuriated. Shaking all over, it faced the boy in a more direct position and fired more salvos:

□You ash of the earth, shame of the inhuman age, sorrow and failure of a slaving household, lame star of your season, the vanquished in the valley of defeat, son of the dead, messenger of slavehood - stop! *Hheen!* where exactly do you think you are and what do you think you are doing? Do you know the forest evil and can you identify the danger of the flaming noon? Look at him! Who had asked you to start to vomit maggots? Insult! What an assault! This is an affront!□ The dwarfish creature thus overturned all Benlilo□s praise annotations against him in reversed orderliness.

Every second, the mysterious figure grew worse by its look and varying dramatisations. Benlilo became mildly upset. The dwarfish being knew this and it was happy at the newest development. As a fighter and an opportunistic maximiser, it must seize every advantage, psychologically, by the slimmest opportunity.

It eyed the boy more resentfully and reversed backward in a few, calculated steps □ thereby sounding its last warning by action and not by words. It fumed all over, boiling the more: it was surely set to deal most ruthlessly with the *boy rebel,* as nobody before it ever did, as it had earlier threatened. How it strongly enthused the hyper-confidence to succeed where countless scores of the powers before it had failed! Its rigid faith grew stronger; it never believed that it could fail at all. In greater vigour and with re-fortified confidence it boasted of power and might:

□Anger collides with danger! Offence is crushed by wrath! Banana is roaming about the bush of ghosts where swords dangle and blood flows like a river. Thunder strikes; the lightening axe smacks into nothing, the no-thing to wait for the killer axe. Where is the armless trespasser to wait for the rolling rock? Terror shoots; horror swallows.

□The ignorant sees death but he does not recognise death. The fool jumps into the bottomless pit. No coffin to house the wasted destiny, his soul and flesh are shattered! Yes! where is the shrub of vegetable to defend itself against the crushing of the baobab tree? The hour of judgement has come □ it is finished □ the zero hour! The dead hour

□See how rage defines a goal; jungle-hot-judgement qualifies it. Tragedy takes stock, celebration crowns it. The arrow for sorrow, this is the morrow. *Aaah-ohoo-hhiii!* - the sacrificial dog has freely walked into the shrine of the gods, a place of gushing blood. The flaming sword is greedy and angry. The evil fire yearns to consume; mercy is never found inside the jungle of the dark. Terror clears the way, as horror ploughs the weed. I tell you, small boy, enough had got to be enough!□ it shouted bitterly in an agonisingly terrific tone and the forest shook to its foundations as if a volcanic activity would happen. It continued, gliding into the realm of self-appraisal the best:

□I am the King of Terror; the Beast of Battle! I have devoured stars and consumed glories,□ further the dwarfish being praised itself. It had not finished, so it rolled out more:

□Son of man, it will be brashly stupid of me to shoot you in the leg. I will and I must shoot you in your heart, and the vulture will feast on your carcase. I am the shooter; I am the striker; I am the vulture □ *aaahaaahah!*□ yet again, the baby ghost exploded into an extra rowdy session of laughter and the totality of the forestry region vibrated to its reinforcements.

□The sheep animal has freely walked inside the leopard□s lair. A destitute helpless and wretched son of man is right inside the den of the lion. The lion will devour him and I am the lion! The blood of the fool must be shed to appease the god and I, Cocoshima I am the god!□ Benlilo continued to watch as it reeled off its self-eulogy further:

□I am the constant shadow that swallows. I am the gallows of human lives, crown glory of cruelty. I am the one and only King of the Night. I am the said beauty of ugliness, the ill destiny of the disobedient child. I am Mother to Calamity and I father Catastrophe. As I have assured you, mercy is dead to me for I am the wilderness of famine. History is about to be made and I am the history maker □ where is your life crying in vain inside my dungeon of callousness?□ The dwarfish warrior thus concluded and the stage was set for Benlilo□s first direct battle inside the mystery forest of adventures.

In a terrific move, the ghostly warrior flew skyward. It descended and rushed towards the lad where he was standing with the suicidal mission to crashing into him and knocking him fiercely onto the ground. However, before it could reach him, Benlilo took a fast dive rightward and the irate being crashed ghastly against the ground. It cried aloud like a wild goat whose two front limbs were, without warning, grabbed by a hunter☐s iron trap. Benlilo was well pleased, as a groaning voice of the powers echoed:

It has happened again and I told you!
This mysterious Benlilo, master dodger
Amoebic portrait of heat up danger
Very slippery, ever cunning ☐ see! See!!
Another tragedy has happened, oh-shrr!

A stooping Benlilo burst into a long-standing season of sneering laughter. The lad☐s sardonic laughter pained the dwarf to no stop. It was also sharp thorns short into the flesh of the powers. Consequently, by that, the lad recorded yet another misdeed against the gods. In the ever-current library of the powers, his file of misbehaviours swelled.

While struggling to regain its balance and be on its feet again, the cold-blooded creature eyed Benlilo, unrepentantly, swearing with the gods to avenge himself of *you my adversary!*

CHAPTER 039

By The Groove Of The Dead

Disabled able bodies of woods
Spirited cowards ruling in despotism by
Divergent scenes rolling in the night of horrors
With renewing hope sustained in flying memories,
Courtesy the expedition reeling into bigger wilderness.

BENLILO CONTINUED TO feast on his harvest of laughters. All of a sudden, he noticed that the baby figure was anchored firmly into the ground by its two shot-out teeth. Alas! the two iron teeth were now sunk deep into the soil - and it was struggling heedlessly thereby to set itself loose. This new detrimental development with the evil creature, to the advantage of the lad, made him to exult. However, without more ado, an invisible sword came down dangling from the wind and it chopped off the baby figure☐s two hands accurately by their wrists.

The boy was pleasingly shocked with the fate of his newest enemy, courtesy of the miraculous sword of judgement. He discovered that instead of blood to gush out of the figure☐s severed parts, the cut surfaces were as dry as apiece of parched wood. Though their water is blood, spirits have no blood. Although they feed on human flesh, they have no flesh except when they invoked fake flesh to cover themselves up in physical appearances. Body, soul and spirit, spirits are spirits.

For what had happened to the attacker the dwarfish ghost, it roared in an incredible eruption of expressive grief. It was greatly baffled at what happened to it because it never expected it. It, the baby figure, crashed onto the ground again, this time backward, before it took a fast and confusedly desperate hop into the midst of the beautiful garden of its flowers.

Beholding its last funny, yet, very sombre action, Benlilo burst into another explosive epoch of disdainful laughter. For a minute, he watched the severely wounded ghost, as it rolled, tumbled and somersaulted inside and across the flowers of the garden on and going on, in severest agony, before it eventually vamoosed. Throughout this tragic episode, demonic stillness lined the forestry mood most dictatorially.

A few seconds after that, there were eruptions of sorrowfulness in some empires of darkness. For the tragedy that had befallen their owner, the flowers became paralysed and their united glory departed immediately. All along, they too had been watching the odious event stage to stage, as it unfolded.

They had enjoyed the master□s winning spots, especially the miracle of the rag from the rod, and its masterly words of oration. In particular, they had believed that it was the master□s mystical power that had made the rod to turn into a piece of rag □ but the never-expected amputation tragedy! The beautiful flowers lost their beauty. They threw away their beauty, unity and cheerfulness. They wore flamboyant robes of combined depression, frustration and confusion in mourning, deep sorrow, disarray and ugliness.

They rejected all entreaties of consolation. Inside the forest, life was victory or defeat, a farmland wherein trees of prosperities grew and withered - hence they burst rowdily into an obituary song:

Bigoted age, untold pains
Service at loss, oh pity!
Hard work of nought
Dedication of no reward
Patriotism of death attune,
As flowing tragedies our paths
On the battlefield of life in the forest!

Benlilo could hear them. He felt the vibrations of the dark ones□ groaning and mourning. He quickly removed his eyes and attention from the enemy□s landscape and ran for his dear life - farther southward of the forest. In the vastness, he could hear boisterous expressions of anguish of hosts and forces of darkness from inside a disorganised conference of an antechamber. They were memorialising an added tragedy. On his part, the lad wished that the tragedies for his enemies would continue and worsen in as much as he remained inside the mystery forest of mysteries against his hope and against his wish.

□Yes, if they would not allow me to get out of the forest, they will have no rest or peace! Calamities for weeping, wailing and mourning must continue to be their portions!□ he assured and declared most authoritatively. He had discovered that finding his way out of the mystery forest might not be an easy task as he had imagined it in the beginning. He could conclude that some invisible and mysterious powers or hands were holding him back from freedom. His conclusion of condemnation fell on the weeping ghost who had earlier-on prophesied this situation negatively but accurately:

□Soon find your way into your father□s compound? What a honey-coated tongue! What a beautiful wish! What a laudable ambition □ visionary - creative thinker, but where□re your legs that will take you out of the forestry prison? Where□re your eyes that will see the way out? Where□s your consciousness that will lead you out of the mysterious captivity into your desired freedom soonest? And where□s your person to know the way out?□

□But why? I belonged to the City of Marpolio and never to this mystery forest or whatever it is called! Why must I be held as a prisoner inside a useless and fearful forest of evil like this, against my desire? What have I done to deserve all these? What sin have I committed?□ it was the outpouring heedful thoughts of Benlilo, as his discernment opened.

Benlilo would see the setting sun in the far distant. This indicated that he was running towards the west and backing the east compass. The setting sun transmitted a reddish beauty into the sky atmosphere. He did not stop running until some mournful roars of the wounded powers had faded away. He halted his race and started to walk hastily while, at the same time, looking back at intervals. He got to the edge of a groove. The groove was sleeping when he arrived there but it soon woke up at the appearance of the lad.

The plain reality was that there was no peace, neither rest nor sleep with the powers. What had actually happened was that the dark powers also invested in pretences as warfare strategies. What they detested, as the cruelly looking shortest ghost had confessed, was an intrusion into their territory. It was a taboo and its punishment was instant retaliation from their cooperative end. They would never tolerate nonsense.

Upon arriving at the edge of the groove, Benlilo too could feel the raw presence of the powers. All the hair on his head stood on ends and they counted odd and even numbers, as his body frames calculated substandard statistics in irksome disorderliness. At times, it seemed as if some invisible hands were about to grip him and squeeze life out of his fragile body. He remembered how the ghosts and ghommids had captured him. He trembled!

At another time, it appeared as if the air he was breathing in and out was decorated with danger signals and voodoo trademarks of looming death. Yet, at the other, it was as if some warriors, who all appeared like the defunct Persian Empire□s soldiers, were approaching his stand fast in order to capture him. Life was terror! It was better defined as a horror! Best imagined than felt.

The name of the place was called *Groove of the Dead*. Spread on sprawling hectares of land, it bordered southward with a river. The river was co-partner to the *Groove*. The deep of the river was a safe haven for demons; fallen angels who had failed to keep their first offices and were cast out of the blissful place. Therein they revelled in sweet glories. They sang. They drummed. They danced.

The evil spirits worked in the groove and they made it thick for plentiful missions. They were all members of out-and-out labour force in the army of His Satanic Majesty. Minor or major, they were commissioned combatant soldiers warring without rest or sleep all nightlong. As they warred, they rendered a peculiar hymn of old:

We are soldiers
Soldiers of our god,
In the name of darkness
We shall conquer□

Background beats of martial music often accompanied the song□s rendition. Then, the greatest memorable moment would come for this section of the hosts and their celebration to run almost without end.

Inside the vast inn of the deep of the river was an enclave called *Deadly Kingdom of Hosts*. It was so-named because it marked the safe abode for thousands of spirits under the authorities of higher demons who carried out missions in defence of the massively networking dark world.

The *Groove of the Dead* had rendered several estates of wealth dead and desolate. It was the abode of hate bartered for love. It was the ranch of beasts for running sorrows and busy-tragedies boundless. It was the groove where multitudes of destinies were manipulated and strangulated. It was the locality where hope was snatched at blazing arrow point. It snatched hopes from the hopeful and dumped him or her ever forgotten inside the valley of despondency.

It was the territory of disasters for humans and a palace of celebrations for the powers. It was the reservoir of talents and ingenuities stolen from the human world. It was the theatre of surgery for human dreams□ abortions. It was an estate of doom for ignoramuses of human generations. It was the point of departure from living into existence. It was called *Groove of the Dead* because it was a showground whereby life exchanged for death and there was neither retribution nor restitution.

Groove of the Dead was an immeasurable place equipped with twenty-one different shrines and twenty-one divergent altars, all in honour of the king. Each shrine and each one altar had its own priest and allocated messengers. The priest was the overseer over the shrine and the altar. The messengers ran errands for the priest in-between the groove and the deep.

Both the priest and the messengers, as operators, were the executors of the shrines and altars□ programmes in the human world with humankind as the primary targets, along with their property, namely: farms, estates, houses, jobs, machines, talents, destinies, careers, stars, glories, professions, etc., as secondary targets.

All the twenty-one altars, taking orders directly from the shrines and carried out by their priests and the messengers, were fortified most inhumanly. They each were equipped with twenty-one brands of curses, twenty-one categories of spells, twenty-one types of jinxes, twenty-one groups of bewitchments, twenty-one kinds of manipulations, twenty-one long and short hindrances, twenty-one crude and modern bondages, twenty-one variegated hypnoses, twenty-one magical enchantments, twenty-one firebrand and slow-poisonous incantations, twenty-one heavy conjurations, and twenty-one death-giving and automatic invocations.

These evil altars were never tired of issuing effervescent curses and abuses, and the receivers or targets of those evils were none other than brood of man in the world. For the targets, several accepted the curses, while only a few always rejected and discarded them.

The air of *Groove of the Dead* was always poisonous for the truth-bearers and oxygenated for all apostles of falsehoods. The music there was often obituaries for the light-bearers and cantatas for agents and couriers to darkness. The groove was always in celebration for raging tragedies that frequently befell people in the human world.

It was the epitomised glory of wickedness in honour of darkness. For twenty-four hours and three hundred and sixty-five days of the year, inside the groove, it was dismal obscurity. Light never therein made a lazy appearance. As long established, it was a great taboo to have light, no matter how fragile, around, not to talk of inside the groove. The most enjoyable feast of the powers and their agents was darkness. The darkness called to darkness and they mixed in faultless conspiracy against man, their only target and achievement for evermore.

A stream flowed through the groove downward into the river. The stream was completely barren of sea creatures but very active in the thing of the spirit, as defined, designed and dedicated by the spirit realm. The stream also served as a linkage between *Groove of the Dead* and *Deadly Kingdom of Hosts*.

It was, for best, harbinger of tears and sorrows. All night unending, it laboured hard to fulfil this arduous mission. The gods and goddesses rejoiced the more and they baptised it with tougher powers. Life was labour and reward.

Benlilo remained standing at the border between the forest and the groove for a few seconds. A python rested at the side of a shrine therein. A giant scorpion had its dwelling place near an altar. Swords, whether single or two edged each, decorated all the altars. An aged crocodile, a strongman of very old witchcraft heritage, hungered for propitiation.

It wanted twelve gallons of human blood and eighty pounds of human flesh. In the earthly place, human being agents of the gods, goddesses and the powers were to supply the needed ingredients. A vampire with a long blood red beak flew round inside the groove and it landed on the stream.

Happily, the stream flowed the vampire bird into the river. It took a dive into the river and the water of the river swallowed it. Some happy voices eulogised the occasion and its players:

Beauty swallowed up by beauty,
Glory vomiting glory of the dark world
Age of harvest and more investments

There was a pressing outburst of jubilation by the hosts of the deep to welcome home the *dynamic* vampire. All animate and inanimate creatures in the environ pretended that they did not see the intruding lad. Their brainy investment in the pretence marked no suspicion. It issued neither smoke nor cloud.

Benlilo was not at all impressed by the goings-on inside the groove. He noticed a whirlwind, an avenger of the powers, raging therein. As the whirlwind raged, it landed atop a mighty silk cotton tree. The greens of the tree caught fire and there was an eruption of jubilation by the hosts of the river to greet the whirlwind. The whirlwind, another messenger of the shrines and the altars, had just carried out a revenge operation against the silk cotton tree on behalf of the powers.

Last night, the silk cotton tree had harboured *evil* against the kingdom. It conspired with prayers of *earthly saints* and the pandemonium in the kingdom of darkness was not a pocket-sized one. In the dark countryside, retaliatory act successfully carried out was a great measure of pride. It lent credibility to the claim of the powers and their ambassadors, while fortifying their strongholds.

As the story further ran, the whole lot of the groove□s victory turned into flooding sorrow, as many of its captives escaped. Still, it was far from the fault or negligence of the silk cotton tree. The fact was that its power could not resist a greater super-firepower. Candlelight could not compete with a thunder strike. The silk cotton power had been rendered helplessly impotent at the visitation of an almighty power.

There was no excuse or forgiveness in that kingdom of darkness. Every mistake or sin was costly and, as such, accompanied with penalty or penalties. That was the golden rule in the *Groove of the Dead!* Therein, ignorance or weakness was no defence at law.

CHAPTER 040

Back To Square Zero

A LION ROARED constantly in the middle of the groove. A range of animals and birds hailed the lion in its *majestic eminence.* The forest stood observant at the passage of the king of all animals. They watched to discover why the eminent personality was out in the open of the night.

Lesser members of the cat family surrounded the imperial lord of the animal world, front, back, and sideways, namely: cats, tigers, leopards, hyenas, jaguars and jacquards. Though they had their individualistic characters and peculiarities, all the wild cats had their common dwelling inside the extra-large cosmic hole that Benlilo had seen in the beginning of the adventure. What had united them was nothing but evil.

The preys that the roaring lion and members of his all-carnivorous entourage were hunting after were not other lesser animals of the forest. They were human beings along with their virtues of wealth, with which the benevolent Creator had endowed and ordained them to survive and to flourish in the world, the forest, as sojourners in the enchanting city of success, mean the earth, as wayfarers on the highway of global life. The lion was the lion of darkness. Either in isolation or as a group, its several bodyguards were all emissaries of the powers and the gods.

Benlilo fled the scene backward and then eastward - still hoping for a way of escape from the treacherous forest. He knew he was a captive of unsympathetic time but he could not explain it off. He might understand that the forest was life, the vastest prison yard, and that his way of escape from it would be a mystery □ like his mysterious appearance therein. Life was the mystery, the crudest adventure.

All of a sudden, shockingly, the lad discovered that the bush to his right hand side was very much troubled. Before he could exclaim, □What!□ the earlier lion-like monster had emerged from the sidestepped location of the *Groove of the Dead*. The beast did not appear alone but in the company of the cat and the he-goat. This mystified Benlilo offensively!

The three beastly creatures now wore fiercer general postures. They made their three different but violently cohesive ways to the direction of the lad□s side but he multiplied the gap in-between them very speedily and tactfully. The entirety of the forestry region was brought to life straight away. It was shocked at the resumption of their pursuit after the boy. All the greens, environmental and elemental forces watched what would happen next. The air wore the ornamentation of sumptuously linens of surprise and suspense. That was how another chapter of the race of life opened and the forest was soon bypassed into a beautiful vineyard of garden eggs.

Too, the hot chasers had no speck of respect whatever for the gorgeous garden. They all ploughed their ways into the model vineyard most resolutely. Benlilo looked backward, timidly, to see the three pursuers bulldozing their ways ruthlessly toward him. He was soon at the foot of a tall erectly standing concrete fence. The very long stretched-out wall blocked his way of moving forward and the powers rejoiced. They could not imagine any way, miraculous or magical, out for him at this point. They concluded that his grisly end has come in their hands.

The boy looked backward and, yet again, he beheld his three unapologetic pursuers: the monster, the cat and the he-goat. Greater discomfiture seized his heart to overwhelming his total being. The concrete wall, very high, prevented him from proceeding further in the task of his escape from the hunting and ever-determined beasts. He could not turn back and run into the jaws of the three beasts.

Running either of the sideways left or of right, he would easily be caught and be devoured by these carnivorous animals. Behind him, the three hungry and angry creatures ploughed their way non-stop towards his direction, as he remained hooked to the spot in indescribable anxiety. The rigid pursuers believed, most obstinately, that he must be caught this time around. Their faith multiplied, as the river of their pessimistic hope banged.

Benlilo too had lost all hope. He had been seeing and hearing of miracles but this was a different instance. He did not know how it came about. He observed a cool wind blow around his person. The whirlwind beclouded the very spot where he was glued to the stonewall, panting like a rabbit nearly inside the trap of a python. The small cloud demarcated his position from the pursuers, as it thickened faster by the second.

All in just a few seconds, the gentle wind grew furious and fiercer. It whirled round and about him terrifically. Then, *fuaam!* at a go, Benlilo saw himself lifted up at the nick of time just as the monster and its co-conspirators were arriving wrathfully at the foot of the rock-strewn and high wall. Benlilo was the recipient of the windily phenomenal reaction, exactly the opposite way for the losers, his pursuers and the powers.

The whirlwind carried and landed him coolly on the fence. Therefore, his pursuers, especially the monster, crashed themselves sadistically against the stonewall. They had aimed at their target with the sole mission to crushing him to the wall, and, there and then, feasting on him battered flesh, bones and blood. Approaching the wall, they had multiplied their speed and so, their collision with the wall was horrifying.

Subsequently, they thereby committed an irreversible blunder whereby they were wounded fatally. Yet, instead of them to repent themselves of their enmity against the boy, their unfriendliness became more aggravated against his person. They were not, in any way, deterred. But for the escapee, he now walked freely on the high wall, as his pursuers watched him in unconditional awkwardness, disgust and amazement - all at the same time.

Escapee Benlilo was over-joyous! *Freedom is truly darling and sweet. Bondage is strong and thorny. It means premature death.* The lad was not lost to the reality that, by now, his fragile life would have been sniffed out for him to serve as raw meat for the three hungry and angry beastly pursuers but for the latest divine intervention.

In celebration of his escape from, and victory over the three archenemies, the boy burst into a song. The song had been heralded by a loud and clear shriek of mockery, as his hunters watched the more with sheer disdain of the uppermost bemusement, stirred rowdily their hearts.

For Benlilo, the atmospheric condition of this mountaintop was most enthralling. Earlier on in the journey, the animalistic beings □ the he-goat and the cat had entertained him musically. He quickly concluded that his turn had come to entertain the three evil hunters. He relaxed, made his person at home and savoured the comforting bath of the caressing breeze. He whistled again and sang:

I am victorious! I am victorious!!
Captivity is bitter! Freedom is sweet!
Joy has no peer, love bedrocks life!
My river of hope flows and it floods
I am victorious! Oh, I am victorious!

What a painful thorn in the flesh, defeat! The monster, the cat and the he-goat heard Benlilo sing joyously, loud and clear. They understood the meaning of his sarcastic song, connotatively and denotatively. Though very helpless, their heads turned and burned; they became bitterer with their prospective captive.

They gnashed their teeth rowdily and groaned in unspeakable agony at their loss. In addition, as another round of salt into their injury, the little escapee now gesticulated and danced more joyously, as he frequently rendered his song of vendetta. He suddenly halted his song□s flow to address the criminal chasers in an invoked voice of a victorious war commander:

□Tell me, evil monster, where is your power? Your brain, where is it □ at your backside or inside your useless thick legs? You bush meat goat, I will slaughter you for feast to entertain all my friends on my next birthday. And you worthless cat of loss, can you not see me on top of this mountain? Powerless beast, impotent goat and senseless cat □ three of a kind: failures of vindictive season, disasters of time, indignities of life □ shame on you all, misery and death unto you idiots!□ With those acidic words of the boy, the gravity of the enmity of his pursuers hit the highest degree against his life.

But, unfortunately, the monster could not grow wings and fly. The he-goat could also not turn itself into a bird and fly after the escapee. Too, the cat lacked the ability to reach him atop the high wall. This disability pained the three inordinate pursuers measurelessly. Their helpless wrath against the far-away lad prospered. They swore never to give up their pursuit. They promised that it was about time for the boy to meet himself inside their top-security prison.

In its incensed fury, the monster stretched forth its long arm to pluck Benlilo down onto the ground but it could not. The arm stretched out the more and all its affected joint-bones cracked to tune in odd places but, still, it could not reach the desired goal. The wall was just too high for it. Noisily, it expressed pains of frustration. It regretted and bemoaned the uncooperative nature of the wall. It withdrew the arm, blaming nature for its ill fate. Its two colleagues, the cat and the he-goat murmured and hissed audibly, nauseatingly.

Nonetheless, the lion-like beast was determined against giving up hope. It invested in hardest struggle but its elasticity expired. It suffered an anklebone crack and it groaned angrily, withdrawing the long limb altogether rather hastily. A watching Benlilo could not help but burst into another moment of time-honoured scathing laughter.

"See him, see him!" a dungeon voice resonated.

"Leave him; leave him alone - he is laughing to weep. He is howling indeed! He is celebrating his obituary!" a consolatory tone whispered.

"By his senseless laughter, he is strengthening our willpower. By his useless laughing, he is fortifying our stronghold of enmity against his poor person. He is set to swallow morsels of bitterness and record a head-on collision with our rock, soonest. What is written cannot be unwritten. The battle line has been drawn long ago and that's final - there's no going back!" it was a lengthy voice of an elderly officer making some militaristic declarations and several voices concurred:

"Agreed!"

"True!"

"Sure!"

"Certain!"

"The truth!"

"Plain straight!"

"And the actual fact!"

As they had openly confessed, the powers never forgave the boy for *this additional sin*. Their strength of mind reinforced, as accompanying wrath maddened. They pledged further that nothing would deter them from dealing with *this stubborn lad the most ruthless manner according to our collective culture.*

Meanwhile, Benlilo decided to boost his *account of transgressions* against the powers. He now walked freely on the thick wall. He danced, whistled and sang his earlier song cheerfully. More he boldly challenged the three enemies to dare come over to the platform of the wall for battle with him. The cool wind continued to blow. The teenager had regained his recently lost love for nature. Again, he was enjoying the best moment of his youthful life, while the stranded pursuers groaned the more in dismal pains!

Yes! according to their sworn word, the pursuers would not give up! Consistency in rigidity with unwavering determination and iron-like faith combined to make a good trait for victory, pessimistic or optimistic. The cat came back to active life. It remembered its order of creation that it was made to climb walls and trees, even rocks, expertly. Then, it made the bold move to climb the wall but at this it failed miserably. The wall was too smooth for its claws to grip.

Therefore, each time it tried to climb the silky-smooth and slippery wall, down it fell onto the ground only to get wounded the more. It groaned in infuriated pains to behold the boy with larger envy and boiling anger at the same time. The he-goat and the lion-like beast mourned the recurring failures of the cat to climb the wall. They hissed bitterly and grumbled angrily. They cursed the boy and abused the wall to its face.

Instead of sympathising with the wounded cat, they looked at it in fuming anger and hatred, for its failure. The wall laughed the three of them all to condescension. With further outburst of sarcastic laughter, Benlilo complimented its effort; he remained super-confident atop the laughing wall.

On the part of the boy, as soon as the over-ambitious cat had started to try to climb the wall, he had strongly resolved that should in case it, in the end, succeeded at it to meet him up there, the animalistic thing would meet itself inside the greatest trouble of its wild life. His brutal kick to its face or a deadly knockout was at the red-alert for the cat to tumble down from the stonewall dead at once.

The monster employed another *viable* option to pluck down Benlilo from the wall. It raised up its long and big head and eyed the escapee with a newly conjured pride. A sure strategy of shooting down the boy had just occurred to it. It enthused an unrivalled self-reliance therefore. It smiled broadly like a true lion soon to be roundly fulfilled on a mission of bloodletting and it eyed the adolescent escapee on the high wall again - just a matter of time...

This was a fresh and guaranteed strategy. Again, it raised up its head and, with its nose, aimed accurately at the prey, its face seemingly transmitting the message: □Have this!□ With the nose and out of it, it blew a hot weighty ball, burgundy red in look and stone solid, at the lad.

Wao! the crude bullet missed its target but the shooter was undaunted in its innovative effort. It smiled the more and exhibited a greater gauge of re-assurance. It looked up again and shot at Benlilo with a set of two different ball-like bullets through the same source, the nose. Yet, again, both bullets, dirty red and super green in colour, missed their lone target, Benlilo.

The two bullets seemed to have flown away to the wrong directions but they soon raced belligerently back. Few seconds after the two arrows had been fired, they dashed down incredibly and thundered into the sides of their owner, the lion-like monster. The beast groaned most agonisingly, as the arrows disappeared into its flesh. It regretted ever firing them at the boy. Life was a harvest of what one had sown in the farm of time.

Everyone is a farmer in this plantation called life. The inevitable *Law of Harvest* is the governor of the farmer along with his farming investments. No farmer runs away from his harvest at the ripe time. Inescapably, the farmer reaps, in bounties, what he had sown. So it proved with the lion-like monster and watching Benlilo was very much pleased with the retributive incident.

CHAPTER 041

Premature Songs Of Victory

The shifting season talks in parables
Communication of dedication by acted wisdom.
Life with the powers irregular unlike day and night
Mystery plain of deeds beyond all imaginations
Whereby impossibility machineries have been dismantled.

THE LAD, ON his part, smiled the better broadly like an orphan who had just been declared the star winner of a big jackpot. On the fence, he walked here and there, to and fro freely like a victorious soldier. Here he sank into deeper relaxation. He also whistled and sang more delightfully. Now, for him, it was Song *of Ridicule* against the unyielding pursuers:

Helpless monster! Foolish goat! Stupid cat!
Down in the valley of time, down! Down, oh, down!
The crafty are gaoled in their own captivity, wao!
All oppressors oppressed in their own oppressions
For life is a harvest! Life is the reward! Life is a fair!
Groaning daft beasts, all in astringent jeopardy of time!

For the recurrent time, the frustrated pursuers listened to Benlilo□s song and they became abundantly enraged. They now boiled with the unbearable annoyance, in fact, wrath. They lust for timely and pungent revenge against the lad intensely. Hence, at this material time, the conspirators□ minds were like a pot of boiling and gushing water that had been under continuous heating over raging fire for hours endlessly. To them, the only alternative was nothing but vengeance: brutality and death to the *recalcitrant* lad!

The lion-like monster□s wounds would matter little to him. It thought for a while. It quickly concluded on another *viable* alternative before it. This time around, it was without a doubt confident of a way out to catch Benlilo and crush him callously, flesh and bones, for the battle to be won by them decisively.

Upon learning of the new warfare alternative, both the watching he-goat and the cat smiled sadistic conformity broadly. They too were super-confident that the latest option would work out. The lion-like beast did not waste any time on this, but, yet again, it concluded very wrongly, and it turned out devastation for its group.

In a terrific force, it had reversed far away backward. Like a dare-devilish Western modern wrestler purposely crashing himself into his opponent, closing all its three eyes half-way, it then ran crazily forward and crashed itself against the wall in a bold attempt to demolish it and have the boy down, but no way! The stonewall did not move an inch.

It was exactly as if the wind had blown a piece of cotton wool at a solid rock. So instead of crumbling into rubbles, the wall angrily but silently, threw the monster back onto the ground assertively. This unexpected action and victorious resistance of the wall was survived by an elongated mockery, of rowdy jesting, delivered by an unseen band of happy hosts around.

The monstrous being could hardly believe what had just happened to it. Here, moreover, the trio☐s tragedy was increased and their pains doubled. For, bitterly confused, the lion-like monster landed on the cat and the he-goat - both that had been lately serving as enthusiastic watchers with vested interest. With the monster☐s fall, both smaller animals turned out to be the primary casualties, having been buried underneath the felled gargantuan beast. Their burial had lasted for minutes under the heavy weight of the beastly master.

When the wounded monster eventually managed to struggle hard and move agonisingly sideways, the little ones made some excruciating cries. They sweated profusely, as they groaned in pains. They crawled on the ground, as they wailed wordlessly. Watching Benlilo had wished that it would take the fallen monster a longer period to stand up so that the two lesser animals would suffocate to death underneath its stony weight. Beautiful! This would have reduced the number of his multitudinous enemies in the forest by two.

Proverbially, the wind greeted the latest development with a song of admonition to the three beasts. All other elemental and environmental forces were surprised that the wind had turned into a futurologist. They listened to the windy song along with the uncivil three animalistic beings:

> *Lion of darkness, goat and cat,*
> *Have you witnessed sleep?*
> *Beware of death!*
> *Do not compare wind with the whirlwind!*
> *Injury is small to tragedy*
> *Quarrel is nothing compared to war*
> *Beware! Beware, less you be consumed!!*

Thus, the wind prophesied. But, alas! counsel is for the prudent. Voice a good advice to the fool, it will hate you. The three beasts rejected the solomonic guidance of the wind; they threw it, in every respect, into the dustbin of history but posterity allotted it as a duty to itself, either to deny or to confirm their joint action. It undertook to vindicate or to condemn the wind for its action, its song of forewarning.

The cat sustained more injuries out of the latest combat investment and flow or throw back of the lion-like monster. The he-goat endured all pains and it, again, crawled about pitiably and wobbly on the ground. Still dazed and seeing various stars in darkness and light, the monster fell flat onto the ground again with all its limbs assembled on one side disorderly.

It would not accept the divine defeat through the wall so easily. Therefore, it struggled to be on its feet again. Benlilo burst into another occasion of backbreaking laughter. Thereafter, he rendered the third stanza of his quickly composed irreverent song:

Victory is sweet, oh how sweet
In the morning of victory!

Freedom is pleasant, oh how pleasant
In the coolly refreshing weather of time!

Useless monster, helpless beasts — uuhuuu!
How sweet inside the valley of dismal defeat?

Like in the recently hurtful past, the pursuers saw and heard Benlilo sing in loud and clear tones. They remained helpless but hopeful. If they had been offended before, now, they were wounded sore! The cat attempted to climb the wall again but on this, it failed once more ridiculously. It wept and lamented, not its recent wound, but the invulnerability of the wall to its traditional art of mountaineering. The he-goat ran helter-skelter about the wall's edge, also powerlessly helpless and running crazy! Both soon resigned themselves to fate but obviously not in surrender as warriors against the boy.

The dejected monster was by now resting from the hard knock it received from the gritty barrier. Backing the vineyard, it sat on the ground; its four limbs arranged riotously forward, it continued to gaze at the boy on the wall curiously, all its three large but different eyes emitting flames and uncontrolled fire. They shone like shooting-rays of the tyrannical sun at the peak of summer in the bone-dry region.

Benlilo remained happy on the wall but not for long. Because of the disturbance that the baking rays from the demonically trifoliate eyes of the lion-like monster had posed, the boy decided to change his position. He started to trace the wall with a temperate run northward but the beasts also pursued him without giving-out an inch of allowance, on a parallel line though, along the ground. The lad kept running, as his pursuers would not stop to pursue and to hope.

On the other hand, alas! without warning, the unexpected happened to the exhilarated elation of the three stubborn pursuers. The cat grew wings and flew towards Benlilo on the run as, at once, the high and thick wall fell down flat. A great number of hosts and forces hailed and eulogised the transformed cat now airborne and the gods who they believed had made its growing emergency wings and the crumbling of the wall possible:

Most elderly of the cats' family,
Weapon of war for war advantages,
The flying beauty of horror and wonder:
Blessed be the gods! All hail the goddesses!

It was most unbelievable an experience for running Benlilo to discover such a thick and rocky wall suddenly turning into rubbles. It was really *out of the usual run of things* luck that saved him from being trapped when the high wall collapsed and its stone rubbles fell, so rapidly, on one another and ruptured like the Indian Ocean Tsunami, issuing out some roars and toxic effluvium.

At that instance, the lad's right leg went in-between three stone heaps, while his left one remained afloat lightly on the fourth. The right leg missed being seized and crushed by the second stone. It was most fortunate for the lad to have re-gained his balance partially so soon, he restarted his race in order to preserve his fragile life.

The three creatures were caught unawares too. None of them least expected, like Benlilo, that the wall could ever fall like that. They too had luckily escaped being crushed alive by the rapidly falling and tumbling rubbles that now covered everywhere. The lad was sorry that the falling heaps of heavy stones had missed crushing his enemies, all the three of them!

Like him, as well, they quickly regained their consciousness for the race to resume and heighten. At the very same minute, a rowdy but classical jazz tune, purposely meant to rejuvenate the hope, faith and vigour of the rigid pursuers and demoralise the pursued boy, burst out in the air and it banged. Benlilo was undeterred, as his hard-bitten enemies were energised.

This was a life opportunity for them to actualise their shared dream. It seemed as if the three unrepentant pursuers had had all their fatal wounds magically healed and their bones grew stronger like those of a mature gorilla. In candidness, it appeared as if they had never sustained any wound.

However, a combination of sorrow and nervousness, in a little while, seized the person of the pursued lad. The now flying cat almost caught up with him on a particular heap of the felled wall. The heat against him multiplied. The he-goat, very enthusiastic and optimistic like a hypocrite and a conspirator combined, which really it was, jumped happily from one heap of the stones to another. The wounded monster had also unbelievably regained its strength so quickly. Amazingly, along with its heavy weight, it was now ploughing its way towards the boy, as it too was running faster than expected on the rocky ruins.

Something inexplicable prevented the cat from catching up with Benlilo at any gainful point. The monster renewed its fierce pursuit and thundering through the way towards him, as the he-goat, on its part, boiled for a snap opportunity for the furthermost settling of scores. All the three excessive chasers had suffered some body damages but they pretended that all was well. They would have loved to double their efforts but the stony rubbles were uncooperative with them in this respect.

At this juncture, another miraculous thing happened. A two-edged sword appeared mid-air and chopped off the two big wings of the flying cat. Blood, which very much looked like a mixture of diesel oil and petroleum, gushed out of the detached parts. The victimised cat somersaulted in the air and crash-landed on the sideway of the rubbles. Groaning with brutal pains, it rolled repeatedly, as it cried, □Mieu! Mieu!! Mieu!!!□ three grief-laden times.

However, Benlilo had no cause to rejoice yet. The struggle and the battle had just started. The monster and the he-goat did not care a hoot about what had just happened to their colleague the cat. What mattered to them most was overtaking the lad, seizing him by whatever part or parts, tearing him into shreds and devouring him there and then.

Though immediately after the two wings of the cat were hacked off by the mysterious sword, the powerful instrument of war, as a warning, had demonstrated acrobatically before them in scientifically-complex conducts beggaring description and they were scared; they were now possessed with broader animosity. They swore that nothing would stop them from dealing, most mercilessly, with the lad upon captivity, which they concluded would be soonest.

For this cause, in unruly rage, they both continued to plough their ways towards him, as he too never, for once, stopped to run with the sole intention of preserving his treasured life. The indefatigable struggle, never giving up faith and hope, is the fuel to run the engine of success and victory, bad and good, in the human life.

Pursued Benlilo prized the unwavering conviction to invest in living and not in dying. He renewed his voting for victory and not for defeat, remembering a native wise saying of his people,

□He who the masquerade is pursuing should endure the pains because as he tires so tires out the heavenly body pursuer.□

CHAPTER 042

In The Sky Of Lake Mystery

BENLILO RAN. HE promised himself never to stop running in as much as his adamant pursuers did not stop to pursue him. Embarrassingly, the boy ran to the end of the road as formed by the heaps of stones — whatever in life that boasts of a beginning must be survived by an ending. He was about to jump onto a supposed dry land when he discovered, to his most pungent embarrassment up to date, that it was a vast lake that bordered downward with the rough rubbles, *whaao!*

All the same, he had only one option before him because the he-goat and the monster were already at his heels. Without a second for a chance of thought or turning sideways therefore, he plunged himself into the lake. Watching him do this, all the three toughened pursuers laughed fiendishly. Their budgeted hope for a condemned end for the boy got greatly improved upon and sustained maximally. No one, not even Benlilo, would imagine that a strangely new thing that had never happened in the adventure of wonders so far was about to happen.

All the stubborn pursuers were fourfold confident that the end of the road had now come for the kill. Their assurance hinged on the fact that the lake and its fullness therein were altogether members of the networking darkness' machinery against the pursued one. They all belonged to the same large family called *Marine Witchcraft Kingdom.*

Here, yet another miracle materialised in good time. Instead of Benlilo to land inside the lake and sink therein lost to the *mercy-never* of its richly in-dwelling carnivorous creatures, the lad landed on the rough head of an enormous crocodile. The reptile must have been nothing short of fifty feet in length - with the vast head a piece of rock-like land.

The crocodile too was caught unawares. It was unprepared. It stirred the deep of the lake angrily and, surprisingly, roared like a forest lion and thrust its very-long head up to seize Benlilo's two legs, drag him onto the bottom of the lake and devour him.

But just without any impediment, the mysterious thing happened — yes! certainly the very first of its kind in the unconventional voyage. As the beset boy's first leg, the right one, was touching the crocodile's head and he realised that it was a water beast, he jumped high forward but instead of landing back into the water, as his pursuers, watchers and enemies had, with conviction, expected, he suddenly developed two big wings. He took off sky bound from the plain of the lake's water akin to a mighty eagle.

The three beastly pursuers — that is the he-goat, the cat and the lion-like monster — all had been watching the scene but, now, they were bitterly frustrated. A minute ago, they had been sincerely convinced, and assertively double sure, that the end of the road had come for the *rascal*. Oh, how painful the boy's narrow yet open escape this time around! They regretted the failure of the crocodile to seize at least one leg of the lad, pull him down into the lake and have him for a free feast.

Thus, a tongue of the powers mourned in bitterest of anguish. What had mattered most to them was death to the common enemy, by whatever means, not really whether they tasted out of his meat and blood or not. But, oh tragedy! the crocodile failed. Subsequently, soon after they saw that the prey had again escaped, by a completely groundbreaking method, they all cursed the mammoth reptile to its face without moderation for the *greatest* miss. Yet, the crocodile was not just a member but also a senior comrade of theirs - another full time agent working for the *Marine Witchcraft Kingdom*.

Mighty crocodile of sure nothing
You have failed on smooth something
When a crown waited for your ugly head
But now your portion in dishonour and indignity
Is assured ere the close of the battle portions!

That was the song rendered for *the disastrous crocodile* from the depth of the lake. Sky-bound Benlilo heard the song and he was joyfully thrilled. The powers wondered on when their agents would stop to commit avoidable mistakes! They pronounced and placed an interconnected curse of gruesome death, not only on the failed crocodile, but on its generations as well. On a specific note, a queen sitting on her high-ranking throne in a palace inside the cosmic belly of the lake vomited a royal curse on the marine beast:

□The night comes and the day goes but your generations shall perish, oh unwisely foolish crocodile!□ Benlilo did not know why, he took note of the queen and other creatures□ cohesive curse on the enormous water reptile.

Nevertheless, the cursed crocodile had not given up that easily. It had manoeuvred its size quickly and the water of the lake had been, to the highest degree, troubled. It had invested in another violent attempt. It shot out and raised up its long, big and horizontal head above the water; it rose high and, again, tried hard to seize one of the ascending legs of Benlilo but it was too late. A host of other crocodiles joined it. They thundered out of the water base like wounded hyenas. Some of them actually launched themselves out of the water into the low sky of the lake, but no way! Alas! none of them could grow wings and fly after the boy. They all landed back inside the water of the lake.

Like the monster, the he-goat and the cat were the most disgusted viewers of the *disgraceful show*. They painfully watched, disgustingly, the escaping enemy doing his flying in the cool air. Still, they remained far-distanced from losing hope. They cursed the wind to its face noisily as if they were capable of making it their permanent enemy. Earlier on, they had commanded it, □not to fly the boy further□ so that he could tumble into the waiting lake as the prey of its carnivorous beasts, but the wind was heedless of their words of command.

□Over our dead bodies!□ they swore never to give up the battle against this wildly hunted Benlilo. This was a direct confrontation to the powers, the gods, their war scientists and technologists, and they quickly accepted the challenge. Indeed, they were battle ready. After all, they had not a few ammunitions in their magazine. Two of their combat strategies were by *suspense* and *surprises*.

That was why, like a super-power□s rocket launched at an enemy at wartime, a golden iron coffin roared terrifically out of the depth of the lake. The bowel of the lagoon bubbled at the rising and launch of the coffin. The coffin had its lid wide opened. Though without wings - yet another magical doing of the powers - it flew energetically and calculatedly high into the sky in pursuit of the airborne and fugitive boy. The powers and their messengers never stopped to celebrate and to eulogise. They cheered the flying coffin with the following accolades:

Coffin the house of the dead
Flying the gate of hell leads
Fly well! Fly better! Fly best!

Swallow him and close your tight,
It is your season□s gift from the gods!

Thus, the flying coffin was greatly energised. It pursued after its only goal, the absconding Benlilo, but right in the air, only its fate knows what happened. It harshly tumbled many times before it got shattered into crumbs. The small pieces of the coffin also reacted speedily to the emergency. They all made hysterical efforts to assemble into another entity, right in the air, and resume its hot pursuit of the flying lad but this turned out an impossible mission.

The iron fragments sank lost into the lake, wounding more than a few scores of living creatures therein □ yet another mystery loop in the adventure. Numberless hosts of ghostly councils burst into an uncontrollable session of tears. For the third time of sadness, the big bowel of the lake was very much disturbed! After this, an era of concentrated mourning and lamentation broke out in the Marine Witchcraft Kingdom.

Benlilo thus recorded another round of victory over the enemies of his life. Conversely, it was a transitory one. The real battles and struggles were still ahead. For, according to their sworn word, the powers refused to give up. They re-invoked the tenets of their blood oath on his life, his star and his destiny. They boasted:

□We are the never tiring warriors of battle!□
□We are the rigid pursuers never fainting!□
□The victory of life is in battle and we□re the fighters!□
□We are the victors!□
□We are the conquerors!□

As soon as his wings miraculously appeared □ a first time experience - automatically, Benlilo had taken off as a jet fighter on a typical air force military runway. Then, he flew into the blues, secured and maintained a comfortable balance. He flew onward, as the wind cooperated fully. It was not quite long after this that a mocking voice boomed across the forestry landscape with the message:

□Benlilo, well done! Well done □ oh, how beautiful! You are surely riding at the back of the tiger and you must soon meet yourself inside its stomach.□

In the space, the lad surveyed everywhere down below, especially the stony relics of the once high wall. His eyes of mind flashed backward and it still baffled him, offensively, how such an adjudged strong wall of hard stones could have collapsed so easily like a pack of cards - just like the Berlin Wall of Shame in miniature! To him, it seemed that his Defender had given him victory plus rest in all sides. He was all gratitude to Providence for his single life to be preserved. By now, as designed by his enemies, he would have been resting inside the bellies of some water reptiles.

The three revolting beings and all the hosts of the crocodiles, along with other sea creatures inside the lake, watched in puzzled dejection and bewilderment. By now, they had nearly all come to the water table of the lake, watching what they had never seen happened before - in gripping repugnance. They renewed the rain of their curses on the crocodile for its grievous miscalculation.

They went crazy - how food, nay, their foe, had escaped! They mourned the greatest opportunity lost, and which would be difficult to regain. They would not help themselves. They bewailed, vociferously, the abortion of their up-to-the-minute effort to kill the giant destiny, the brilliant star and the trail-blazing glory. How they lamented and regretted their miss of the greatest advantage to set the boy□s treasure of life afire! Yet, they swore never to stop to treasure hope.

The hope, either productive or unproductive, remained the only oil to run the engine of their common life. That such hope in their life was flat negative was irrelevant. The end justified the means.

CHAPTER 043

Life As Reoccurrences

Whirlwinds against his soul
The winds go as they have come.
Oh rest, beauty of life, where art thou?
Missing on land and in the air somewhere,
Chased about into the hiding consign of nowhere!

FOR THE SECOND time in the adventure, the extraordinarily dazzling star appeared and it was directly atop the flying lad Benlilo. This could only have promoted the annoyance and irritation of the helplessly watching powers, the gods and their agents, because this was the very star that they had been massively hunting after for destruction ever since the commencement of the journeying. The adventure was specifically organised for the purpose of witch hunting after the star, overpowering and killing it.

They and their agents that populated the depth of the lake and the three evil pursuers, namely the he-goat, the lion-like monster and the cat watched in sheer disgust, as the boy maintained his admirable flying along with the star in the cool air overboard the lake. How the star and the flying boy displayed clarity of cultural exhibition in the air! They faced each other; they danced; they laughed; they sang:

Unity by faith, unity of oneness
Victory love of joy era of success
Partnership of fulfilment, oh glory -
We□re the victorious achievers of life!

Not quite long after the air travel had taken off and he secured an enhanced comfortable balance in the sky of the vast lake, that Benlilo recorded another shocking discovery. The cat had magically recovered its lost two big wings and it was now flying after him in all furiousness. All the hosts of the accursed crocodiles, the lake□s innumerable living creatures with the watching beast and the he-goat rejoiced in mischievous sanguinity. They praised the deities for the wings□ recovery for the warring cat.

Their roars of jubilation thundered into the sky and the warring cat was best energised in its projected retribution. This time around, they were surely confident that the renegade would be caught by the flying cat and be yanked down the lake into the hungry mouths and bellies of the waiting crocodiles. The expectant lake remained awake to the good expectation. All the eaters of flesh and drinkers of blood in its bowel were full of eyes, rampaging hunger and burning thirst.

The boy, on his own part, manoeuvred his course in flight, as the cat also displayed its fabulous dexterousness. He turned rounds and whirled, as the flying cat also did the same thing with all attendant proficiency very much unexpected of a flying animal by Benlilo. As was customary of them, rendition of cheers for the hero, that is the cat, roared high and higher from hosts of the night:

Deadly warrior, well done.
Air power! Fire power!
You are the magic wonder of all ages
Employ your flying attack! Overtake him!

The flying cat, on its part, pursued Benlilo in fierce flying over the lake, as if it had much longed for their battle to take place right there in the sky, having been powerfully energised by its colleagues□ drumming eulogies. The ploy was still the same: that the boy be plucked into the lake. This was certainly advantageous to the powers and their ambassadorial warrior the cat did not want to miss the opportunity.

Its other colleagues: the he-goat, the monster and the crocodiles and other water creatures - all continued to watch with committed interest, and to hail it largely. At a point, the cat was almost catching up with the boy in the air but another thing occurred: accurately with military precision, a bullet of fire roared out of Benlilo□s arm and it thundered into the heart of the cat, exploded therein and shattered its whole body into inconsequential bits.

Among all the eyewitnesses, Benlilo could not the least explain how this had happened. Too, the watching powers were more than baffled! The devastated cat□s pieces of flesh raced wrathfully down and they all sank deep into the lake, while its feathers got scattered, floating thereon. The lake hymned noisily. It grumbled mind-bogglingly, as it received the crumbs of the *martyred cat*. The crocodiles and other hosts of the lake, the he-goat and the monster made unforeseeable lamentations over the conquest of the bafflingly flying cat, but the end of the struggles and battles was still very far. The dark powers□ reaction to the most recent development was renewal of their undertaking never to give up:

□In as much as life continues, the battle is endless,□ so they concluded. For as the inn of the deep received the remains of the downed cat, with intensifying grumbling and unhappiness, another entirely unanticipated thing happened. A tilapia fish, bronzed in colour and from the distance downward the lake, shot up with two appropriate wings. It took to the air intolerantly after the boy.

Benlilo laughed at the latest reaction of his pursuers. *If the flying cat failed tragically, the same destiny awaits the newest attacker □ a minor fish for that matter!* Yet, again, all the studious hosts had their hope resuscitated. They believed, surprisingly, that the air-warring fish could tackle the escaping lad most notoriously and victoriously. They treasured the hope that, inexplicably, the flying fish would achieve the goal at which the crushed coffin and the shattered cat had fumbled tragically.

However, as it was nearing Benlilo in the sky, a hot east wind blew at the fish. It boiled and roasted to ashes in seconds. The ashes were dispersed by the same wind on the lake before they sank boisterously therein. The bowel of the lake was extremely troubled, as it sorrowfully received the remains of the downed fish in ashes.

Another record shock, the fish□s bits were as cumbersome as iron pieces. This went to show how important an officer the destroyed personality was in the *Marine Witchcraft Kingdom*. In the Queen□s Kingdom, attending practicalities spoke workers□ variable grades the loudest. Sharing positions in the hierarchy did not go by size and neither by name nor fame.

The innumerable hosts inside the lake resumed their session of sadness; they had never been tired of weeping and sobbing. Benlilo viewed the latest development with an unlimited conclusion of happiness. He intensified on his flight to cross the vast lake into safety. He hoped that, soon, he would be inside his much-beloved father□s compound in Marpolio. This remained his greatest desire, nothing less. Meanwhile, the watching and saddened powers kept their deadly but cold and coded silence.

No doubt, they were making some calculations and projections. Soon after this, the soaring youngster manoeuvred deftly and landed at the other edge of the lake □ far distanced from the stony rubbles. Upon landing, his two wings disappeared. He meditated and marvelled at the mode of his hottest escape from the strong-minded enemies. In particular, the authenticity of his growing crisis wings and towering in a mysterious flight majestically in cool blues dawned on him. He shook!

Wonderful Providence, fountain of mercy
Cool marvel my escape from the enemies
You□re wonderful! You□re marvellous!

He quavered! He rejoiced inmost his spirit. Then, more, the current escape□s method thrilled him immeasurably. How could he understand how it had happened, how it was so easily possible that he could convert into a big bird flying just like that in *this sky?* He had looked bemusedly into the sky and shouted his last statement on top of his voice. His hope reacquired active boosting; an air of reassurance flowed tranquilly across his merry mind.

Now with a brand new freedom in a spanking new environment, he walked leisurely on the lakeshore made up of tiny but sharp pure white sand. The white sand was alluringly silvery. It was a paradise of sand. The immaculately white sand seemed to be chorally singing a welcome song to the newcomer Benlilo immediately he had stepped his feet on it.

There was no shrub or tree by the lakeside where the previously flying lad had now landed. Everywhere appeared pleasingly plain and fear of whatever kind had no part to play with the most recent atmosphere. But for his never envisaged escape this far, the gods were exasperated. In a while, a solemn dirge filled their crazed air. The wind fluted in drearily conflicting tones and tunes:

Thou powerless powers, your tall glory?
See your prey walking free in pleasure
Morning of conquest turned tragic
Milk of the adventure soured
Differing will at variance to realities□

For the derisive song, the powers were worse angered. Life stood on edging; glory at stake. The beauty of a season became the shame of the grave land. Tombs therein cried to the heavenlies for rescue, but the heavenlies shunned their pleas.

A rainfall started to bombard the earth□s surface and everywhere, in a little while, turned ice-cold. But instead of the boy to be drenched, the rain did not touch him. How this had happened was another miracle of the classic mission. A sun-circle materialised from nowhere and it overshadowed the lad, as he onward journeyed along the path of the unknown.

The mysterious rain stopped. The air ungenerously began to current in sweet rhythms. The floods rejoiced exuberantly. The gods had accepted defeat? No disbelief, they were covered in humiliation and reproach. They mourned their fate but for how long? Of what stuff was life furthermore to Benlilo the explorer in the wilderness of loss? Only the same phenomenon named time could have told the story□ An excessively livid voice thundered across the horizon and Benlilo heard it plainly:

□The gods are the gods! It is a taboo - the gods will never accept defeat! The powers never shall surrender!□ The newest voice was poison into the ointment of the wayfaring boy.

Nevertheless, for the young man Benlilo, he was overwhelmed with flowing happiness. He was excited that the over-ambitious cat had been destroyed. He was glad that his two remaining major enemies, the he-goat and the monster were now completely cut off on the extreme side of the lake, stranded on those stony rubbles of miserable defeat. He recollected that the lion-like monster had, in the beginning, emerged out of a river to pursue him almost to no end, and he shivered visibly! He concluded that there was no difference between a lake and a river. Both of them stood for water.

Too, he never lost the inner sight of the hurtful reality that, somehow, the crocodile could cross to this side of the lake in a flash of swimming - no matter how far away - in order to catch him and redeem its battered reputation, and remove those curses from its head. It was this realistically logical reason plus the fact that the crocodile family was a skilled swimmer, which compelled the schoolboy Benlilo to distance himself hurriedly from the lake□s shore so as to ensure his permanent safety.

But where was the insurance cover for the enduring security? Where was the secure ground, the safety itself?

CHAPTER 044

A New Woodland Of Life

Spring of amazement action-packed
A heavenly body arrives the scene for
Both in the dark and holy worlds, life is renewal,
Hope sustained goodly invested resources
By fixed faith as tough-strong as rock-hard iron.

BENLILO SURVEYED THE new environment. He admired the multifaceted nature of life in celebration of his newfound freedom. He breathed a healthier air and ran for joy, all alone though, on the white sand as neat as a new pin. For him, it was truly a moment to memorialise. Every step into or towards freedom is celebration worthy.

The adventurous lad was still celebrating his new-found-life when a completely new detrimental interruption erupted □ the powers had never slept. They had never rested or relaxed. They lived on their revered swearword not to allow him a molecule of rest or peace. Hardly had they been caught unawares. Their armoury of surprising methodologies was never exhausted. For the sarcastic song and untold shame from failures, especially the latest letdown attending their warfare paths, they then pulled a new strategy □ what cropped up?

A cruel looking masquerade emerged from nowhere and it started to pursue the boy. The masquerade was very huge and terribly formidable. Its feet stamped the ground like those of a raging hippopotamus. The awfulness of its movement terrorised the meek sand and the whole environment in all unruliness. The air ceased on its singing and it started to watch like all other elemental forces.

The masquerade□s heavy movement made the background to tremble, as if a locomotive train was in jagged passage. It was so fast and fierce! Its movement emitted horror. It was an epitome of terror and panic. It seemed to be a generator and distributor of turmoil and embarrassment at the same time. Grave pandemonium conquered the atmosphere, as a newly invoked horror co-ordinated the obscene show of absurdity. More than that, the pursuing avenger presented himself as an agent of clear-cut death!

The masquerade□s head was that of a mature crocodile well equipped with two sets of sharp-pointing extensive teeth. That□s why, sighting it, the first thought that came to Benlilo□s mind was whether it was the angered crocodile that had materialised in the form of the masquerade. With the powers, all magical evils were possible.

The masquerade□s head, veiled in a leather cap, housed a curved horn with a petite opening stuffed with something like iron-thorns. Its body was in the form of that of a human being but, all over, it was covered with fresh and old dry palm fronds and loutish clothes that gave out such an offensive odour.

It wore raggedy gloves on its two hands, while its feet were in a pair of mismatched and polluted socks. This masquerade was criminally swift in action like a swooping fowler. It growled like a leopard. Worth mentioning, it was armed with a long bunch of many small wooden sticks, which burned like mad at their cooperative end to make a potable bonfire with which it now pursued Benlilo in unimaginable excitement and furore.

Simply put, the boy could not understand! Against whom had he sinned so much that he had rarely met a friend but plentiful sworn-enemies in the wild adventure? What on earth had he done to earn him all these open cruelties from these faceless enemies? Could it be possible that the lion-like monster had materialised from nowhere in the format of the masquerade? Alternatively, could it be that one of the crocodiles inside the lake had transformed itself into this masquerade? Benlilo had realised that in the territory of endless mysteries, anything and everything was possible.

He was lost, but even so, he had only one option before him, the old and up-to-the-minute selection: he took to his heels. He ran as fast as his two legs could carry him but the masquerade too was not out for play. It pursued him desperately and most indomitably. The lad ran and ran farther from the lake□s shore, as the masquerade pursued him non-stop. He remembered the unexpectedly collapsed wall of stone. He prayed that the soil did not cave in for fear that he could be swallowed up alive to the gladness of his enemies. He remembered Laala and his reprehensible end inside the bowel of the earth.

Somehow, luck was on the side of the boy. For whenever the masquerade was about to catch up with him, something of an invisible force would propel him forward and he seemed to be on a pair of the heels of winds. He continued to run for escape, facing somewhere but heading for nowhere really. Too, the over-ambitious chaser intensified on its effort with its bonfire burning consistently like its taut determination.

Benlilo sighted an averagely big tree afar off. He ran determinedly towards it with all his remaining energy □ still treasuring the hope that he would live. On the other hand, the masquerade□s hope boosted. It pursued him. Getting to the tree, the boy saw a moderately thick and strong rope, rough in outlook, dangling from the treetop.

Hurriedly and expertly, he seized the rope with both hands. He started to use it to climb the tall tree, while rolling up the cord at the same time progressively. Wisdom had told him that should he fail to roll up the rope, when the masquerade would arrive the foot of the tree, it would use the same rope to pluck him like an unripe fruit onto the now-dreaded ground. Then, the verdict would have been emphatically pronounced and the rest slipped into unsightly history.

Soon, he had climbed the tree to the top. He first ensured that he tied the long line securely somewhere. He then sat on a thick branch, holding another bough with one hand and resting his back on another, breathing oddly like a middle-aged alligator that had just fortunately survived a bush inferno. Later, from this vantage position, he surveyed his immediate environment in all inquisitiveness.

The masquerade arrived at the foot of the tree. It turned and raised its long head to look up at the escapee lad who, thanks to his youthful exuberance, waved at it with both hands. The angrier masquerade tried to shake off Benlilo down earth but the tree was too strong for such a child□s play. Its pain modified into agony.

It gnashed its teeth to produce a raucous sound very offensive to the ear. It groaned in visible regrets of loss. Nevertheless, it swore, in a strange language, never to leave the foot of the tree until the boy would come down. The masquerade was serious, as it stood purposefully by its word. The purpose was getting the head of the boy and it would settle for nothing else.

Some revelations rolled by as soon as Benlilo had settled down atop the tree, his mental eyes having been opened. Far away, inside an *Enclave of no Mercy,* a group of widows and orphans sang a *Song of Abandonment.* But nearby, positivism manifested: a young man left the land of *not enough* for the territory of *more than enough.* In other words, he had just plucked the juicy fruit of good success in the garden of breakthrough.

The fruit of fortune in success and victory is available for plucking inside the garden of mercy, wisdom and hard work. On the other hand, the fruit of misfortune, in failure and defeat, is harvested in the vineyard of wickedness, foolishness and laziness. Sorrow grows therein like a prosperous tree by the river of failure, as that of joy stands strongly rooted into the rich soil by the river of success. Harvests of both fruitful trees are reaped bountifully in their seasons. The seasons would not fail.

Failure cried for belonging on the street of life. Majority of sons and daughters of man said they did not want him around but, in due course, an overwhelming majority of them had him as their indispensable associate in the business of life. Success longed for a home in which to settle and prosper like that tree planted by the riverside. Almost all human beings scrambled for his friendship but, in due course, few had him.

Both the handsome and ugly sides of life canvassed for attentions. Forces of poverty and riches were never inactive. Life remained the sharp contrast. Benlilo was not afforded the slightest opportunity to discover the stories behind the lamenting widows and orphans and the fortunate man. Neither was he led in wishful explorations to discover the deeps of the success stories, nor the experiences establishing actualities behind those of the failures. His eyes roved on.

The two eyes stumbled on a dreadfully breath-taking scene of an immobilised ghommid tied to a tree. The ill-fated ghommid was *so wickedly tied* that there was no way it could escape unless its captors had mercy on it and they loosed it. Why the ghommid was so *cruelly* maltreated Benlilo would not know. It was also far beyond his human understanding who and what could have done that *cruelty* to it.

Yet, the tied ghommid was an uncommon giant. It stood stoutly at nothing short of nine and a half feet in height. The aberrant being's two arms were longer than its lone leg, which had sprouted directly out of the position of the anus in an archetypal human being.

The two long arms were tied wide apart with steel fetters onto the tree's two branches. The lone leg was as bulky and long as a piece of wood. The foot and its toes were like those of the elephant. Were it to be free, how it would be walking with its single leg must have been a fascinating act to behold.

It appeared on the stake only in a pair of khaki shorts and nothing more. Its head and body were full of hair and they would have been as white as snow but for many stripe cuts decorating its flesh that had produced blood stains. For this, it groaned - more so that its lips were perforated and padlocked with an iron key.

The chained ghommid's two ears were as big as those of an elephant were. They flapped and swung uncontrollably left and right, south and north. Its mouth was like that of a Somaliland games reserve wolf that was nearing its grave. With the mouth, though it was dumb and deaf, it hissed and murmured irritatingly. It struggled edgily to free itself from the bondage but its shackles of iron were stronger than it.

Streams of sweats ran freely down its body in trivial runs. It had a nose like that of a rattlesnake. Beyond that, the chained ghommid had an eye directly into its forehead. The lone eye radiated antagonism and reprisal, even in its wholesale captivity. It transmitted vehemence and violence in wildest imaginations. These all the lone eye did with two identical red rays that shone like the headlamps of a brand new Italian made trailer.

Underneath the dangling legs of the grieving ghommid were uncountable number of dry bones of human beings and spent shells of some water creatures. All these formed a rich collection of its achievements while operating in the human world. But now, the *commendable achievement* had been turned into *condemnable sin* against it.

The congregation of human bones and water creatures' spent shells issued out fragile lights and thin flames that stung like bees and as poisonous arrows. Thus was the creature tormented sore continually day and night. It regretted its sorrowful existence and bemoaned its unfortunate lot. Its song became funeral hymn, as its body frames were adorned generously with sores.

Directly in front of the hanging ghommid, most of the time, was the like of a Brazilian Amazon Forest Kangaroo. This Kangaroo was a marvellous dancer and so it danced around the chained ghommid some of the time. The Kangaroo's assignment was to make constant jests of the chained ghommid and ridicule it persistently. In other words, it was serving as the representative of the torturers of the chained hostage. Continually it recited some rhythmical verses of its taunting words:

Undisciplined ghommid, soul acidic
Led into captivity by his own antic
Oh! how fair in the dungeon of life
Where your might never again strive
Chained to a stake in strict torture
And all the pains you must endure?

Hated useless ghommid of ill-fortune
When little loyalty you know not attune
Here you are under chains and lock
Tortured sore by imperceptible shocks
Day and night for an all-time season
Till, off your sins, you turn to reason.

Benlilo remained pleased on the treetop, as his adversary the masquerade doggedly waited at the tree□s foot to effect its retaliation. The schoolchild peeped further. He saw a tall palm tree with two heads, swinging here and there to the cuddle of the cool wind. The peculiar palm tree was inside a wilderness demarcated with a stream-flow from a forest. The wilderness rendered, joyously, a mantra of loss and want. The stream sang a song of hope and despondency, while the forest chanted a chorus of famine and plenty.

The forest harboured mighty trees of spotted natures and other green plants, all of which, it seemed, were in ardent conspiracy to colonise their immediate sky. The stream reared no other creature beside snakes and crabs. The wilderness pastured rattlesnakes, scorpions and insects □ all in their multitudes.

Birds of variegated species found their havens inside the latest forest. Some sang in dissimilar odd and beautiful tunes, while others were in search of their daily food rations. They were all happy, fulfilled and contended. In one way or the other, they glorified Creation or re-creation.

Then, the standing masquerade did one thing that staggered Benlilo beautifully. It changed the position of its cluster of fire to the right hand. It dipped its left hand into the chest pocket of its gown and brought out a cellular phone. It was all portrayal of seriousness. Having first pulled out its antenna for excellent reception, it dialled a number, put the phone machine close to its left ear and entered into a conversation with an unknown spirit or person or a fellow masquerade.

It soon winded off the curt conversation and returned the miniaturised computer to place. Benlilo did not hear the wordings of the masquerade□s dialogue but he suspected that it must have been conversing in the language of the outer world. Since, according to the mythological credence of Marpolians, the masquerade was a heavenly body, the lad wondered whether *heavenly people* were using phone!

A new round of fear gripped him tight as to whether the cruel masquerade was actually calling for re-enforcements for his sake. He could not guess what next would happen. He continued to hold on to the treetop, still hoping for the very best of life. Yet, again, he remembered his supper-dramatic escape from his enemies at the other side of the lake. He shivered, as his hope to overcome obstacles, no matter how insurmountable it looked, of life boomed.

The life is a drama, a wonder!

Continued in Volume Five.

$$ * $$

<u>Blurb – For Back Cover Only</u>

Universally satirising, THE mystery forest is alluringly beautiful and inordinately ugly. The uncommon experience is thrilling and horrifying an extraordinary adventure. Decorated culturally with high-class dramatic, musical and cinematographic outplays, this is, figuratively, the super-complex story of the student man☐s struggles, battles and journeying through unwinding labyrinths of the *University of Life*. Time☐s recorded observations and interpretations are coded heavy in abstract planes, racing scenes and flying acts. Boisterous and thunderous seasons run along paths of eras, as history for posterity pursues unendingly. Refluxes of retribution. Harvests. Testimonies. Bizarre even obscene deeds are meaningful messages to humankind. Rooted epically in the collective African Mythology, this is the narrative of Benlilo in a dead night yet virgin day of wonders and mysteries. Weighty words and active actions through lucid prose, singing poetries and striking dramas tell philosophies. Night and day, light surviving darkness. Symbols, images, allegories, metaphors, parables and proverbs - all represent multifaceted life and the earthly place belongs to both the living and the dead. Terror! Thunder and lightening! Horror! Fear! Bitterness and joy! Ultimate dynamics of power! Coal is for fire, as pearl is for beauty. A field of silver, diamond and gold. Vision flies, as mission runs. Messages relay, unlike ambitions in displays. Excellences compete with extreme cruelties. What of affiliations and diversifications? A fiesta of fast, lethargic and rolling events! This train of awe-inspiring revelations is the hot narrative of love and lust, war and peace, hope and despair, successes and failures plus tragedies, as juxtaposed with comedies through amoebic layers of wonderful surprises and action-packed suspense spots ☐Yes! this is *Operation QMC-UKDDC* the superstar account: galaxy of a thousand stars and a thousand thorns. Beauty and crown glory of the African storytelling culture, with its volume at well over two million words, *Midnight of Horrors!* is the biggest, most complex and longest storyline; largest, greatest(?) and richest(?) literature novel that has ever come out of Africa ☐ and you reserve the right to find out why ☐

www.ingramcontent.com/pod-product-compliance
Lightning Source LLC
Chambersburg PA
CBHW081003130726
48004CB00008BA/1838